**"What is the real woman like
beneath that breathtaking facade?"
Cade demanded.**

Lita averted her eyes from his, but his hand reached out to tilt her chin back toward him. He went on, "I've seen the ice and some of the spirit. But is there fire stirring in your blood?"

His face came closer—the hand at her chin now lightly touching the silky skin of her neck. "Is there desire burning hotly inside this cool, disinterested body?" The heat glowing in his eyes could easily have scorched her, Lita thought.

Without waiting for her reply he covered her mouth with his, absorbing her fragile lips, consuming her until her mouth opened to his insatiable hunger. When she pulled away Lita was gasping for air, dizzy from his unexpectedly devastating attack.

He murmured her name as his hands caressed her arms but she slipped away and walked to the edge of the ocean. She didn't want a one-night stand, and she didn't need an affair, she thought. In a moment he was there beside her, and she appealed to him with her eyes to leave her alone, to halt his seduction. But he would have none of it.

Don't plead with those enormous velvet eyes, he thought. *I'm not going to allow you to escape. Someone shot my brother, and I think it was you. . . .*

WHAT ARE *LOVESWEPT* ROMANCES?

They are stories of true romance and touching emotion. We believe those two very important ingredients are constants in our highly sensual and very believable stories in the *LOVESWEPT* line. Our goal is to give you, the reader, stories of consistently high quality that may sometimes make you laugh, sometimes make you cry, but are always fresh and creative and contain many delightful surprises within their pages.

Most romance fans read an enormous number of books. Those they truly love, they keep. Others may be traded with friends and soon forgotten. We hope that each *LOVESWEPT* romance will be a treasure—a "keeper." We will always try to publish

LOVE STORIES YOU'LL NEVER FORGET
BY AUTHORS YOU'LL ALWAYS REMEMBER

The Editors

LOVESWEPT® · 104

Millie Grey
Suspicion

 BANTAM BOOKS
TORONTO · NEW YORK · LONDON · SYDNEY · AUCKLAND

SUSPICION

A Bantam Book / August 1985

*LOVESWEPT® and the wave device are registered
trademarks of Bantam Books, Inc. Registered in U.S. Patent
and Trademark Office and elsewhere.*

ISBN 0-553-21674-0

Published simultaneously in the United States and Canada

Bantam Books are published by Bantam Books, Inc. Its
trademark, consisting of the words "Bantam Books" and
the portrayal of a rooster, is Registered in U.S. Patent and
Trademark Office and in other countries. Marca Registrada.
Bantam Books, Inc., 666 Fifth Avenue, New York, New
York 10103.

PRINTED IN THE UNITED STATES OF AMERICA

O   0 9 8 7 6 5 4 3 2 1

One

Cade Hamilton sipped his Scotch, one hand clenched into a fist as raucous music blared from a loudspeaker behind his table. It was humid in the honky-tonk atmosphere and he longed to shed his Hamilton Exclusive suit jacket. But then, he had no intention of staying for the entire performance.

Across from him sat the private investigator who had walked in with him only minutes ago. The man would stay to point out one person from among the twenty beautiful women, in various states of undress, now dancing on the stage. Cade's six-month search had finally come to an end in San Juan.

"Which one?" he asked, scrutinizing each woman.

"The sexy redhead in the last row, second from the right. The dish with those delicious long legs."

Cade nodded, his eyes narrowing. "I'll take it from here," he said. His companion raised his brows, stood up, and walked briskly away from the table.

The willowy young woman was dancing sensuously, executing a series of graceful movements and high kicks. Sparkling silver rhinestone briefs flowed over her slender hips, leaving little to the imagination. Narrow straps, crisscrossed above and below her breasts, allowed the firm, milk-white skin and rosy tips to remain bare. Cade watched the sultry movements as the young woman kicked high, then moved to the center of the stage. Her glittering headdress added a queenly elegance to her Titian hair.

His blood ignited, simmered, then blazed through his veins. "Damn you," he muttered, glaring at the young woman known to him only as Lita Jamison. "You left him to die."

He observed the slim hips and waist, the expressive swaying motion of her hands, the pasted-on smile that did nothing for his libido. By far one of the most gorgeous women he had ever seen, she struck him as being totally devoid of emotion. It was as though she had been formed from a block of ice. She kept her eyes at a level just below the ceiling behind him, never once looking at the quiet men ogling the bodies performing for their pleasure. There were a number of women present in the audience; a few giggling, others obviously bored by the gyrations on the stage. The young woman never missed a step, but Cade had the distinct feeling that her mind was far from the dance routine.

The music ebbed and a new instrumental took its place, and the chorus line moved to the wings. The fire-eating act that followed was excellent, but the lone man, drumming his fingers on the table, waited impatiently for its finale.

The curtains finally closed, then reopened on six dancers undulating before the lusty-eyed audience. But the woman he sought was not among them. Cade arose slowly, reached into his pocket for a bill, and dropped it on the table beside the empty glass. How would he approach her? Time was of the essence.

In a flash of intuition, he knew what *modus operandi* was required to induce Lita Jamison to accompany him to Florida. He smiled callously, intent on his ruthless mission.

Lita grabbed a towel from the young female stagehand

and wiped the perspiration from her face, then draped the towel around her shoulders and over her breasts. As she walked wearily to the dressing room, reliving the night's performance, she realized that every second on that stage was an eternity spent in the presence of lust. The only way she could go on dancing six nights a week in the abbreviated costume was to force her thoughts to Jeremy—that wild young man who had taken her silly dreams and smashed them.

Six months had passed since then and it was an effort to re-create those days and the brief heartbreak that had followed. She knew, deep in her soul, that her love for Jeremy had been the quick, impassioned kind, like lightning striking a young willow tree. But the electrical flash had diminished just as rapidly when he had shown his true colors.

Ignoring the chatter of the other girls, she quickly stepped into panties and an emerald-green cotton jumpsuit. After combing the auburn mass of hair that flowed to her shoulders, she used a tissue to remove most of the vivid eye makeup that emphasized her enormous apple-green eyes.

"There's someone here for you," the young stagehand said.

"For me?" she asked. The chattering subsided and Lita was aware of the interest of the other dancers. "I'll be right out," she said stiffly, avoiding the stares of her coworkers.

Since she had joined the troupe, only the stage girl had given her a welcome of any kind. The dancers were a close-knit group, mostly former Las Vegas show girls who had been robbed of their youthful beauty, but were still attractive beneath the subdued lighting of the Mariposa Club. They seemed to resent Lita's dewy skin and vivid coloring, but she had to ignore their hostility. This was the only job she was suited for in the land of perpetual sunshine.

Hanging up her costume for the daily inspection by the wardrobe mistress, she tossed her head like a young filly, then slipped out of the room.

"Miss Jamison?" The voice behind the bouquet of

flowers was rich and warm, a slight southern drawl giving his tone a mellifluous quality.

But it was the eyes above the lovely blossoms that caught and held her gaze. She felt the conscious need to swallow, as though a smoldering flame had scorched the moist skin of her throat.

He lowered the flowers and delicately wrapped her fingers around the expensive yellow roses. His features were handsomely masculine and he seemed to be looking down his straight aristocratic nose at her.

"I saw you dance tonight and wanted to meet you," he said.

A Stage-Door Johnnie, she thought, and frowned. "I'm not accustomed to speaking to the customers. So if you'll excuse me—"

A smile curved one side of his mouth. "You won't escape me that easily," he said, his tone soft and seductive. "Come, my car is at the stage door."

She hesitated, then shook her head, almost dropping the flowers in her haste to escape the warm, possessive hand on her arm.

"I'm Cade Thomas," he said, his fingers moving in tiny circles against her wrist. "I'd like you to share dinner with me. Dancers don't usually eat before a performance, do they?"

"I don't," she murmured, caught between the strong desire to go with him and her usual caution.

"Please," he whispered huskily. "I promise to have you home"—he checked his watch—"in two hours."

Plenty of time for a seduction. "I'm sorry," she said quite firmly, "but I'm expected."

"Another date, hmmm?" he teased, his white, even teeth barely evident in the darkly tanned face.

Lita was drawn to him. There was something so easy, so familiar about him, yet she was certain she had never met or seen him before.

"No, I promised my aunt I'd be home on time." Hot blood charged through her body as she recalled her near-nakedness on the stage and guessed what he must think of her. No man could have pure thoughts of any woman who performed in such a lust-provoking show.

Sometimes, since starting the job, she had felt no better than a call girl.

"Excuse me." She brushed past him. "And thank you for the flowers. Or"—she paused, extending the bouquet—"perhaps you would like to give them to one of the other girls."

When he shook his head, she drew them to her. She *had* offered him an alternative. His trim-fitting clothes spoke of wealth and a certain bearing. She was sure that a dozen roses wouldn't dent this man's bankroll.

"Can I take you home?" he persisted.

"No thanks," she said softly, walking through the stage door and into the alley. Unchaining her bicycle, she was aware of his eyes on her. After tossing her purse and the flowers into the basket behind the seat, she hopped on and started pedaling away from the club. Was he following her? Something told her he would not.

Using side streets, she kept away from the heavy traffic, avoiding the cab drivers that sometimes drove as though the devil were sitting in the backseat. "Devil," she muttered, then smiled. If Satan had jet-black hair, finely molded ears, and a complexion like copper, then perhaps Cade Thomas was indeed the occupant of one of those darting autos. Although he had said, "My car . . ." But then, rich folks liked to use the possessive case in most instances.

Where was he from? His voice held a trace of a drawl. A tourist from the glorious South, no doubt, spending his money on women and at the numerous large hotels that catered to gamblers. Oh, well, she would never see him again.

The smells permeating the air in Old San Juan were different from the clean, fresh scents in the newer part of San Juan, where the club was located. Although she had few acquaintances, those local people she had met were warm and friendly. One of them had put in a good word for her with the owner of the Mariposa Club.

Lita unlocked the iron gate to the three-story building where her aunt and four other families lived. The building was clean and neat, but in need of repair. Stucco had chipped off in places; a coat of paint would have brightened the walls of the courtyard.

As she stepped into the courtyard, the scent of roses was like a powerful aphrodisiac. She rested her bicycle quietly against a wall and made her way to her aunt's apartment, tiptoeing past the woman's door and into her own tiny room that was at once a sanctuary and a prison.

Aunt Maria was a loving, good-hearted woman, who had welcomed Lita into her home in spite of her own poverty. Lita felt she owed her a great deal, and had given her aunt her first paychecks, reserving only a few dollars for herself. Lita sighed as she filled a jar with water and arranged the fragrant yellow roses in it.

Stripping quickly, she stepped beneath the ancient shower, the driving force of cool water a welcome stimulation. She felt the tiredness begin to dissolve, then remembered that she must conserve water. The old fixtures seemed to groan and complain as she turned them off.

As she slipped beneath the sheet, she was grateful for the trade winds that swept in from the northeast. Down in the harbor, the sleek cruise ships would be departing for new Caribbean destinations. Was Cade Thomas aboard one of them? She fell asleep dreaming of vivid azure eyes and a soft, drawling voice that called to her.

Hours later, the steady hum of voices in the courtyard awakened her. Lita rolled over, thankful for the first good night's sleep since her arrival in San Juan. The temperature was already in the high seventies, with warmer temperatures predicted.

She stretched and groaned. Every muscle ached. She slipped on a pair of white shorts and a shirt that tied beneath her breasts, then went into the tiny kitchenette. Inhaling the aroma of strong Puerto Rican coffee, she dropped a slice of bread into the toaster.

Maria came in to ask how she was feeling. "You poor darling," she said, "you must get very tired dancing all evening on that stage."

From her five-foot-eight-inch height, Lita looked down at the tiny woman who had no idea that the club catered to tourists and featured a seminude show. Although her aunt knew such places existed, it would never occur to her that *her* niece would *ever. . .*

"Who brought the flowers?" Maria asked.

Lita shrugged. "Just a man."

One eyebrow lifted. "A Don Juan, eh?"

"We call them Stage-Door Johnnies in the States."

"Rich?"

"I suppose."

"You were made for a rich man, Lita," Maria said, pouring coffee into two cups.

"I don't want wealth," Lita murmured. "I've been through all that. Rich people lead a different kind of life. There's no sincerity or kindness. Whatever they give is only with a greater return in mind. Love is a scarce commodity."

"You are saying this because of Jeremy Hamilton."

"Definitely. And my parents," Lita said solemnly. "But don't be concerned about me. I have no feelings left where Jeremy is concerned."

Maria shrugged. "I hope that's true." She made no comment about Lita's reference to her parents—Maria's sister and brother-in-law.

Unaware of her beloved aunt's worried glances, Lita cleared the table and washed the dishes. Today she would help Maria with the wash and with cleaning the apartment. Then she would rest for a few hours before the first performance.

At seven-thirty, Lita got on her bike and began pedaling toward the Mariposa Club, aware of the delightful scent of flowers and the jukeboxes blaring rock and spirited Spanish music. When she arrived, she parked the bicycle and hurried to the stage entrance.

Once inside the dressing room, she removed her clothes and snapped on the skintight briefs and the bra that exposed her high, firm breasts. Catching a glimpse of her body in the mirror as she adjusted the glittering headdress, she drew a sharp breath. How she hated herself for allowing her talents to wither in a sleazy nightclub. With all the inner strength she could muster, she tried to erase all thoughts from her mind.

Focusing on a dark spot on the ceiling, she counted: nine, eight, seven. . . Closing her eyes, breathing deeply, she felt a wave of calmness wash over her. Soon she was ready for another performance. Covering herself with a towel, she walked toward the stage.

The other members of the troupe were quietly milling around, exercising, adjusting their costumes. For some reason, Lita peeked through the curtain and quickly surveyed the crowd. Tossing the towel to the young stagehand, she breathed a sigh of relief when she realized Cade Thomas was not there.

At a signal from the stage manager, the dancers stepped to their places. The introductory music started and the curtains parted. An uncanny sensation trickled down Lita's spine, one that seemed a forewarning. As she went through the dance sequences, she scrutinized the audience, something she had always tried to avoid doing before.

Her heart thudded in her chest as she caught sight of Cade Thomas in the far corner of the room. She watched him sip from a glass, then their eyes met. Excitement clutched at her stomach. She flinched as though he had reached out to touch her.

Lita felt the unsteadiness of her limbs and tore her gaze from his. When the curtains closed, she tried desperately to regain her composure. Cade Thomas had penetrated her defenses, leaving her completely vulnerable.

Offstage, staring at a spot on the ceiling, she suddenly became aware of the young stagehand standing by her side. "That man is here again," the teenager said softly.

"I know," Lita murmured.

"If he asks to come backstage, do you want to see him?"

"No."

The girl nodded and walked off. Cade Thomas would not be rebuffed twice, Lita was sure. There were too many other lovely women to choose from to chance another unsatisfied night.

After the last show, she put on her jumpsuit and stepped out the stage door. Her bicycle was nowhere in sight. Stolen!

How would she get home? A taxi? She fingered the few coins in her cotton purse. It was an emergency. As she started down the alley toward the front of the building, she heard the muffled sound of a car motor. She began to run, and had almost reached the corner when a shiny black Rolls-Royce pulled up beside her.

"I'll drive you home, Lita." She heard the soft-spoken drawl and halted in her tracks.

"No thanks," she managed to say. Her stomach churned and lurched as though it had received a sharp blow.

He laughed throatily. "I'm harmless. I promise I won't touch your lovely body or try to seduce you."

Why did she suddenly feel a sense of trust when her brain kept sending alarm signals? "You'll take me right home?"

"Yes. Unless . . ." He paused. "Would you like to have dinner with me? I'm very hungry."

She felt her stomach tighten. Hungry for food or for her? she wondered. Ignoring her better judgment, she stepped toward the vehicle just as Cade leaned forward to push open the door. Lita eased into the plush seat and pulled the door shut.

"Where to?" he asked.

"I could do with something light to eat," she said. "Anything except Puerto Rican cuisine." After six months on the island, she was ready for a change. Aunt Maria was an excellent cook, but one accustomed to great variety in food could only take so much black bean soup and *pasteles* without rebelling.

He nodded, then revved the engine and pulled into the street.

"I'm not dressed for anyplace fancy," she said.

"Relax, Lita. There's a restaurant a few miles out run by an American whose food is very good." Glancing at her, he added, "You look just fine."

She smiled, rather feebly.

The night sky was filled with stars that could be seen through the open roof. The cool breeze was welcome after the strenuous performances. Lita glanced at Cade covertly. What did he expect of her? she wondered. A one-night stand? She hadn't allowed any man to touch her since Jeremy. She'd found she had no desire for physical contact.

"This is a lovely car," she murmured, her fingers tracing the plush upholstery. "Did you have the sunroof installed?"

"Why do you ask?"

"I didn't think that Rolls-Royce made an open-topped model."

He seemed to hesitate. "I take it you've been in one before?"

"Why, yes. Several, in fact." Lita's parents had wealthy friends who doted on the most expensive European cars.

"Men friends?" he asked, a certain hoarseness to his tone.

She shrugged. "Not particularly."

The air between them tingled with unspoken words. The pressure of his foot on the gas pedal seemed to increase.

"Where are you from?" he asked.

"Several places."

"Like where?"

"Oh. . .Miami, New York, Los Angeles, London."

"You've traveled—as a dancer?"

"Yes." She felt as tightly wound as a coiled spring.

"Do you have a valid passport?"

She nodded, puzzled at his question.

"What caused you to come here?"

She hesitated. "Escape, I guess."

"Do you enjoy your job?"

"No." *I hate it. The degradation and the sense of barrenness pervade my soul.*

"There must be places other than a dump like the Mariposa Club where a beautiful dancer can find work."

"Why do *you* go there?" she asked defensively, feeling warmth rush to her cheeks.

"It's a favorite tourist spot. The entertainment is good. Besides that, I happen to know the owner's wife."

"And you just happen to enjoy watching women prancing around with very little in the way of costumes."

"Lita," he said patiently, "I'm not a young boy. I've seen my share of naked women."

"Of course."

"And you've seen your share of naked men."

Something in his tone sent a shiver skipping down her spine. "Really?" Her voice rose. "How would you know?"

"It only makes sense that a woman who can bare her flesh for all to see. . ." His voice trailed off.

She felt her stomach twist into knots. "In other cultures, and in places like Las Vegas, it's an accepted form of art, and considered in good taste on beaches throughout the world."

"Sorry. I didn't mean to condemn you."

"You're dead wrong about me," she blurted out. "If you think that the price of a meal and a ride home is worth spending the night with you—"

"I'll say it again," he interrupted. "I'm sorry if I've given that impression. I really don't need a woman that badly."

She lapsed into silence, her knuckles whitening. When he pulled into a parking space in front of a restaurant, her body was ramrod taut. It took all of her restraint not to flinch when he touched her arm as she alighted from the car.

"I think you'll like the Champ's food," he said, walking beside her to the entrance. They were greeted by a tall man, with the pummeled features of a prize fighter.

"My friend," he said joyfully, pumping Cade's hand. "And the lovely lady."

Lita smiled, small white teeth gleaming in her oval face. "Hello, Champ," she said, extending her slender hand.

They were seated at a small table by a wall of windows that overlooked the bay. A mass of twinkling lights reflected on the water.

"I never heard of this place before," Lita said. "It's lovely." She felt the warmth of Cade's eyes before she looked up to meet his penetrating glance. She took the menu from his outstretched hand and looked down at the list of enticing dishes.

"Champ serves excellent food," he said. "What would you like?"

"You order for me." At the moment, Lita felt anything but hungry. While Cade studied the menu, she covertly studied him: a snow-white cotton shirt, the diminutive print on the classic tie, the light beige suit jacket that clung to his broad shoulders.

Her gaze focused on the tiny nerve throbbing in his cheek and she realized that he was not as unruffled as he sounded. The mere thought that he might be somewhat disturbed by her presence gave her a sense of confidence.

He ordered Southern Comforts, prime ribs, baked potatoes, and salad. The waiter gave her a slow flirtatious wink before departing for the kitchen.

"Tell me about yourself, Cade," she said evenly. "Where are you from?"

"The East—the South."

"Specifically?"

"I have a place in Florida."

"What line of work are you in?"

"I'm affiliated with a distributorship for food, drink, clothing."

Although he gave her polite answers, she sensed a certain evasiveness. After the waiter placed their drinks before them, she looked directly at Cade. "Am I asking questions you'd rather not answer?"

He stared at her for a long moment. "You're rather forthright," he said. "Do you always say what's on your mind?"

Her eyes narrowed. "I believe in shooting from the hip."

He paled visibly. She watched as he tossed the liquor down, his hand unsteady. "Do you mean that literally?"

"It's just a figure of speech," she replied cautiously. She sensed that something was wrong—but what? "I'd like to ask a question that has disturbed me since you first appeared at the club." She picked up her glass and sipped. The liquid had a cooling effect as it slid down her throat. Then she felt the warmth radiating through her chest. He gestured for her to proceed.

"Why did you choose me out of all those dancers in the club? And for what purpose?"

He leaned forward, his hands gripping the edge of the table. "You really don't beat around the bush, do you?"

She settled back in her chair, her fingers tightening

around the glass. She intended to wait for his reply, not to speak until he had revealed his motives.

"Would you believe," he said, "that of all the dancers in that troupe you stood out as more beautiful, classier, than all the others put together?"

She shrugged, waiting for the second question to be answered. Before he could reply, the waiter arrived with their orders. She looked up expectantly when they were alone again.

"What I'd like to do"—he lowered his voice—"is make love to you until sunrise." He sighed. "My other alternative is to take you home and kiss you at your door."

Lita watched his mouth as the words poured forth, the sensuous, full lower lip and the thin upper one that she sensed could smile or sneer with equal aplomb.

"At least you're honest about it," she said, her voice breathy, her pulse racing in staccato beats.

"Why shouldn't I be?" He half-smiled. "I've always found it more profitable to lay my cards on the table. It's up to you to make the choice."

"There's no question of choice, Cade," she said softly. "I don't go in for sexual calisthenics with strange men."

"You've known me for two days. I should no longer be a stranger."

"Let's see." She glanced at her watch. "I've been with you for exactly one hour, including last night. You've told me almost nothing about yourself. Only a highly immoral individual would hop into bed with you under those circumstances."

"Immoral?" He sat erect in the chair, his blue eyes darkening to cobalt as he stared at her. He seemed to be struggling with pride and another emotion she was at a loss to interpret. "Perhaps you'll get to know me better in the next few days. I think you'll change your opinion of me."

"You're staying on in San Juan?"

"Let's say I have no immediate plans for returning to Florida."

"Business?"

"Pleasure." He grinned and she couldn't help smiling in return.

At his change of demeanor, the magnetism that she

had tried so hard to ignore began to exert its power over her. Cade had seemed almost grim at times—tortured might have been the better description. But now the feeling that flowed between them was no longer filled with suspense. Lita felt herself relax beneath his undemanding gaze.

Suddenly the food became more palatable, and she speared a piece of tender meat and brought it slowly to her mouth. Cade watched each of her movements, focusing on her lips as she chewed.

They discussed San Juan's beautiful countryside and its less desirable areas. Cade had obviously been on the island before. Lita was so engrossed that she never noticed how he was manipulating the conversation.

"My aunt says that rural electrification has brought washing machines and color television to the poor and to the isolated people in the mountains," she told him as she devoured a wedge of Black Forest chocolate cake. She sighed, and put her fork down. There was not a crumb left on her plate. "That dessert was fantastic."

"Didn't I tell you that Champ had an excellent chef?" He reached across the table to cover her hand lightly. "Does your aunt have a color TV and a washing machine?"

Lita shook her head. "No. Maria is very independent. She only buys what she can afford. She was provided with a small trust fund many years ago. That was before inflation."

"Do you miss television?"

"Heavens, no." She laughed. "I don't really have time to watch."

When he removed his hand to pick up his glass, she felt strangely abandoned. You should be used to that feeling, she told herself.

"Would the señorita care for anything else?" asked the brash young waiter, who had openly flirted with Lita throughout the meal.

"No, thank you." She gave him a big smile. "Everything was delicious."

"Stop trying to steal this beautiful lady, my macho friend," Cade warned jokingly.

The waiter grinned. "What chance would I have against the wealthy señor?"

"Why don't you become a politician," Cade teased. "Then you'll be able to compete with anyone."

"Sí," the young man agreed. "Or a baseball player."

After chatting a few minutes with Champ, Cade and Lita left the cozy restaurant. He opened the door of the Rolls for her, and after she was seated, walked around to the front of the car.

The balmy breeze which came through the sunroof tossed her hair. The meal had been satisfying—the company likewise. She leaned against the headrest, glad that she had accepted Cade's invitation.

She's beginning to trust me, he thought. *Perhaps it won't be so difficult getting her to leave with me. The aunt could be a stumbling block, though. I'll have to work on that.*

"What are you doing tomorrow?" he asked later, as they walked toward the iron gate of the courtyard.

"It's my one day off. I usually sleep."

"How about coming with me to a beach?" His eyes glittered with anticipation. "I'll provide the basket lunch."

She hesitated, but only momentarily. For the first time in many months, she was intrigued by a handsome, charismatic man, one who seemed to be edging his way into her life.

"It sounds just lovely," she said, inserting the key into the lock.

He searched the depths of her eyes before drawing her lightly to him. His head came down, his mouth covering hers, his tongue leisurely nuzzling her lips. As though hypnotized by his warmth and moistness, she allowed his tongue to enter her mouth, becoming deeply aroused as he explored its recesses.

The urgency of his hard thighs filled her with heated desire. He crushed her to him, one hand dancing erotically over her breast, soothing it, sending ripples of hot sensations to the center of her femininity. Her hands flew to his neck, and she grasped his dark hair tightly with her fingers. His vibrant kiss rocked her and she seemed to be losing herself in the tightening pressure of his arms.

Without warning, he tore his lips from hers and stepped away from her, breathing heavily. Thoroughly shaken by the intensity of his sensual assault, she felt the weakening of her limbs and the rapid thudding of her heart against her rib cage.

"I'll see you about one o'clock," he said huskily.

When her tongue flicked over the lips he had devoured only moments before, his eyes seemed to glaze over. She felt suddenly chilly in the warm Caribbean night.

"I'll see you then," she murmured, sadness and excitement mingling at his departure.

He's dangerous. The warning throbbed in her brain.

"But if he is," she whispered as he walked to the elegant car, "then I have no one to blame but myself."

Moments later, the signal light blinked and the Rolls-Royce and its occupant sped down the steep hill and out of sight.

Two

Lita stretched and tumbled out of the twin bed. She had just enough time to dress, straighten the room, and grab a cup of coffee before Cade was due. Would he actually come?

The effect of his mouth on hers the night before had greatly disturbed her rest. Although self-hypnosis enabled her to perform in the show, to set aside for a few hours at least some of her principles, Lita refused to use it as a crutch in her daily life.

She put on a sky-blue cotton dress over a matching bikini. After brushing her hair until it shone with auburn and brown highlights, she added a touch of lip gloss.

Maria smiled when Lita entered the tiny kitchen minutes later. "Beautiful," the woman murmured.

"*Gracias.*" Lita touched her lips to Maria's cheek.

"You did not come home until quite late."

"That same man who brought the flowers"—she gestured uncertainly—"took me to dinner."

"The rich one." Maria nodded approvingly.

"I suppose you might say that. He's involved in some

kind of distributorship." She met Maria's gaze. "Money isn't important. I told you that before." She poured the dark brown coffee into a cup and added a dash of milk.

"When one doesn't have it, it is *most* important, little one."

Lita looked up sharply. "You could have accepted money from my mother, but you chose independence instead."

"It makes a difference who does the offering," Maria said softly. "I have accepted your assistance, have I not?"

Lita let the question slide by. She had never understood the rivalry between the two sisters, but she definitely knew which of them she had always preferred.

"He's coming to pick me up soon." She heard the faint tremor in her own voice. "Would you like to meet him?"

"But of course." Maria laughed. "I must give my approval to this suitor."

Lita smiled. "The time of the duenna is long past. Today a woman fends for herself."

Maria sighed. "Unfortunately, this is so."

The sound of people in the courtyard caught their attention. Then a tapping sound brought Maria to her feet. Lita heard the door open, but refused to turn around.

"Señora," the deep voice said.

"You are here for my niece?"

Lita rose and stepped behind Maria. "This is Mr. Thomas," she said. "Please come in. This is my aunt, Señora Vargas."

Her aunt's expression was almost comical as Lita introduced them, petite Maria staring up at over six feet of rugged masculinity.

"May I get you a cup of coffee?" Lita offered, glancing away from the handsome features. She hadn't been able to erase the memory of his hot, throbbing mouth, and here he was again to challenge her senses. She felt his gaze on her as she gestured for him to sit down and poured the steaming liquid into a cup. Strangely tongue-tied, she was grateful for Maria's chatter.

Sipping on the strong, black aromatic coffee, Cade answered her aunt's subtle interrogation with amused replies, relating only the same information he had given Lita the previous night.

"How long are you staying, Señor Thomas?"

"I'm not sure at this point." Glancing at Lita, he added, "It depends on . . . shall we say . . . circumstances."

"Ah," Maria said, all-knowing. "And where are you staying?"

"At the Hilton."

Maria nodded, her mouth curving upward. Without a doubt, her aunt approved of this man. Well, Lita thought, *she* didn't make snap judgments about people anymore. She had had her lesson in trust with Jeremy.

"Perhaps we should get started?" she suggested.

Cade rose, thanking Maria, obviously enchanting her when he kissed her hand. Oh, he really knew how to charm a woman. *Beware, Lita*, a tiny voice warned.

An hour later, they were traveling past large houses, tiny, humble homes, and miles of palm trees that grew along both sides of the highway.

"I think of all the trees in Puerto Rico, the royal poinciana is the most beautiful," Lita said. She felt his gaze on her profile.

"Is that because the flame trees enhance your lovely hair or because they stir the fiery blood that thunders in your veins?"

"Wow," she whispered. "That's almost poetic."

He chuckled. "The company inspires me."

They found a tiny, palm-fringed cove washed by the surf of the Atlantic Ocean. Their only companions were the gulls and a harmless lizard. Cade placed the lunch basket on the sand, then spread a colorful blanket. When he started to undress, Lita kicked off her sandals and turned away to watch the waves crashing against the offshore rocks, casting spray high into the air.

Slowly she unbuttoned the sleeveless dress and allowed it to slip from her body. Then she walked to the edge of the water. The foam that lapped against her feet felt cool and inviting. Cade had already swum out toward a boulder and was now cutting smoothly back through the waves to her side. Something irritated her at the typical demonstration of male prowess.

"The water's cold but invigorating," he said. His gaze slid down the length of her and back up to her face.

That cool, calculating look made her feel almost naked. A tiny chill scudded down her backbone. With much the same appraisal as he had given her, Lita allowed her slow gaze to take in his broad shoulders and the crop of chest hair that came to a V at his navel. Then she lazily scanned the tri-color briefs that covered his masculinity so enticingly.

Drops of water on his muscled thighs were already evaporating as she continued her thorough perusal all the way down to the feet that were partially hidden in sand.

"Have you decided to swim?" he asked.

"Well, I thought I'd wait until the Olympic champ was through with his performance," she said mockingly.

One eyebrow lifted. "Are you calling me a show-off?"

She raised her chin. "I've never appreciated men who had to be one cut above everybody else . . . in sports or otherwise."

His hands moved to his hips, the stance now coolly arrogant. "It's only natural for a man to try to become a hero to the woman he's trying to win."

At least he doesn't deny it, she thought. "Or to whatever woman happens to be around."

"At the moment, I only have eyes for one beautiful, desirable woman."

Her nonchalant shrug, belied the excited flutter in her heart. "Why don't I race you to that boulder?" she suggested.

His glittering gaze seemed to strip away the tiny patches of fabric that covered her. "What do I get if I win?"

"What do I get?" she retorted.

"Maybe"—his voice became almost a whisper—"we can each reciprocate with a stimulating reward."

Flames shot to her cheeks. In order to avoid the lust in his eyes, Lita leaped into a wave and heard the splash as Cade joined her.

He was an excellent swimmer, but she matched him stroke for stroke. She hadn't come within a hairs-breadth of capturing a national title without some expertise. She had tried so hard, she remembered, hoping to win her parents' love and approval.

Their hands reached out for the boulder at the same moment. Neither had won. But neither had lost. They raised themselves to sit on the rock.

"You're good," he said with an air of restrained surprise.

"You're not bad yourself," she admitted, breathing heavily.

She looked out across the distance they had swum. When a finger caressed her cheek, she turned to face Cade. His vibrant blue eyes were focused on hers, his lips parted as though he were hesitant to speak.

"Even with your hair plastered to your head, you're so lovely. You don't need that makeup for the stage. Lita Jamison would stand out in any crowd of women."

"Thanks."

"But what is the real woman like, the woman beneath that breathtaking facade?"

She averted her eyes. He turned her chin so that she had to face him fully.

"I've seen the ice and some of the spirit. But I wonder, is there fire stirring in your blood? I haven't been privileged to see that yet."

His face moved closer, the hand at her chin now lightly touching the silky skin of her neck. "Is there desire burning inside this cool frame?" The heat glowing in his eyes could easily have scorched her.

Without waiting for her reply, he covered her mouth with his, moving his head from side to side as he absorbed her fragile lips, consuming her until her mouth opened to his greedy tongue. When she pulled away, Lita was gasping for air, dizzy from his unexpected and devastating attack.

He murmured her name as his hands caressed her arms, but she slipped away and into the frothy water that cooled her heated body. Stroke, stroke. She didn't want a one-night stand. Stroke, stroke. She didn't need an affair. He'd be gone in a few days.

When she reached shallow water and waded to the sand, he was there beside her. She appealed to him with her eyes to leave her alone, to stop this throbbing seduction. But he would have none of it.

Don't plead with those enormous velvet eyes, he said silently. *I'm not going to allow you to escape. Someone shot my brother and I think it was you.* Cade forcefully grasped her waist with one arm and led her to the blanket.

But what if he was wrong about her? he thought suddenly. There was something dark and forbidding in the whole sordid affair. He might never find out the truth until he confronted his brother with Lita. The sand in the hourglass was quickly running out for Jeremy . . .

"How old are you?" Cade asked as he lay down on the blanket.

"Twenty-six." She kneeled and let herself fall forward.

"How long have you been . . . dancing?"

"You mean seminude?"

The slight flaring of her nostrils and her spirited reply caught him by surprise. There was a great deal about this young woman he had yet to find out. She was so outspoken when he least expected it, so demure and innocent at other times.

"Where are your parents?" he asked.

She seemed to flinch at his question. "Probably stoking Satan's fires."

He swallowed hard at her cold, unemotional reply. "They're dead?" he asked carefully.

"Killed in a boat accident in South America."

"How long ago?"

She bit her lower lip. "Six years."

He hesitated before asking, "You miss them?"

She sat up quickly, all patience gone. "Like a guppy misses its mother," she said, bitterness apparent in her tone.

He seemed taken aback by the harshness of her words, and she watched as he closed his eyes, his chest rising and falling rapidly. When he continued to be silent for the longest time, she finally lay back on the blanket. What was he thinking? she wondered. That she was hard and bitter? Never that. Too soft and trusting was the problem.

"I don't think I understand you."

She heard his voice as though from a distance. How could he understand what an unwanted child feels like? "I shouldn't have said that," she murmured, swallowing hard. "It's just that when all the other kids' parents would show up for a school activity, mine were never around or wouldn't take the time to go. They always treated me as though I were only a sweet little puppy who deserved a pat on the head once in a while."

"I had loving parents, so it's difficult for me to put myself in your place."

"Don't bother trying, Cade," she said, overreacting to the misery that always encompassed her when she thought of her parents.

"And if I want to try?"

"Why should you?"

"Maybe because I'm intrigued. Perhaps even a little in love with you."

Lita's breathing seemed to stop. Love? Was love real? Or was it just a fascination that held two people together for a moment in time? Hadn't she pleaded for love as a child, hungered for it in her teen years amongst friends and acquaintances, and finally believed she had shared the elusive emotion with Jeremy?

"I'm afraid you'll have to use a different tactic," she said honestly. "I don't believe there really is such a thing as love—lasting love."

Cade writhed uncomfortably beside her. He hadn't meant to mention love, but it had slipped out. What was he thinking of? A man of his background, knowing what she had done, would not allow himself to fall in love. Dammit, man, he told himself, use your head!

He rose to his feet. "Let's have some of that delectable food and wine." He laughed without mirth. "We've been much too serious." Uncorking the bottle, he poured sparkling Pinot Chardonnay into wineglasses.

Lita unwrapped corned beef sandwiches and set tubs of mustard, pickles, and potato salad on the blanket. "All this and mixed fruit," she said. "I'll bet these delicacies come from the one and only Champ."

"Right." He smiled, his teeth a brilliant white against copper skin.

Lita sucked in her breath, one hand raised in midair

at the shock of seeing the contrast. He was two separate personalities; one dark and mysterious, the other like sunlight filtering through a massive cloud.

"Tell me," he urged.

"Tell you what?"

"Why your face suddenly changed from cold to warm?"

She laughed. "I was thinking the same about you. You're like—" She hesitated. "Like Laurel and Hardy. Remember those movies where one was so happy-go-lucky, the other deadpan?"

He studied her for a few moments. "I've been called many things in my lifetime, but never a comedy team."

She shrugged. "I don't really think you're what you present yourself to be." She saw him start.

"We make quite a pair," he said, averting his eyes.

Lita nodded, sinking her teeth into a poppyseed roll chockful of paper-thin slices of beef.

A half hour later, replete with delicious food, she suddenly realized Cade hadn't commented on her appraisal of him. Was he what he seemed—a businessman from Florida with pleasure on his mind?

They stretched out on the blanket, the sun simmering on their backs. "I think," he whispered, his breath warm and moist against her neck, "that you will need some tanning lotion. We wouldn't want that luscious skin to be burned. What would your customers say if you turned up two-toned for your performance?"

She turned her head to face him, their mouths only inches apart. "I don't like to think of them as customers. That connotation brings to mind an entirely different variety of entertainment."

"Does it bother you to perform before those lecherous eyes?"

Her nostrils flared slightly. "Right now, it bothers me more to be discussing it with you."

A slow smile spread across his face. "I can think of better things to talk about. But first, how about that suntan lotion?"

They gazed at each other for a silent minute. His eyes were mesmerizing, almost hypnotic, in their vivid intensity.

"Okay," she finally said.

Cade reached behind him, then straddled her hips. Lita took in a deep, troubled breath, grasping the edge of the blanket as his weight pressed into her fleshy buttocks. Before she could protest, he flipped open both ties of her bikini top. With swirling motions, his palms spread the warm liquid over her back.

As he kneaded the muscles of her shoulders and the tense cords of her neck, she felt herself slowly drifting off. His touch was gentle . . . warm . . . relaxing.

Then, with a jolt, her consciousness resurfaced as two bold hands traced a fiery path over the sides of her breasts. She felt the muscles of his thighs tighten, heard him suck in air with a hissing sound.

"Turn over," he whispered, his voice thick with desire.

"No way," she murmured, pressing her arms against her sides, stilling the erotic sensations he was creating within her.

"Lita," he breathed.

"What?"

"Don't pretend I haven't excited you."

"I'm not pretending," she managed to say, desperately attempting to quell the throbbing in her lower stomach.

"There's no one around," he said hoarsely. "Just the two of us."

She felt as though she were melting beneath the whisper-soft touch of his hands as they again began their rhythmic seduction. In one swift movement he was beside her.

"Turn over, Lita," he implored, his voice rough with emotion. "Answer me."

Her lids felt as though they were encased in cement, so achingly did they lift to meet his gaze.

"Let me love you," he said urgently. "Since I met you, I've wanted this, to touch you, to hold you, to feel your body beneath mine."

"Don't. Please don't," she begged, her plea sounding like a ragged sigh.

He pressed his face into the blanket and his body stirred restlessly. For endless minutes he seemed to be in agony. Then, gradually, his breathing returned to normal. His long length quivered and an exhausted sigh left his lips.

Finally he turned to face her, his gaze clouded, frustrated, watchful. "Tell me one thing," he said, his voice hushed, tormented.

Her eyes were riveted to his.

"That you're not just holding out to punish me for what I said about you dancing nude."

"Not nude, Cade," she corrected him. "Seminude. And no." She leaned forward to kiss him feather-light on his mouth. "I'm not looking for revenge and I don't play games."

He nodded, releasing a deep breath. "Let's pack up and go," he said.

She was still wary of his motives as he retied the bikini top, scooped up the towels and basket, and headed back to San Juan.

"I'd like to take you dining and dancing tonight," he said as they approached the old section of the city. "Oh." He laughed. "That's like a busman's holiday. Well, how about dining, anyway?"

An inner voice kept nudging her, but she was deaf to its warning. "I'd like that," she said.

As the car drew up beside the iron gate, she quickly hopped out. "What time?" she asked, her heart thumping loudly.

"Is eight o'clock all right?" When she nodded, he added, "It can't be soon enough for me."

After the sleek car had disappeared down the side street, she stood at the gate for some time, fumbling with the keys. "I don't want to fall in love with him," she said emphatically, then looked around to be sure no one had heard. Her mind was caught in a tangled web. It would be insane to react positively to him. Would she be put to the ultimate test tonight, fighting the raw magnetism he exuded? She wasn't sure she would win.

She placed the key in the lock, mumbling to herself that the chemical attraction between them would sizzle and eventually evaporate. "I hope," she added for reassurance.

Three hours of soul-searching passed. Lita tried to act natural, for Maria's sake, but the woman seemed to have a sixth sense where her niece was concerned.

"This man is becoming important to you," she said during their early evening tea.

"I don't want that." Lita's voice was husky with unconcealed emotion.

"This one could be the right one, my child. You must give him a chance."

"What if I give my heart and he stomps on it?" She felt a sob rise in her throat, but muffled it in a napkin.

"I did not know your Jeremy, but I would say this man has integrity, a basic honesty." She paused, as though not quite certain of what she was about to say. "Yet somehow I feel a sense of hesitation. He tries to hide it, but something is bothering him."

"You mean something to do with me?"

Maria laughed. "I may be intuitive, but I am not a mind reader."

Someone rang the bell at the courtyard gate. Lita froze, but Maria rose and headed for the door. Moments later, her aunt ushered Cade Thomas into the room.

"You're early," Lita said.

"Not too early, I hope." He handed her a single yellow rose and sat down across from her. Maria busied herself clearing the table.

Lita nodded her thanks for the flower. "I'm ready."

"And lovely too." His sensuous glance took in the full-length emerald-green dress. Its Grecian bodice emphasized her firm breasts and the color seemed to magnify the size of her eyes.

"I thought we could go for a ride along the coast and stop for dinner at a new nightclub I just heard about today."

"Sounds delightful," she murmured.

As he glanced at his watch, she caught a glimpse of it and felt the color drain from her face. Jeremy had one like it, there could be no doubt about its unusual shape. He had told her the Swiss manufacturer had made only a limited number of them.

"Your watch," she said faintly. "It's . . . different."

"There were only about one hundred of them made. I was lucky to get one."

So was Jeremy. Lita was aware of the hair on the nape of her neck rising.

"Shall we go?" Cade said in the sudden silence that surrounded them.

"Yes," she murmured. She kissed her aunt's cheek, picked up her purse and the rose, then walked out into the courtyard. A lady waved from an upstairs window. Lita smiled back at her.

"Will you miss this place?" Cade asked as he held the gate open for her.

"Why should I be missing it?"

"When you come away with me." His gaze never left her face. "I just thought you might have become attached to these people."

Lita must have held her breath. She couldn't for the life of her recall getting into the car or leaving the congested city behind.

"Lita?"

She looked up at him.

"I asked you a question fifteen minutes ago," he said softly.

"I'm not going anywhere with you." Her tone was so low, it was almost inaudible. She felt herself shiver in the warm breeze that came through the roof opening.

"We both know differently, don't we?" His voice had a purring sound, like that of a contented jungle cat.

"I came to escape Je—" She stopped in mid-sentence. "I'm not returning to the States."

"I want you to come with me," he said gently. "I can give you whatever you want. You won't have to work in the club again."

"No." Panic edged the single word. The air between them crackled like live, hot wires.

"I thought you didn't like working at the club."

"I don't," she said quickly.

"This is a chance to escape all that, Lita."

"I'm not that desperate."

They had left the city lights behind. A sickle moon was reflected on the ocean. The road was dark, with only an occasional car passing in the opposite direction. Lita crushed her purse tightly in her hands. What did she know about this man?

"I was hoping you would say you wanted to come—to be with me."

"I don't even know you." Her voice rose. "No matter what my personal feelings are, I have no intention of becoming a rich man's mistress."

He was quiet for a few minutes. "You would display your . . . charms before all those lustful men rather than come with me and share a good life?"

Lita laughed harshly. "That's what it all comes down to, doesn't it? Baring my breasts to them or baring all to you." She caught her lower lip with sharp teeth. "You want to use my body—use me. Well"—she swallowed—"you won't." She gave a strangled sob. "Let's turn around and go back to San Juan."

His hand reached for her trembling fingers and held fast. "I'm sorry," he said. "I shouldn't have rushed you. It's . . . only that I must return soon and I don't want to lose you. As for using you, you're an adult woman. I could no more use you than you could use me."

She tried to clear her throat quietly, but it was impossible. She couldn't have uttered a word if her life had depended on it.

"Let's enjoy our dinner," he said, pulling into a well-lighted parking area. "We won't discuss it again tonight."

He leaned toward her. His kiss was soft and warm, engulfing her in a delicious sense of pain. She wouldn't become entangled with another man, she told herself. At least not one as handsome and sure of himself as this one was.

She watched him take the keys from the ignition, open the door, and walk gracefully around the front of the Rolls-Royce. When he opened her door and offered his hand, she stepped out and into his arms.

"Tell me you're going to enjoy your meal, that you'll think only of good things and of me." He touched her chin and lightly caressed her lips with his. "Come, my lovely señorita. Do me the honor of being my attentive companion tonight."

Her suspicious gaze collided with his. She didn't believe for one minute that he had changed whatever plans he had for her. But then, she wasn't a simpering idiot who would allow a man to lead her by the nose.

She nodded. She would enjoy this evening. She might

even flirt with him. But this was the end. After tonight she would never see him again. Tossing her lovely dark-flamed hair, she accepted his arm as he led her into the enchanting restaurant.

A Puerto Rican string trio serenaded the diners and Lita ate heartily of the delicate lobster dish. She saucily tapped Cade's glass each time she raised the excellent wine to her lips. She hadn't flirted with a man in a long time, and this was her night to shine. Amused at first, Cade entered into her bright-eyed chatter, delivering rapid-fire responses to her quips and sparkling humor. But now and then she caught his puzzled glance.

Later, as he led her in a rumba, she tried to bewitch him with her eyes. His half smile told her he was not fooled. During a slow number, he held her tightly to his hard chest, burying his face in her glowing tresses. The pressure of his muscled thighs against her soft ones turned her legs to butter. His manly endowments left nothing to her imagination.

This was a virile male, and he meant to have her tonight. But there would be one totally dissatisfied man at the Hilton Hotel when dawn approached.

Sipping on a margarita in the lounge, she fingered the money through the fabric of her purse. There was enough to take a taxi from his hotel to Aunt Maria's house. Enjoy yourself, Señor Cade Thomas from Florida, she bid him silently. No man will ever command Lita Jamison's emotions—not ever again.

But as the evening progressed, she felt a strange, wistful sensation enshroud her. Breathing deeply, aware of a flutter in her throat, she experienced a new sense of fear.

Would the night end as she had vowed?

Three

"I can see why you chose dancing as a career," Cade said as he led Lita to their table. "You're so graceful. As light on your feet as the feathery tuft of a dandelion."

"You're rather good yourself," she said, lifting her lashes, then lowering them demurely.

"You're also a little flirt," he teased, increasing the pressure on her waist.

"Oh." She pouted. "You noticed."

"If you do that again," he murmured huskily, "I'll ravish you in full view of the customers."

"Come now," she said quickly, turning aside to hide the color she felt creeping up her cheeks. "You're more civilized than that."

"A man becomes primitive when he's aroused sufficiently." His pale blue lightweight suit emphasized eyes that smoldered with passion.

"Have you tried saltpeter in your food?" she asked, throwing him a mischievous glance. "I'm told it takes care of those male bursts of energy."

He laughed softly, pulling out her chair and nibbling seductively on her earlobe. Sitting close beside her, he said, "We won't need either stimulants or suppressants tonight, my love. We're going to experience pure sensual pleasures."

"You're certain of that?"

His glazed eyes slowly, tantalizingly, roamed over the silky material that caressed her breasts. He would never forget the beauty of her slender body as she performed on the stage. He felt a tightening of his jaw and a touch of anger at the thought of other men lusting after her body. No one else should ever see her nakedness, he thought possessively. No one but himself.

But as he suddenly recalled the image of Jeremy lying in a hospital bed, he was twisted with hostility. No matter what he wanted to believe about Lita, the gut feeling that she was guilty persisted. His heart and mind warred over the belief that she had injured his brother. There were times when he was filled with self-loathing at his ambivalence.

Lita Jamison must spend her life behind bars or be imprisoned in his arms. He didn't quite know how he would accomplish either. He also didn't know if he could go through with the punishment he had in mind to appease the rage he felt at the thought of his brother bleeding from a gunshot wound. But the hatred he had initially felt for her seemed to have waned.

"Let's leave now," he said, rising from his chair.

"One more dance," she whispered.

In the center of the floor, Lita writhed and dipped in a dance of passion, her brilliant eyes never leaving his as she enticed and retreated, then tempted him anew.

Her lovely swaying arms, lightly kissed by the sun at the beach, reached for Cade, then subtly spurned him. Unable to stop himself from grasping her waist, he drew her to his body. "You're an enchantress, a Lorelei," he said, panting slightly against her ear. The music stopped and still he held her tightly. "It's time to discover what other talents you possess."

"I never claimed to have any."

"Nor did I," he said, but Lita knew the promise of his virile expertise was there in every movement of his lithe, athletic frame.

What have I done? she asked herself as he led her

past the tables to their own. She was neither a temptress nor an innocent. But Cade couldn't know that she had seldom used her charms to entice a man.

Tonight was different. She felt almost angry at his taking her for granted. His attitude was one of telling, not asking. But who would be the loser when she slipped away from him? Cade or herself?

He said nothing when they left the nightclub. His arm curved around her waist as he assisted her into the car. The Rolls-Royce purred out of the parking area. He turned on the tape deck and the melancholy strains of a love song mingled softly with the wind from the open roof. Cade pulled her close, his hand warm and caressing on her shoulder. Lita clung to the single yellow rose.

She felt wistful, close to tears. Her emotions coursed from acceptance of this man to total rejection. She wanted him, probably as much as he wanted her. But desire had led her astray once before—and she had been betrayed.

With her thoughts tossed in a whirlwind, she was barely aware of the city lights, the heavy stream of traffic, and then the parking valet assisting her from the car. The lobby of the Caribe Hilton, the classy hotel near Old San Juan, was brightly lit, and the Club Caribe was alive with a floor show, the place milling with visitors and guests. Lita had once ventured to the first level of the hotel, where she'd played the quarter one-armed bandits. She guessed the casino was now filled with quiet, feverish gamblers. The well-dressed men and women gave the place an air of elegance.

She didn't look at Cade as he escorted her into an elevator and pressed the twelfth floor button. His features were set, determined, and he stared straight ahead. What was he thinking? she wondered. That he had a "sure thing" in Lita Jamison? Her mouth curved up, but the smile disappeared as the doors slid open and Cade's hand grasped her arm.

Matching his steps as they walked down the plushly carpeted hall, she looked away when he opened the door. Then he stared down at her and her glance met his. He smiled, a tantalizingly beautiful smile for a man so intent on one purpose. His tone was gentle and warm as his "Come, Lita," urged her into the elegant room.

"Would you care for a drink?" he asked.

"No, thanks," she murmured. Despite her trembling legs, she managed to walk to the windows that overlooked the moon-silvered rippling ocean.

Then Cade was behind her, his hands on her waist, his warm breath nuzzling the nape of her neck. She closed her eyes, reveling in the gentle pressure of his hands kneading the soft flesh of her stomach.

But when she heard the rasp of her zipper, she pulled up sharply, aware that the time had come to put her plan into effect. He turned her toward him, his tongue making crazy sweeps across her lips and over her cheeks. When it hotly invaded her mouth, she heard herself moan and leaned into him.

"I was beginning to wonder if I'd ever get you up here," he said softly. "The evening was endless."

"And you can't wait to get a woman into your bed."

"Mmmm, not just any woman." He crushed her closer to his throbbing desire. "I never wanted a woman as much as I want you."

She turned in his arms to gaze out the window again. His caressing fingers sent a tremor of pure pleasure through her. Hard thighs, moving sensuously against her buttocks, stirred an eager response.

"Does it feel good?" he murmured behind her ear. His hands danced intoxicatingly over her breasts.

When she molded the hard tips into his palms, he chuckled softly.

"You're coming with me to Florida?" he asked, raising the issue that had troubled her deeply since he had first mentioned it. If he thought this was the opportune time to extract a promise from her, he was sadly mistaken.

"You have a one-track mind," she teased lightly.

"When I want something, I go after it."

"And you want me." She felt his body tense. A frown crossed her brow.

"Why shouldn't I want you? Haven't dozens of men pursued you in the past? Your eyes are like luscious new leaves in springtime. You smell absolutely delicious. A wood nymph bewitching me with her charms."

He sensed her hesitation, and wondered if he was babbling too much. He felt as though his tongue was liquid fire, the words slipping from his lips without effort.

"I want you, Lita. It's not lust, although how can I deny that that must be one of the reasons my brain is ·eeling?" How could he tell her that one part of his mind was devoted to seeking revenge? This was no time to think of Jeremy, he admonished himself. Somehow, at this moment, nothing else mattered but the promise of their lovemaking, the hot, steamy invitation of her body that would release passion.

Lita's mind was slowly going blank. But she fought to hold on. She wanted to turn to Cade, to see the fringe of dark lashes, the tiny laugh lines at the corners of his eyes. The need to be possessed by him was so strong, she felt weak from resisting it.

"If you'll turn on the shower, I'll join you in a few minutes," she promised, almost breathless with desire as his persistent kisses fell on her neck and his low murmuring set her mind ablaze. When he turned her in his arms, she saw the questioning look in his eyes.

"Yes," he said, moving away from her, his gaze filled with a throbbing warmth that set her blood on fire. He walked into the bathroom and she waited until she heard the water running before moving. Her heart was hammering against her ribs, her palms so moist, she wanted to wipe them on something.

Glancing at the yellow rose in her hand, she pulled back the cover on the bed and placed the lovely blossom on the pillow. Pausing for a moment, she was startled to see Cade poised in the doorway, watching her. From where he stood, he couldn't possibly see the flower.

"Yes?" The word caught in her throat.

"I just wanted one last look at you in that lovely dress," he said softly.

Her teeth grabbed for her lower lip. Her heart was leaping in her chest. What was he thinking? Did he suspect that she might try to leave? A doubting Thomas? She wanted to giggle—anything to relieve the suffocating sensation in her chest and head.

But the eyes that glittered in his handsome face were

far from distrustful. He extended one hand in loving entreaty.

"I'll be right with you," she said huskily.

His hand fell to his side and he nodded, giving her a half smile that tore at her heartstrings. He stepped back into the bathroom.

Seconds later, as she slipped noiselessly past the open door, she saw Cade disrobing, his back to her. A tear trickled down her cheek as she reached the door to the hall.

"You fool," she chastised herself aloud. The night with him would have been wonderful, but she seemed to have no control over the footsteps that carried her past the threshold and away from this exciting man.

Lita rubbed sleep from her eyes and stared up at Aunt Maria.

"Someone left your bicycle chained to the gate."

"Impossible," Lita murmured.

"Come look for yourself. I found this key inside, as though someone had thrown it through the bars."

Lita slipped her legs over the edge of the bed and pulled on the robe Maria extended. Following her aunt into the courtyard and through the gate, she was amazed to find the old, battered bicycle with one drooping yellow rose between the spokes of the front wheel.

Cade!

She took the key from Maria's hand and slid it into the new lock. Even the chain had been replaced. Cade had taken her bicycle! He must have returned it after she'd left the hotel room. But why? Any other man would have dumped it into San Juan Bay.

Aunt Maria was studying her with the strangest look. Then her face brightened and she started cooing like a dove on a spring morning. What was the woman thinking? Lita let it all slip past.

She wheeled the bicycle into the courtyard, staring at it with unseeing eyes. What had he thought when he came out of the bathroom to find her gone? Had he smoldered in rage? Most men would have reacted that way.

A strange, sinister chill raced down her spine. He had stolen the bicycle so that she would have no choice but to ride with him. "I don't understand him," she said aloud. "I wonder if I want to."

"What are you talking about?"

"Oh, nothing. I can't understand why they brought it back. But I'm glad it's here. What would I have used to go to work tonight?"

Maria, still shaking her head, preceded her into the kitchen. "Cade Thomas brought you a yellow flower last night." Shrewd brown eyes watched Lita's reaction.

"Coincidence," she murmured.

"Hmmm," came the suspicious reply.

The sun was overhead when Lita entered the kitchen and placed a bag of food on the table. She sniffed the heady scent of the frangipani tree that filled one corner of the courtyard with its velvety star-shaped flowers.

She sat down on a chair. If Cade was feeling vengeful, he might convince the owners of the Mariposa Club to fire her. She had been thinking about that possibility for the last hour as she walked past the crowded cafés, hearing the excited conversations, of San Juan's inhabitants.

The sidewalks had been teeming with tourists from the two cruise ships anchored in the harbor. Once she thought she saw someone who resembled Cade, but the man disappeared among the shoppers. Several times she had felt a prickling sensation on her neck, but when she turned around, no one familiar was in sight.

She curled a lock of hair around her finger. How long would she search the crowds for him?

Her thoughts were still on Cade when she entered the dressing room of the club at eight o'clock that evening. She slipped on the skimpy costume and slung a towel over her shoulders. Then she walked into the wings, sat down on the one available chair, and leaned back against the wall.

Needing time alone, away from the chattering women,

she slowly drew in and expelled air. She realized, with a frown, that her heart was beating against her ribs. Damn that man! Surely he wouldn't be here tonight. And even if he was, he'd be looking for another woman.

Ten minutes before curtain time, the stage girl approached her. "I have something for you." She presented Lita with a long, narrow box. "It was delivered to the owner's office."

The color drained from Lita's face. Had she been standing, her legs would have buckled. As though in a dream, she opened the box to find one perfect yellow long-stemmed rose cradled in tissue paper.

She looked down at the blossom, bewildered and uncertain. She didn't see or hear the stage manager's signal. One of the dancers kicked her foot and hissed at her. Dropping the box on the chair, she struggled to her position in the last row.

The curtains opened slowly and the dancers went into their routine. Lita peered at the far corner where Cade had sat before. The seat was empty. She looked down at the front row of grinning men and almost missed a step. She had forgotten to concentrate, and the shock of finding herself without any defense against that leering audience made her stomach churn.

At the end of the number, she stumbled into the wings, grabbed the towel, and wiped the perspiration from her face and body. The single seat had remained unoccupied; the florist's box was nowhere in sight. She collapsed into a chair in the dressing room. Only then did she spot the box beside her purse.

She tried to relax, staring at a spot on the ceiling, then counting backward. Gradually she felt calmness steal over her. She would be all right. Hang Cade Thomas and his roses. Somehow, she had to get through the evening.

Fifteen minutes before the last show was over, Cade slipped into a vacant seat reserved for the owners and their friends. He was certain Lita hadn't noticed him, for her vacant stare was focused above the audience. It had taken him a full day to come to terms with himself.

The night before he had stepped out of the bathroom when five minutes had elapsed to find that she had vanished. That slip of a girl had put one over on him. In anger, he had taken the flower and bicycle to her building. Unsure as to whether he would bang on the gate until she answered, then calmly wrap both items around her neck, or sweep her into his arms and force his attentions on her, he had done neither.

His plan to get her to Florida would not be accomplished if he revealed his true feelings. Later he would wreak his vengeance. But now, appearing all-forgiving and understanding—while gritting his teeth—would be the best procedure to follow.

Cade watched her gyrations, the dance steps that seemed intricate, the way her willowy body swayed to the music. "I still want her," he muttered. "More than ever." He looked down at his hands, amazed to find them shaking.

A half hour later, when she walked through the stage door and headed for her bike, Cade moved out of the darkness to stand behind her. She stooped to unlock the chain, but must have seen his shadow. She jerked upright, her eyes enormous in her lovely oval face.

"You scared me!" she whispered.

"Leave the bike," he said. "We'll come back for it later."

She didn't argue, merely nodded and walked beside him to the expensive black car. She hadn't expected him, so the element of surprise was in his favor. She slipped into the seat like a whipped puppy, her luminous eyes conveying a mixture of emotions.

When Cade started the engine and headed in the opposite direction from his hotel, she breathed a silent sigh of relief. Twenty wordless minutes later, he pulled into an area overlooking the Atlantic. Turning off the ignition, he sat back, watching the ocean swells as they surged toward shore. The final phase of a sickle moon rode in the sky above them.

"Why?" he asked simply.

She didn't have to be a mind reader to know what he was referring to. "You didn't ask—you *told* me what would happen. I decided it wouldn't be as you wanted it."

"So you ran out." His voice was flat, devoid of anger. "You might have considered my feelings."

She breathed deeply, filling her tortured lungs with the cool ocean air that swept in through the sun roof. "Did you consider mine?" She glimpsed the handsome profile, aware of a moment of panic.

"You weren't honest. You flirted, gave me every indication that you were as aroused as I was."

"Would you have taken no for an answer?"

"I've never forced myself on a woman. I wouldn't have done it last night."

She pondered that for a minute. "I don't go in for one-night stands."

"I was hoping for more than that," he said grimly.

"You'll be gone in a few days. I don't want an emotional attachment to someone who's just passing through. That kind of involvement is not for me."

"You know this is different, Lita."

She couldn't meet his gaze. She stared straight ahead, seeing the pounding surf and whitecaps through misted eyes. "I know that I'm vulnerable with you." Impulsively she added, "I had one man dump me and it hurt very badly." She heard his sharp intake of breath.

"Who was he, Lita?"

"It doesn't matter."

"If it happened to you, it does matter. Why don't you tell me about it." He twisted in his seat to face her.

"Let's leave things as they are—no personal secrets revealed, just a pleasant relationship with no strings and no one getting hurt."

His hand tenderly caught her rigid chin. He turned her face toward his. "Come to Florida with me." His tone was soft, sexy, stimulating. "I want to show you how I feel. It takes time to establish a relationship. We can leave tomorrow."

She looked at him, her eyes glowing with unshed tears. She had to admit there was magic between them. Perhaps this man was different. Should she listen to her heart?

She felt herself relax, but that was only momentary. When he took her in his arms. his warm breath near her mouth, she responded to the enchantment of their romantic surroundings and the thrilling strength of his arms. She gave a tiny sigh as his lips came alive on her own.

When her hands slid up his chest, she was intoxicatingly aware of the pounding of his heart through several layers of clothing. His kiss was insistent, urgent, and then his tongue teased its way into her mouth. She gave herself up to him, her need becoming more important than the doubts that plagued her.

When he pulled away from her and settled back in his seat, she felt bereft and bewildered.

"I'm not going to rush you," he said wearily, rubbing the back of his neck. He knew he could have had her—her resistance to him was slipping—but something held him back.

It was difficult to separate his emotions from the hard, cold facts that had led him to Puerto Rico and Lita. The evidence against her was circumstantial, and he was constantly reminded of her soft, innocent eyes.

He had thought he would derive a sense of satisfaction from finding her. What a fool you are, he chided himself. Softening toward this woman was probably the biggest mistake he had ever made.

She was beginning to haunt him with her unusual beauty. He found himself waking at night from dreams of her lissome body molded to his, the taste of her skin. And each time he was on the verge of entering her, he was jolted awake. It was pure agony to lay his head on the pillow and attempt to sleep.

He'd never cared deeply for a woman before. Could this lovely creature be his undoing? The warmth of her body was seriously tempting him.

Remembering the raw pain etched on Jeremy's face filled him with blinding resentment. He had to find the truth, to inflict just punishment on the person who had ended Jeremy's zest for life.

How many times in the past few days had he asked himself if it was only satisfaction he wanted? Were his motives sincere in avenging his brother's crippling injury? Battered by warring emotions, he felt weariness wash over him as he attempted to weigh his feelings of attraction and a sense of repulsion.

"Cade?"

He snapped back to reality at the sound of his name. "I'll take you home now," he said. Starting the motor, he reversed the car and pulled onto the road. "Can I see you for the next few days?" It was a mistake to ask, but then he couldn't seem to stop himself.

"Yes," she breathed.

"You won't run out on me?"

"I ran once. I'm not about to do that again."

You had every reason to run from Jeremy, he thought. Attempted murder is not an act to be taken lightly. "Tomorrow afternoon you can show me the fort, okay?"

El Morro, the fortress dominating the sea approach to San Juan, was within walking distance of Aunt Maria's apartment. Guarding the harbor with its stately magnificence, the historical landmark was a popular tourist attraction.

"Okay." It was one thing to believe that a decision to pursue the relationship would probably lead to grief, but quite another to cease further contact with this enigmatic man.

When they reached Maria's home, he pulled into a parking space near the gate. He kissed her lightly, then reached across her to open the passenger door. His arm grazed her breasts, and at his touch she felt the stir of passion in her loins.

Her glance locked with his. "Thank you for returning my bicycle. Although, I guess we forgot to pick it up tonight."

He laughed, almost guiltily. "It was the least I could do, since I arranged to have it stolen. I'll bring it for you tomorrow."

"It wasn't worth much."

"To someone who doesn't have a great deal it could mean a lot."

She gave him a half smile. Wouldn't he be surprised if he knew the extent of her parents' bequest? "Good night," she whispered quickly, stepping out and closing the car door.

Cade raised his hand in farewell and eased the car into the street. Shaking her head, she hoped he would remember to return the bicycle before she had to leave for work. Then she shrugged. That was the least of her problems. . . .

Mid-morning the next day, Lita returned to the house with milk and bread to find the bicycle in the courtyard. Cade must have kept an extra key for the lock, she thought. He and Maria were sitting at the kitchen table eating the Danish pastry he had obviously brought and drinking her aunt's delicious Puerto Rican coffee.

He stood when she entered, taking the bag from her arms. In a surprise move, he kissed her gently. Lita felt the blood thud in her veins. He pulled out a chair for her while Maria poured coffee into a cup.

"What have you two been discussing?" Lita asked hesitantly.

"You," Cade said.

At Lita's quick frown, Maria reached for her hand. "It is only natural for a man to want to talk about a beautiful woman."

Cade laughed. "I asked your aunt if she would like to come with us to Florida."

Her puzzled eyes took in the two of them. "You what?"

"I thought she might like to see Miami again. It's been years since she moved here."

Lita swallowed the lump in her throat. How dare he come to this house and discuss such a personal matter with her aunt! He was pushy, like most men, trying to force her to agree to leave with him.

"You can go if you like, Maria. I'm staying here," she said.

Maria looked at Cade, then at Lita. "But I thought—"

Lita shoved back the chair and rose, her hands quivering as she grasped the table. Eyes widened with distrust and rage, she faced him. "Last night you said you wouldn't rush me. Today you're inviting my family. How dare you, Cade? I've known you for what . . . three days? And you're already trying to run my life."

Maria gathered up the dishes, placed them in the sink, and scurried from the room. Cade's face was a mask of confusion. In a way, she regretted having confronted him in Maria's presence, but as uncontrollable rage had flashed over her, she'd felt the urgent need to vent it.

"I told you once before that I don't understand you, and I'm finding it more difficult each hour." She clasped her hands together. "I think you'd better leave now." Pausing to catch her breath, she added, "I don't want to see you again." A fierce sensation clutched at her chest. Pivoting abruptly, she made for the door.

"Lita!"

She halted, her shoulders stiffening.

"Please come here," he pleaded.

She turned to face him, relaxing at the sight of eyes that were now cloudy blue, partially opened lips that seemed to hesitate.

"Come," he whispered, opening his arms.

Step by faltering step, as though in slow motion, she walked to him. He enfolded her in his arms, drawing her head against his chest, murmuring soothing words near her cheek.

"Forgive me for being presumptuous. I want us to be together so very much that I'm really using less common sense than I normally do." He tilted her chin up. "Give me another chance."

Held against him, his hands feathering her back, she knew that she cared too deeply. She wanted him, needed him with a growing passion. She could smell the tangy scent of his after-shave, feel the athletic muscles of his thighs pressed against hers. His quickened breathing stimulated every nerve ending.

How had she allowed this to happen after the terrible experience with Jeremy? What difference did it make? she asked silently, and nestled her face into the throbbing warmth of his neck.

Four

Cade and Lita strolled from Maria's home to the lush green lawns leading to El Morro Fort. To the right, the brisk spray splashed against the rocks. Ahead lay the tunnel-laced bastion, standing on the craggy promontory that dominated San Juan Bay.

They walked past walls that were twenty feet thick, climbed and descended dozens of stone steps. The wailful cries of gulls and the crash of surf against the rocks one hundred forty feet below added to the awesome sight. Far out at sea, an occasional yacht bobbed on the horizon.

"This island is steeped in history," Lita said. "Wouldn't it have been exciting to watch from these ramparts as Sir Francis Drake's attack was repulsed in 1595?" She made a sputtering sound like a machine gun.

"Are you trying to storm the bastion?" he teased, pulling her close to his chest.

"Heck, no." She giggled. "I'm defending it."

"I would hope you'd be manning a cannon. I'm afraid the machine gun wasn't invented until more than two hundred years later." The word *gun* triggered a chilling response in him and he released her quickly. "It must be the Latin in you getting all fired up for a good fight."

She grimaced. "I'm only one-fourth Spanish. My mother and Maria were half sisters. Their father came from Spain and settled in the States."

"Then, of course, you didn't inherit the fiery Latin temperament," he said.

She ignored the innuendo. "I'm very proud of my grandfather. He was good, honest, fair. He was also tall and extremely handsome. Even though he died when I was very young, I always adored the portrait over the fireplace."

"Is that the kind of man you dreamed of finding one day?"

She shrugged. "Maybe unconsciously. I never really thought about it. I figured it would just happen, and when it did—"

He waited for her to continue, to reveal something of her relationship with Jeremy. But she suddenly became silent, a pained expression on her lovely face. Was this gorgeous creature capable of aiming a gun at his brother and pulling the trigger? Why had Jeremy rejected her? More and more he wondered about that. He had seen a bit of her temper surface, but not enough to determine how she might react under distressing circumstances.

"I don't want to talk about him," she said.

"It's all right. You don't have to discuss anything you don't want to." There would be time later, when she stepped aboard his yacht.

She nodded, grateful that he seemed to understand.

After several hours of investigating every corner of the giant fortress, they sat on a grassy slope overlooking the ocean. The welcoming breeze wafted over them, lifting Lita's hair away from her face. She knew Cade's eyes were on her and reacted with a slight flare of her nostrils.

Some of the strain between them had dissipated when she had gone into his arms earlier. A part of her, however, was still disturbed at his discussion with Maria. What must her aunt think? That Lita made a habit of going off with any man after knowing him only a few days? Maria was the only person who had ever given her real affection, and it was important that she understand the circumstances.

"Does it bother you to have men stare at your body?" Cade asked suddenly.

"Like you're doing now?" She kept her gaze seaward.

"Like I'm doing now," he echoed. "You have on far more clothing than when you're dancing."

"I'm on stage physically"—her voice quavered—"but not mentally."

"I sensed that."

She faced him fully. "Would you feel comfortable performing for an audience with your . . . er, male endowments exposed?"

His laughter held an element of surprise. "Your candidness always affects me like an undertow at a beach—my underpinnings are momentarily knocked out from under me." He lowered his voice. "I have to say you're the first woman I've met who seems entirely guileless, without the game-playing that's part of most relationships."

"Perhaps no one taught me the rules."

His finger traced a circle on her cheek. "I find that heart-warming," he said huskily, his eyes a smoky, passion-filled blue. "As honest as you seem to be, I wonder if you would tell me how you really feel . . . about me."

How could she respond to that? Her lashes lowered. "If I were certain of my feelings, I doubt that I would have any reservations about being completely sincere." She plucked a blade of grass and looked at it intently. "Of course I would expect the same in return."

He nodded. Why had he asked her that? Was he falling under her spell? He was thirty-five years old and had never asked any other woman to level with him. Why was his subconscious putting words in his mouth?

"Of course," he murmured. He knew this woman fascinated him to the point of distraction. After asking a leading question like that, would she now expect him to confess his feelings for her?

Lita saved him from further introspection by glancing

at her watch and announcing it was time for her to leave. He breathed a sigh of relief as she nimbly leaped to her feet and brushed dried grass off her mint-green skirt.

They walked to her home in silence, both absorbed in their own thoughts. Lita was totally aware of his lithe frame, the way his slender fingers squeezed and caressed her hand. Covertly, she observed the sea-blue knit shirt that molded his chest and the tight white slacks that outlined his virility. What did he want from her? she wondered. Would he press her to go with him, or was that a means of getting her into his bed? Well, a few more days would tell the story. She wasn't sure she would particularly care for the last chapter.

At midnight, Lita glanced at her watch. The curtain would close in a few minutes. Cade wasn't at his usual table, nor had he said anything about meeting her tonight. That afternoon he had merely placed a chaste kiss on her cheek, gotten into his car, and sped off.

After the last number she quickly removed her costume and dressed. When she reached the stage door and looked up the dimly lit alley, there were no cars in sight. Why hadn't he come? Was he with someone else? Another woman?

The hollow thump of her heart expressed the empty sensation that flowed over her. Tossing her hair, she walked to the bike, unchained it, and pedaled down the alley to the street.

Should I go to his hotel? she asked herself. *No, I won't. If he wanted to see me, he should have been here.* She proceeded toward Old San Juan. She wouldn't want to embarrass Cade or herself if he was with another woman.

She felt a wrenching pain in her chest at the thought of him making love to some other flaming beauty, and took a deep breath to relieve the pressure. He might even be with one of the dancers at the club . . .

By the time she reached home, she was in a complete tizzy. "I'm not falling in love with him," she said severely, trying to ignore the twisting pain in her stomach and the dull ache in the region of her heart.

An hour later, she was tossing and turning on the hard bed in her room, unable to explain her feelings of loss. Finding a dark spot on the ceiling to focus on, she started counting, then stopped. "I don't need to live my life in a soporific state," she said aloud.

The next things she was aware of were bright sunlight, a hand gently shaking her, and the persistent calling of her name. "Please wake up," Maria said. "I've already given him three cups of coffee."

Lita tried to shake the fuzz balls from her brain. "Who?"

Maria smiled. "Cade Thomas. He is waiting for you and I am running out of conversation."

Cade was here! Lita jumped out of bed and slipped into her robe. Hurrying to the bathroom, she glanced at her patient aunt. "That's impossible," she said, grabbing her toothbrush and toothpaste. "There's no end to your ability to talk." Joy sprang to her heart. Cade had come!

Maria grinned. "There is no need for makeup," she teased. "Your cheeks and eyes are in full bloom."

Five minutes later, dressed in a lacy apricot camisole and matching slacks, Lita stepped into the kitchen. Cade arose and came toward her.

"Good morning, lovely." He kissed the full, unglossed lips.

"Good morning," she said breathlessly.

He pulled out a chair for her. Maria dished out scrambled eggs and warm muffins. "Señor Thomas brought these for your breakfast." She pointed toward the scrumptious baked goods. "You like a woman with more meat on her bones, eh?" she said to Cade.

Lita laughed. "If you bring any more goodies, I'll burst right out of my cos . . . tume—" Crimson flushed her cheeks.

Cade seemed to catch the slip. She had forgotten to tell him that Maria didn't know about the Mariposa Club and its girly shows.

When Lita only took a small portion of eggs, Cade spooned the rest onto his plate. "I like what I see right now," he said, slipping his hand under the table to touch her thigh. "Although a few pounds would add a new dimension to Lita's lovely figure."

She reached down to brush his hand away. Maria wasn't used to modern ways. "I wondered where you were last night."

He looked up, then a smile curved his mouth. "Another woman would have talked around that. You simply put it bluntly."

"It doesn't seem to do much good," she complained. "I never get a straight answer." Maria moved across the room and out to the courtyard.

"Did you miss me?" he asked.

She thought for a moment. Cade seemed sure of himself. Perhaps she shouldn't add to that arrogance. "Yes," she said quietly.

"I missed you too."

Well, so much for evasive answers. She looked at him and waited. If he thought she was going to add anything, he was wrong.

"I have a yacht available," he said. "Would you like to sail with me?"

"Yes." She hesitated. "If I can be back on time for work."

He smiled, his white teeth shiny and straight. "I promise."

An hour later, the *Sea Sprite* headed into the waves. From his position on the fly bridge, located above the saloon, Cade had deftly maneuvered the forty-foot yacht from its slip.

Gulls flew overhead and sea spray flicked against Lita's cheeks as a frothy trail of water was left behind. When only the distant outline of land remained, Cade cut the engine, climbed down the ladder, and joined her on deck.

"Champ made us some southern fried chicken and Virginia ham sandwiches. There are a couple of salads and desserts and wine—"

"Stop!" She put her hands over her ears. "I could gain ten pounds just thinking about all that food."

"You're too active to gain weight," he said. "Why, I can span that tiny waist"—he proceeded to demonstrate—"with my hands."

Aware of the darkening of her eyes, he dropped his hands to his sides. "Let me show you around," he suggested, allowing her to precede him into the cabin.

The interior was decorated in a nautical theme of white and blue with touches of red. Paneled in teak, the saloon was furnished with a stereo, a color television, two barrel chairs, and a sofa. She was surprised to find the galley fully equipped, including a refrigerator-freezer. In the pointed bow, along the walls, were two bunks with drawers underneath. Cade opened the door of a full-length locker which was half-filled with men's clothing.

"This is so lovely," Lita murmured, following him back to the saloon.

A wave of erotic heat rushed through Cade's body as he observed her pleasure in the yacht. Gazing at her face, he drew a deep breath, suffocatingly aware that she had never looked lovelier. The light breeze lifted her hair in gentle waves; her skin held a slight honey cast.

Close-fitting slacks emphasized every curve of her long legs and slender thighs. He found himself staring in awe at the full breasts beneath the lacy camisole. A symphony of rushing swells and ebbs swept through his body as his imagination played havoc with his libido. Swallowing hard, he clenched his hands to keep from grabbing that enticing form.

His body was reacting to primitive emotions as intense heat raced through his veins. Hold it, he warned himself. Do something. Eat. That was it.

"Why don't we have a snack and then sun ourselves for a while," he suggested. She nodded in agreement.

Food was the farthest thing from her mind, but she made a good show of interest as she helped him place the dishes on the table. She kept her eyes lowered, aware of the unmasked desire in his.

Barely tasting the chicken and salads, she waited for something to happen. She was certain that today would be a turning point in their relationship. Was she ready for it? Was a starving kitten ready to lap up a bowl of milk?

"You're very quiet," he said, breaking the silence.

She smiled. "Just deep in thought."

His heart did a double flip. "Have you had enough food?"

She nodded, picking up the plates and clearing the table. "Ready for some sun?" she asked.

His eyes told her he was ready for much more than that. When he placed his arm around her to lead her to the deck, he touched a sensitive spot. She flinched and laughed. She giggled again as he purposely tickled her. Then, suddenly, as she saw the smoldering passion in his gaze, she gasped and the smile died on her lips.

When he lowered his lips to hers, she met him half-way, eager to be absorbed by his moist warmth. His tongue explored the soft inner flesh of her mouth. She leaned into him as she lost all strength in her legs.

"Lita," he groaned. "Let me love you."

Her lashes lifted and her gaze held pain, uncertainty.

"I need your love," he whispered. "Please say yes."

"Oh, Cade," she murmured, feeling the thud of his heart against her palms.

As the trim ship bobbed in the ocean currents, he held her close to him, so close she could barely breathe.

"Don't refuse me," he pleaded. "I can't go on like this."

"It isn't right," she said breathlessly.

"Whatever two adults agree to do is right, if it doesn't hurt anyone. You can't allow that old love to keep you from a new one."

Old love? she thought. Jeremy? She had never really loved him. Who was Jeremy, anyway?

"I know you need me, Lita. A woman with your stormy passion can't deny herself. And for what reason?" A shudder went through him. "We need each other."

Her heart raced at the sound of his seductive voice. She felt as vulnerable as flotsam on a gale-tossed sea. How many other women had he said the same words to? she wondered. Then she put her thoughts into words and told him exactly what she was thinking.

"You're wrong," he said, kissing her cheek and nibbling on her earlobe. She felt her own heart beat in rhythm with his as he continued. "If I wanted just any woman, I could have had a dozen today."

"I thought you had—last night."

"Oh, Lita." He laughed huskily. "I can't believe you said that."

"It's what I was thinking."

"I only hope you'll always be this honest with me." *Always.* In their case, always could be a very short time . . .

His warm mouth roved over her neck until she felt dizzy. Clinging to him as though she would never let him go, she responded with her own fiery brand of kisses.

"Devour me, darling," he begged, his hands slipping the spaghetti straps from her shoulders. "Let me see them." He groaned in tormented pleasure. "I've wanted to hold your lovely breasts, kiss them, absorb their beauty."

"Oh, Cade." Her head writhed back and forth as he took one pink tip in his mouth and caressed the other with his thumb and forefinger. A wild, throbbing sensation soared through her body, ending in her sensitive femininity with a jolt that arched her body against his.

"Oh, love," he moaned, unbuttoning her slacks, then sliding them over her hips. He unhooked the camisole and eased it off her shoulders, his eyes glorying in her beauty. Then, with his thumbs, he pushed down the silky bikini panties and watched as they fluttered to the deck. She stood before him—naked, unbelievably lovely, enticing.

Scooping her into his arms, he carried her to the bulky terry cloth pillows spread on the deck. Burying his head between the milk-white mounds, he tore at his shirt, the buttons popping as hot uncontrollable urges flared through him. He quickly discarded the rest of his clothing, then was beside her, teasing each breast, tasting the delicate salty flavor of her skin. He hungrily caressed her with his lips, whispering incoherently as he blazed a torrid trail across her creamy flesh.

After days of yearning for him, Lita felt the rising tide of her responsiveness. The scent of him heightened her emotions: the tingling mixture of after-shave and masculine perspiration tempted her primitive senses. She let herself drift, feel, taste, touch, love.

One of his hands crept to the delicate flesh below her lush coppery triangle, gently rubbing, tantalizing her until she groaned in pleasure. All doubts were brushed aside as though a gentle breeze had cleansed her mind, allowing only the tempting play of slender fingers and the tormenting blaze of Cade's mouth to enter her awareness.

Her throbbing lips and tongue thanked him silently for ignoring his own needs in order to arouse her to the fullest. At the precise moment she thought she would explode with passion if he did not take her, he nudged her legs apart and penetrated her warm moistness. The age-old thrusts and counterthrusts spiraled them to the edge of fulfillment, then, finally, to a shuddering surrender of incredible emotions that left them spent and exquisitely gratified.

Cade kept her imprisoned beneath him as his mouth possessed hers in a hot, wet kiss. When tears flowed freely from her eyes, she felt him grow rigid and he slid to the cushions.

"What is it?" he whispered tightly.

A sensation of tenderness caught in her throat and she could only shake her head.

"Please tell me," he urged, his voice low and concerned.

"I don't know," she said, opening her eyes.

"You're not . . . sorry we made love?"

"No, no," she murmured. "It was . . . it was . . ."

"I wanted it to be good for you, better than with any other man who has ever possessed you." His gaze reflected uncertainty.

In her wildest thoughts she would never have pictured Cade insecure in his ability to arouse a woman to the pinnacle of her desire. "It was wonderful," she said, her fingers caressing his shoulders.

"I'm so glad." His gentle smile warmed her banked fires of passion. "It's what I wanted for you—your pleasure first."

"Oh, Cade." She sighed and nestled against his frame.

She was his, he thought. Fingertips stroked her face

and neck, working down to her breasts and stomach, then his hand cupped the soft triangle protectively. Leisurely this time, he rekindled the tiny embers, adding fuel to the flame with gentle nips at her shoulder. He felt the simmering warmth within her, and he teased the delicate spots until she raised herself off the pillows in a blaze of scorching desire.

"Cade," she cried out, clutching at his muscled shoulders, pleading for another soaring journey to celestial heights.

"Trust me," he murmured as he melted into her and gave her much, much more than she had begged for.

The cool breezes wafted over them as they lay in each other's arms beneath the soothing Caribbean sun. Slumber nudged them gently and Cade protectively placed a towel over her, then joined her in sleep.

An hour later, he shook her. "Lita, we have to head back to San Juan."

She jolted upright, urging the wispy effects of Cade's lovemaking to be cleared from her head. Glancing at her watch, she jumped to her feet. "I'll be late for work!"

"I'll get you there on time," he promised, grabbing his jeans and racing up the ladder to the fly bridge. When the engine started with a roar, she gave a silent sigh of thanks. Easing into her clothes, she looked down at their bed of love, recalling the deliriously happy afternoon they had shared. Was this the beginning of a relationship with Cade, or the end? He had asked her to trust him, she remembered in a haze of thrilled emotions. But she couldn't forget that her simple questions had been met with evasion or silence.

The yacht whizzed over the waves toward port as Lita climbed up the ladder to join Cade. His back was to her, one leg poised to pull on his jeans. When she slipped her arms around his waist, he paused to allow her to place her head against his back.

He chuckled softly. "If you want me to get you to San Juan, we won't have any more time today for that."

Her hands slid lower. "Too bad," she teased.

He sucked in his breath. "I'll take you to work and pick you up later, okay?"

"Mmmm," she murmured.

"Oh, God, Lita, don't touch me again or I swear I'll stop this craft and ravish you."

She tickled him and he yelped. "That was so you won't forget me while I'm working."

He turned to face her, his hands on her shoulders. "Forgetting you would be impossible."

"I'm glad."

His mouth brushed hers as he pulled up the jeans and zipped them. "Now, I'm afraid I'll have to concentrate on getting us safely to shore."

As Cade sat down to operate the controls of the *Sea Sprite*, Lita smiled with satisfaction. Playfully, she came up behind him and nipped his ear. That should hold him until midnight, she thought. Then the happy thoughts faded. How long would she be able to keep him interested after tonight?

Thirty minutes after midnight, Lita and Cade were in his hotel room, snacking on delicacies and sipping imported champagne. Lita sighed. "I must have been hungry."

"I still am." He removed the glass from her hand and pressed her into the couch.

As his mouth consumed hers, she threaded her fingers through his thick hair. When he pulled back she looked up at him, her eyes glowing like polished jade, her soft lips open and waiting.

"Come, my sweet," he murmured against her ear. "Let's make sensual music together."

Lita soared on wings of love to his bed. Is this marvelous man real? she asked herself.

As she lay beneath his masterful body, he answered her question with positive action. Cade Thomas was very, very real.

Lita pinched herself to be sure she wasn't still dreaming. Glancing at her watch, she saw it was noon. She lay back in her bed, thinking of Cade and their glorious day and night together. "I must be in love," she said aloud, thrilled at the sound of her own words. Was he planning to come for her this afternoon? He hadn't said, although she rather took it for granted that he would.

She showered, then dressed in white shorts and a bright red knit pullover. The color rioted with her hair, but she laughed off the thought. Having auburn hair wasn't like being a carrot top.

She leaped up at the sound of the bell and raced for the door. It was a visitor for one of the other tenants. Disappointed, she roamed around the courtyard, picking an occasional weed out of the flower beds. A tiny lizard scurried for shelter. She wasn't able to sit down for more than five minutes.

Sighing heavily, she did some warm-up exercises. Maria had gone visiting and the neighbors were probably taking their siestas. Disillusionment was building inside her as she kept an eye on the clock. Wasn't he coming?

She sat in the shade at a table in the courtyard supposedly reading. But the hero's name was always Cade and the heroine's Lita. "I wish we had a telephone," she grumbled as the book fell from her hand.

Maria returned at six o'clock to find her niece pacing the kitchen floor. "What's wrong?" she asked in a worried tone.

"I haven't heard from Cade."

Maria flung herself into a chair and sighed. "Ah, you young people have such problems. He didn't come. Did he promise?"

"No."

"So?" She shrugged. "He is a businessman. He has other things on his mind besides women."

Lita grunted. "I'm going to take a shower."

"Make it a cold one," Maria teased. Then the bathroom door slammed shut.

At ten minutes past midnight, Lita charged out of the stage door expectantly, only to come to a halt when she saw that the Rolls-Royce was nowhere in sight. Where was Cade? She tried to swallow her disappointment, but could do nothing to dispel the lump in her throat.

Unlocking the bicycle, she pedaled down the alley and

into the busy street, suddenly worried that something had happened to him. She decided to check his hotel. Perhaps he was tied up with a customer.

A nerve throbbed in her neck as she parked the bike outside the Caribe Hilton. One of the attendants told her she could not leave it there. When she pushed a dollar bill into his hand, he grumblingly allowed her to wheel it into the parking area.

Lita could hear the sound of music from the Club Caribe as she hurried to the reception desk. "Señor Thomas," she said. "Is he in?"

The young man looked down the registry. "We have no one by that name."

Nervously, Lita gave him the room number.

"We have a new occupant registered in there since this afternoon," the clerk said.

"But I have to find him," she blurted out.

The clerk gave her an odd glance and asked her to wait a minute. After conversing with one of the other room clerks, he returned to her. "I am sorry, but that room was vacated early this morning."

A pain shot through her heart. Lita nodded and stumbled away. Checked out. Cade had left? She shook her head, feeling the pressure building behind her lids. It was a mistake. It had to be.

She whirled toward the elevators, oblivious to the strange looks she was getting from the hotel personnel. Maybe she had asked for the wrong room number.

Moments later, she found herself on the twelfth floor. At the end of the hall, more certain than ever that the room number was correct, she tapped softly on the door. After several more attempts, she turned to leave, but just then the door opened. A middle-aged man looked at her inquiringly.

"Is Señor Thomas here?" she asked hopefully.

He shook his head, beady eyes taking in her lovely face and figure. "There is no one here by that name." He paused. "Perhaps you would like to join me for some champagne?"

Lita just stared at him, her eyes wide with distress. "No, thank you, señor," she whispered.

"But"—he laughed caustically—"a man, any man, is better than none, eh?"

Straightening her shoulders, she swallowed her disillusionment. "No, señor," she said, tossing her head. "I'm afraid just *any* man won't do." She spun away, aware that he had not closed the door.

Cade had left without a word. Tears stung her lids, pain stabbed at her chest. Stoically, her head held high, Lita Jamison walked toward the elevators.

Five

Lita collapsed on her bed, burying her tear-stained face in the pillow. Now she was sure that Cade's only intention, from his first glimpse of her on the stage at the Mariposa Club, had been to make her come alive in his arms. Misery filled her tired body. By resisting his advances, she had piqued his male ego. Now he had won and gone on to the next challenge.

Unwilling to awaken Maria, she cried softly, battering the pillow with her fists. She wanted to hate him, but could not. She had thought she'd made an impression on him. He had even said "Trust me" in a seemingly sincere way. How could she have allowed herself to be sucked into a situation that was a repeat of, but much more severe than, the situation six months ago?

"If I could find a way to pay him back," she murmured into the shadows, "I would do it—eagerly." But he probably had no intention of returning to San Juan and she certainly would not seek him out in Florida.

"Admit your defeat and go on from there." But it was easier whispering the words than implementing them. You're strong, she told herself, gripping the pillow for support. You came through once before, and you can again. "If I live to be one hundred," she vowed aloud, "I'll never trust another man."

The memory of other rejections stormed into her consciousness. It had always been this way.

"You'll have to act like a grown-up," Elva Jamison had told her thirteen-year-old daughter. "We can't be here for your dance recital. You know how important this expedition is for your father and me. Why, we'll be the first to bring back that species of Amazon flower . . ."

Lita pulled her thoughts back to the present, but something deep inside her wanted to review those unhappy childhood days. She felt herself slipping back. She was seventeen . . .

"The housekeeper will bring you and your date back from the prom, if you have no means of transportation. Why did you choose a young man who's had his license revoked?

"We won't be able to attend your graduation, but here's a little gift from both of us." She remembered the check for a thousand dollars that had fluttered to the floor when her mother's back was turned.

"We can't be with you when you're at the swim meet. What's so important about it? You'd think you were competing for a national title." And when she had actually swum her heart out and won second place in the big event, her parents hadn't been there to cheer her on and see her triumph.

We can't be there, we won't be there, rang in her ears until she clapped her hands over them to ease the remembered pain. She had never been important enough to the famous botanists for them to make an effort to love or care about her.

Elva Jamison had been so different from her sister, Maria. The comparison was shocking. Where one was vain and cold, the other was selfless and warm.

I almost accepted Cade's offer to leave with him, she thought. *I know I never consciously accepted, but the thought was always stirring inside, a little ray of hope that couldn't be smothered. Until now.*

When pearly shafts of light heralded a new day, Lita finally slept.

*　　*　　*

At noon, she was sitting on the grassy bank of the fort above the swirling surf, trying to fathom the reason for Cade's departure. A steady line of visitors came and went at the fort as she recalled, with bitterness, the lovely afternoon spent with him there. Why had he tried so hard to persuade her to join him on the trip to Florida? Was it just to instill confidence in her?

At three o'clock, she biked back to Maria's. Being alone wasn't the proper therapy. Her aunt's chatter was preferable to the haunting sound of the breakers.

As she found herself scrutinizing every sleek black car, she realized that she was automatically searching for Cade. That had to stop. She would not let him drive her insane, she vowed silently. Unlocking the gate, she wheeled the bicycle into the quiet courtyard.

Maria had gone to the market and in a way she was glad. She suddenly felt exhausted, as though she could sleep for days. She let herself into the apartment, swallowed a few aspirins, and closed the door to her room. Stripping off her clothes, she sprawled on the bed and pulled a sheet over her.

"I'll forget him," she promised herself aloud. "I will, I will. . ."

Cade Hamilton flipped through his wallet for his telephone credit card and reached for the phone. Should he try to call Lita at the club? She might be hurt and angry if the owner learned of their involvement. Slowly, his hand slumped to his side.

His mother and sister-in-law were waiting down the corridor of the hospital and there had been no opportunity to consider any other way of contacting Lita. The hours since his arrival in Miami had been spent keeping a vigil with his family at the bedside of his younger brother, Jeremy. Fortunate enough to obtain a seat on the first plane out of San Juan, he had had only a short time in which to pack and get to the airport.

What was Lita thinking? Surely she would understand an emergency situation. Wait. He could send her a telegram. Why hadn't he thought of it before? But before he could do so, he was interrupted.

"Jeremy is awake and wants to see you," his sister-in-law, Debbie Hamilton, said, interrupting his thoughts. "The doctor says that the immediate crisis is over."

"Thank God," Cade said, briskly accompanying the dark-haired young woman down the hall.

"He's going to be all right, isn't he?" Her misty eyes were seeking reassurance.

Cade stopped to look at her. "We both know that the bullet lodged in his spine is moving into a dangerous position. It may only be a matter of time." She nodded and he heard her swallow hard.

The police had declared the shooting an accidentally inflicted wound. Although others had accepted that explanation, he could not. His wild young brother loved life and women far too much to "accidentally" commit such an act. He was always happy, secure, even though his devil-may-care attitude did make him a bit lax in his responsibilities to the family business.

Jeremy should be enjoying life—flying over the waves in his hydroplane, speeding along the track in his racing car. He had been so flamboyant, so carefree, until he had taken up with that sexy redhead.

Cade's heart leaped into his throat at the thought of Lita. He couldn't blame his brother for falling for the sorceress. He felt a tenderness so intense, it left him breathless. Lately a new kind of doubt niggled at him. What if he was wrong about her and someone totally unsuspected was guilty? He wanted to believe in Lita's innocence, yet all the clues seemed to point to her—the redhead seen leaving in Jeremy's car, abandoning her job without notice, taking a flight to Puerto Rico later that afternoon, and her continued refusal to speak about the man she had cared for.

He pushed open the door to Jeremy's room. His brother's eyes were half closed, his lips moving soundlessly. Cade was overwhelmed by searing pain. As Debbie came forward to touch his hand gingerly, Jeremy focused fully on her. A tortured groan passed his lips.

"Mother should be back from the cafeteria shortly,"

Cade told Jeremy. Then to Debbie, "I'd like five minutes alone with him, if you don't mind."

Debbie hesitated, then nodded and left.

"Jeremy," Cade said in a low voice, "please tell me if Lita Jamison is the one who fired the bullet. I have to square this with her if she is."

Jeremy slowly turned his head from side to side. "She wasn't the one?" Cade pressed. "Or you're not telling? Which?"

His brother did not respond.

"I know where she is, Jeremy. I've seen her, spoken to her."

Cade's brother lifted a hand and extended two fingers.

"You're not telling me, right?" Cade sighed as Jeremy closed his eyes. "Damn," he whispered softly. "You're still protecting her—or someone else." He paused. "Jeremy?"

Cade unclenched his hands, feeling a terrible sense of helplessness sweep over him. He walked out of the room with heavy steps. "He's sleeping again," he said to Debbie. One trembling hand whipped over his dark hair, then dropped to his side. A nerve jumped in his cheek.

Watching life slowly ebb from the brother he loved was like being torn apart. The stress of dividing his loyalties between Jeremy, whom he'd felt deep affection for all his life and the young woman he'd met just days ago was sapping his strength.

"I don't suppose there's much use in your being here now that the crisis point has been passed," Debbie said. "Ray is flying in from the Coast today."

"I'm glad he'll be with you," he said. "You need his comfort."

Cade had always thought that Debbie would marry Jeremy. But one summer, after a rapid courtship, she had accepted Ray's proposal. Perhaps she had decided that Jeremy was not as stable as his older brother.

Calm, determined Ray was a rather stark contrast to flashy, exuberant Jeremy. Recently, Cade had wondered at his older brother's mood swings and why he had suddenly decided to move to California. He had thrown himself feverishly into Hamilton Industries' West Coast operation.

Cade swore under his breath. What difference did it make? Never in his whole life had he felt so vulnerable, and part of it had to do with that siren in San Juan.

"Perhaps you're right, Debbie," he said, "Maybe I should return to Puerto Rico and continue negotiations with that shirt manufacturer. Since Jeremy isn't in immediate danger now, I'm not really needed here. Besides, Jeremy might be happier if I'm not here to grill him about the shooting."

Six doctors had held consultations regarding his brother's condition. He might lie in this hospital bed for years.

Debbie nodded sadly, but beneath the sadness on her face, Cade detected another emotion that he couldn't identify.

He bent to kiss his sister-in-law's cheek. "I'll find Mother downstairs. Keep me informed," he murmured, and hurried to the elevator.

Five hours later, his plane touched down at San Juan International Airport. He would have time to catch a taxi to the hotel, then meet Lita after her performance. Would he be able to hide the renewed suspicion that festered in him? Why wouldn't Jeremy acknowledge her innocence or guilt?

Cade knew that when he saw her again, all the old allegiances would dim and he would once again be lost in her charms. After the other day on the boat and the night at the hotel, he was certain that she had irreversibly heated his blood and seduced his mind.

He was forced to admit that no other woman had ever come close to piercing the armor he wore around his heart. Why it was there had always been a mystery. Perhaps he was just unemotional, but that hypothesis would have to be discarded. What he felt for Lita was a driving need, an overwhelming sense of both contentment and excitement in her presence.

It was something that could not be set aside or ignored. She was the very foundation of all that he previously hadn't bothered to consider for his future—a wife, a family, a home.

At eleven forty-five, he entered the Mariposa Club, waved to his friends, and ordered a drink at the bar. The place was packed with patrons, many with the name of a cruise ship on their lapels. It was a package deal—two drinks and the floor show for one price.

Eagerly, he awaited the end of the act on stage, hungry for a glimpse of the woman who caused his heart to pound. He supposed he had asked for this, being so wound up in his brother's welfare that he was driven to return to Puerto Rico to come up with an answer.

Cade thought back on their conversations. Each time Lita had started to loosen up and seemed about to speak of Jeremy, she had caught herself before she revealed anything about their affair. She had a temper which was apparently held in check. She also seemed sincere, loving, and had the most delectably seductive body he had ever seen.

His experience with women was certainly not minimal. He had had his share of them. Now he was forced to question his motives regarding Lita. His fingers drummed on the bar, matching the beat of his heart against his rib cage. His stomach was in a tightly wound knot. Adding to his frustration was the realization that Lita hadn't given much indication of her feelings for him. He couldn't remember ever needing to know from any other woman how she felt about him.

But knowing would create another problem between them. He would have to admit his feelings for her. One hand raked through his thick hair. What was so special about her anyway? He scanned the room, observing other lovely ladies. Then it came to him. It was her warmth, the sympathetic nature of Lita. The expression in her soft green eyes when she looked at him told him *he* was special to her.

The applause brought him back to the present. As the curtains opened, he felt his heart flip over. She was in her usual position on the stage and he watched her go through the routine. But there was something different about her tonight. Her mask of nonchalance had slipped. The cold, unaffected smile had been replaced by a hardened, almost bitter one. She stared above the heads of the crowd.

Cade felt the stirring in his loins. You're thirty-five, not eighteen, you fool, he thought.

As the performance ended and some of the men in the front rows clapped and yelled for an encore, Cade arose, hiked up his slacks, and buttoned the expensive jacket. He would have a few minutes in which to purchase a flower.

But when he picked up his car and drove into the alley fifteen minutes later, Lita's bicycle was gone. She couldn't have traveled far. Taking the main street, he circled back to the club and tried another route.

Then he saw her, riding the dilapidated bike, her resplendent hair flowing in the breeze. He passed her slowly, hoping to catch her attention, but she continued down the street, oblivious to any vehicle or person.

He pulled into a parking space and waited for her, only pushing open the door and stepping into her path when she was about ten feet from him. He heard her gasp, and the next thing he knew, she had fallen into his arms and the bicycle was careening drunkenly across the street.

"Gee, honey, that was some greeting," he said, laughing, when his breath had returned. He set her on her feet, aware of the disbelief in her gaze.

"You came back," she said hollowly, her breasts rising and falling in agitated rhythm.

"Of course," he murmured huskily.

"Why?" she asked in her usual forthright manner. She seemed to take in his elegant silk suit and soft Italian shoes in a single glance.

"Do you think I could forget you?" His eyes shone with unexplained wickedness.

"Very easily." Her chin rose.

"Then I'll have to prove how wrong you are."

"Two days without a word from you." Was it a question or a statement?

"I can explain." He put her away from him and motioned for her to slide across to the passenger seat. Then he raced down the street and picked up the bicycle, opened the trunk, and slid it in.

"I'm afraid the trunk will have to remain open," he said, climbing into the car. "I'm really famished after my flight from Miami. How does a quick meal at Champ's sound?"

She nodded, biting her lip. It was as though he did this every day, she thought. Leaving without a word, then expecting her to welcome him. He didn't owe her anything, but she had thought . . .

She felt his gaze on her from time to time as the Rolls sped along the streets. She could hear the bicycle rattling in the trunk. Fifteen minutes later, they were seated in a secluded booth, their orders taken, an air of suspense hovering between them. Cade reached across the table to capture her hand.

"I'm sorry I couldn't notify you," he began, aware of the tightening in his throat, the flutter of her lashes as she looked away. "I received an emergency call that night after I returned to the hotel. One of my . . . relatives is critically ill."

"I'm sorry," she murmured, wondering at his hesitation before the word *relatives*. Suspicion chased all logic from her mind. Was it a woman? Someone he was deeply involved with? A wife?

"Except for a quick shower and change of clothes, I've been at the hospital since I arrived in Miami."

"How is she?" Lita asked, meeting his gaze.

Cade gave her a half smile. "It's a *he*, and the prognosis is the same. He may not have too much time left, but this crisis is over, thank God." The words choked him.

"I'm sorry," she repeated.

He nodded. "If you've ever watched someone slowly die . . ."

She turned her palm to meet his, her natural warmth and compassion surfacing. What she found herself holding was a trembling hand. Only then did she notice the tired lines near his mouth, the purple shadows beneath his eyes.

She wanted to believe him. "Why didn't you leave word at the club?"

"I didn't know how you would feel about that, since the owners are friends of mine."

"Or perhaps"—she hesitated—"you didn't want them to know you're interested in one of their lowly dancers?"

He withdrew the warmth of his hand from hers and

leaned back in his seat. For the first time since they had met, his features displayed a taut line of anger. She had obviously drawn one too many conclusions and her honesty had forced the emotion to surface.

"I shouldn't have said that," she said quickly. "I realize you're tired. I doubt that you need any accusations tonight."

His eyes noted the sincerity in hers, the soft, pliable lips, the straight, proud nose. Her makeup was a great deal heavier than usual. Was she covering the ravages of a sleepless night, two days of wondering why he hadn't tried to contact her? She cared. He would bet his last dollar on it.

The waiter arrived with their meal; his jokes were met with silence. Easing away, he seemed to hover covertly. Cade had been anything but cold and unresponsive to the young man the last time. Lita flashed him a gentle smile, then toyed with the food.

"I'm sorry," Cade said finally. "As you say, I'm exhausted from lack of sleep and worry."

She wanted to ask why he had come back. Unfinished business? Was it something to do with his distributing firm—or could it be her? Don't be stupid, she chastised herself. Who would travel all those miles for Lita Jamison?

"Has anyone ever tried to jump on the stage while the dancers are performing?" he asked suddenly.

A frown crossed her forehead, quickly hidden. "Not since I've been there."

"How long is that?" he asked, buttering a roll.

"Uh, four weeks."

"Isn't it dangerous for a woman to be cycling in the streets alone after midnight?"

"I suppose," she said. "But I've never been approached."

"That's difficult to believe."

Why was he baiting her? she wondered. That awful feeling of rejection clawed at her chest. There had to be a reason for his bringing up the subject. It was almost as though he regretted picking her up tonight.

"Then you'll have to disbelieve it." The words came out slowly, tonelessly. She was aware of anger building in her, of a flush that seemed to rise from her throat. She didn't need his brand of degradation. Or any man's. Perhaps her job was not of the highest moral quality, but it provided an honest living.

Her chin rose, wide snapping eyes meeting his. "You know something, Cade." She leaned forward so he couldn't mistake what she was about to say. "I don't give a damn whether you believe me or not! Quite suddenly, it occurs to me that you're really not that important in my life!"

She stood up, grabbed her purse, and headed for a telephone booth. Before she could lift the receiver to call a cab, however, Cade caught her hand and held it against his heart.

"I'm sorry, love," he said huskily. "I'm just not myself tonight."

He was so handsome, so totally vulnerable, she could have cried. She nodded, quick to forgive. "Why don't we leave now?" she suggested. "You'll feel much better after a decent night's sleep."

"If you'll spend it with me . . ."

She shook her head. As much as she wanted to be with him, she felt her decision was wisest.

While Cade paid the bill and conversed with Champ, she slipped into the rest room. Maybe she was better off without him, she thought. She sighed wearily and applied a fresh coat of lipstick. Dealing with Cade certainly took a lot out of her. If she didn't feel so much for him . . .

In the twenty minutes it took to reach her neighborhood, there was an uneasy silence between them. When the Rolls drew up in front of her home, Cade got out, removed the bicycle, and wheeled it toward her. She had already unlocked the gate when he pulled her against his hard body.

"Just let me hold you," he murmured. They stood in each other's arms for several minutes before he stepped back. "Good night, Lita," he said, running a hand through his dark hair.

She pulled the gate shut behind her, her eyes troubled and sad. "Good-bye, Cade," she whispered.

He nodded and walked around the front of the car.

Moments later the Rolls purred down the street. Lita parked the bike, releasing a heartfelt sigh. Her lower lip quivered. Brushing one hand over her cheek impatiently, she opened the door of Maria's apartment.

"I guess it wasn't meant for me to understand you," she whispered.

"I want you to come back to Florida with me." Cade tipped Lita's chin up to gaze fully at her. His tall, lithe frame took up a good part of the small kitchen.

"Oh, no. That's . . . not possible."

"Why not? You only have a job holding you back."

She laughed nervously. "It's much more than that." He waited for her to continue. "I made one very bad mistake in choosing a man. I don't really think I could survive another."

"You never told me anything about that."

"Because there's not much to tell."

He eyed her skeptically. "You ran away?"

"I guess you could call it that."

"Why don't you want to talk about it? I have an exceptionally sympathetic ear."

"Why dig up an old love affair?"

"To get it out of your system. Exorcise your ghosts."

She bit into her lower lip. "He said he didn't love me anymore, that there was someone else. I went a little crazy."

"Yes?" he pressed. Was he holding his breath? "What did you do then?"

"I don't . . . really remember too much."

"Because you don't want to?"

"No, no," she whispered, overcome by the horror of that day. She felt the blood drain from her face, those weird images that she hadn't visualized in months returning to haunt her. *The car.* She had been in an accident. "I don't want to talk about it anymore," she said.

"All right," he agreed lightly. "We won't discuss it now. But you do know that in order to commit yourself fully to any other man, the old love must be erased."

"No." She shook her head. "I don't want a commitment."

"You don't?"

"No."

"What *do* you want?" he asked brusquely.

"I said good-bye to you last night, Cade. Didn't you hear me?"

He nodded, his eyes narrowing. "I realized this morning what you had said. Last night, it felt like I had giant hammers pounding in my head." He held her to him. "I can't let you go, Lita. You mean too much to me." *We also have to clear up a mighty important question.*

He heard her breathy sigh. "I'm not asking anything of you," she said quietly.

He studied her, then leaned forward, his tongue exploring her sensual earlobe, both hands pulling her thighs to his. Fanning the fires of her passion, he nibbled at the fine skin of her throat and stroked her shoulders. When he reached beneath her loose top with one hand, her breath came in tiny, quick pants.

"Honey, let's get away from here," he said. "We'll spend the afternoon on the *Sea Sprite*."

Aroused and rocking from the emotions he had evoked, commanded by the brilliant eyes she was constantly aware of, she didn't resist his suggestion. She wanted him—as much as he seemed to want her.

With his arm firmly about her waist, Cade led her through the courtyard to the car parked at the curb. When she was seated, he strode around to the driver's side.

"Is there some other reason you want to remain on the island?" he asked. The engine roared to life.

"I don't want to leave Aunt Maria," she said. "She means a great deal to me . . . the only relative who cares whether I live or die."

"I offered to take her with us," he reminded her. "Or have her join us later."

"You should know how proud these people are, Cade. Maria doesn't take handouts."

"Good Lord." He swore under his breath. "I can certainly afford the air fare for her. It's not as though it's a hardship."

"I can imagine her feelings. To her it would be as though she owed you something that was not repayable."

"Have you asked her?"

Lita's head swung to meet his gaze. She hadn't discussed the matter with Maria. "No. I didn't have to."

Cade let out a long sigh.

An hour later, the trim yacht was humming over the calm Atlantic, a condition highly unusual for that normally wave-tossed body of water. Cade's eyes held hers as she stood beside him in the cockpit, and he only occasionally looked away to check his instruments.

He had thought about their relationship from the time he awoke with a pounding head to the first glimpse of her at noon. He desperately wanted an affair with her. If he was successful in persuading her to come to Florida, she would have to quit her job. Would he feel responsible for disrupting her life? He abruptly reminded himself of the main reason for his pursuit. Sometimes he seemed to lose all his objectivity when it came to Lita.

He smiled at her. "I brought champagne. We're going to feast on the goodies Champ packed. Do you remember that last time we left most of them?"

He had ordered the food beforehand; he'd been sure of convincing her to come with him, she realized. "Yes, I remember," she murmured, visualizing the promise of the cushions on the rear deck and the sensuous movement of their bodies.

"We're going to do it right this time."

She grinned impishly. "I didn't realize we'd done anything wrong last time."

"Ummm." He growled low in his throat, reaching for her. "Everything was perfect." He squeezed her waist and dropped a kiss on her breast. "They're beautiful." His eyes devoured the fabric covering the high, firm mounds of flesh. "I'm jealous that other men can view them. I want to feast on them, to bring you to the highest point of arousal."

Lita licked her lips and swallowed. His words were so visual, she squirmed, unable to still the pounding in the lower part of her body. Almost in a frenzy, she reached down to nibble his lips, incapable of controlling the hot flashes that seared her veins.

Her tongue penetrated his mouth and she fell forward, collapsing in his arms. "Hurry," she whispered. "Hurry."

His hand shot out to the controls, and the next instant all was quiet and serene. Only the sound of the swells lapping against the hull broke the silence. But the inanimate objects were the only ones that were tranquil. Two bodies moved hastily down the ladder and onto the deck.

Lita kicked off her crepe-soled shoes. Her eyes, liquid with love, never left Cade, and his mouth came down to cover hers while he unbuttoned her shirt. As he peeled it off her, his eyes glazed over. Unzipping the white cotton shorts, he pushed them down over her hips. They slid to the deck noiselessly. Lace panties were eased down her legs and he stooped to lift her feet and toss them aside.

"Let me," she breathed as he started to remove his T-shirt. Beginning at his navel, she brazenly kissed each inch of his flesh as the fabric was lifted to his neck. When she flipped it over his head, she grabbed him, clinging to his lips with her feverish ones, drawing on the hot, moist skin of his mouth.

Easing her hands from his shoulders, past the coarse dark hair of his chest to the button of his jeans, she undid it, poking her finger through the hole and tickling him.

She heard the rumble in his throat and knew she could tarry no longer. There was a rasp of the zipper and the slow descent of his jeans. Stepping out of them quickly, he pulled her down to the cushions. Lita barely felt the heat of the sun on the terry cloth covers, her own flesh was so fiery with desire. She pressed a hand to her forehead to still a wave of dizziness that washed over her.

"Cade," she pleaded. "I can't wait!"

Straddling her, he unleashed the throbbing heat, fusing them together. She felt his sublime and meaningful need like a loving torch as his thrusts became more frenzied.

Spiraling upward in an unending moment of glory,

she whirled with him in tenderness and ardor. Dazed with their shared bliss, they clung together, happy sighs mingling.

Cradled in each other's arms, they lay in breathless wonder, Cade's passion-filled eyes gazing into hers. The sea breeze swept the moistness from their bodies; the sun lovingly caressed them.

So touched was she by their gloriously uplifting union, she rubbed her lips against his. "Cade," she murmured, oblivious to her own vulnerability or anything except the presence of this marvelous man. "Do you believe that I was born to share this moment in time with you?"

He breathed deeply and sighed her name. He pressed his frame to hers and Lita felt the velvet throb against her leg. "I believe," he whispered huskily.

Six

Radiant from several exquisitely passionate bouts of lovemaking, Lita observed Cade as he slept. Long, silky lashes lay against his bronzed cheeks; the shallow murmur of his breath, inches away, caressed her ears. He was beautiful—so masculine, so much of everything she wanted in a mate.

Could she have him? Was it possible for a man who had so long remained single—although she wasn't certain of that—to settle down with just one woman? Love burst from her like blossoms on a warm summer morning.

He had asked her several times to come with him, to share his life. What he hadn't mentioned was for how long. She had made no commitment, letting him think she was uncertain and reluctant to disrupt her life a second time.

But *time* was running out. She knew he could not stay on the island much longer. The fact that he had returned should have convinced her to accept his offer. She was in love with him. Just how deeply she didn't yet know, but enough to make her heart flutter at the mere thought of him.

Her senses were filled with Cade: his musky male scent, the rough texture of the thick, jet hair on his chest, the salty-sweet taste of his firm skin. She loved to hear him murmur against her hair, to behold his gorgeous naked body. He made her feel alive, a woman in every sense of the word. If that alone wasn't love . . .

When his lashes lifted, he smiled at her. She wanted to cry, to laugh, to shout out her feelings.

"I'm glad you covered yourself," he said lazily, gazing at the clothing she had spread to protect herself from the sun.

At the Mariposa Club, her milk-white skin was her fortune. But if she decided to leave with him, that would no longer be a problem. She could bask beneath the Caribbean sky and forget the daily torture of exposing herself to lascivious eyes.

"Ask me again, Cade," she murmured without considering the consequences.

He studied her for lengthy seconds. "I want you to come with me."

She nodded. "I will."

He pulled her closer, absorbing her mouth with his. "Somehow, I knew you would."

"I'll have to give notice."

His eyes clouded. "A day or two more is all the time I can spare."

"I'll talk to the owners tonight," she promised. "They were good enough to give me a chance. I owe them something."

"Of course. But I'm sure they can readily replace you." His fingertips trailed across her lips. "I take that back. No one could replace you." He brushed her clothes aside, bending to take the pink tip of her breast into his mouth, his tongue swirling around it.

"I can't believe I still want more of you!" she cried softly, arching against him.

"I'll make certain you get all you want and then some."

She glanced at her watch. "We should leave, so I can get to the club earlier."

"Ten more minutes." He nuzzled the soft skin of her

stomach. His hands trembled as he lovingly smoothed the silky auburn strands of her hair splayed across the cushions. Inhaling the clean scent, he combed his fingers through the lustrous tresses before raising them to his lips. Then he let them drift back to the pillows.

Gazing into her hauntingly lovely eyes, now filled with passion, he couldn't imagine not having her beside him. Nameless emotions tore through him, overshadowing whatever nebulous thoughts he might have had for his future.

Lita shivered as his lips left a trail of embers over her body. She strained toward him and his swell of arousal burned into her flesh. A low moan, beginning deep in her throat, escaped her lips at the ancient mystery that held them in its tender grasp. He shuddered and groaned, then covered her body with his. With a primitive cry of mastery, he spread her soft thighs. Astonished at the sensations that his entry created, she gripped his shoulders, smothering his mouth, allowing the wild and whirling tensions to overwhelm her.

She responded with total abandon to the magic of his body as he urged her ever upward, withholding his own physical needs to heighten her pleasure. At last, in a rhythmic blending of desire, he exploded the hot, racing passion within her. His name was torn from her lips as the engulfing sensations peaked, then slowly, slowly waned. He hugged her close as he reluctantly whispered that they must leave their love nest to return to San Juan.

But her mouth opened once more and his skillful, pulsating tongue branded her as his again. Offering her love selflessly, she had accepted all he had to offer, silently wishing for something beyond even their exquisite passion.

An hour before the first performance, Lita entered the club through the stage door. Even though this job had been a degrading experience, she had second thoughts about quitting.

The owner's wife was at first surprised that she was

giving her notice. "I had my eye on you for a solo spot," she admitted quite frankly. "You are good—very good."

Lita expressed her thanks and started to leave, but the woman had more to say. "If you should return to the island, be sure to stop in. We might create an opening. It is refreshing to have someone do a job well without the griping that usually goes on. I know those girls—they have not made it easy for you. Yet you never said a word."

Lita smiled. "I suppose it's because I'm used to being rejected."

The woman shook her head, her eyes taking in Lita's features and shape. "You tell me you are going to Miami with a friend—a man, I suppose. This man will not reject you. He would be a fool if he did."

Lita nodded her thanks. "I hope you're right." Concerned that she might be leaving the club shorthanded, she asked, "You're sure you have a replacement for the day after tomorrow?"

"Do not worry. We will manage."

"I'm sorry to—"

"You are leaving with your man. That is as it should be."

Smiling, Lita ducked out the door. Would her employer feel that way if she knew it was Cade Thomas she was leaving with? Somehow, knowing her time on stage was limited to two performances each for only two more nights made the ordeal easier. Keeping her eyes focused above the crowd, she went through the routines.

Cade had business to attend to, so he wasn't at the club. But when he picked her up after the show, they spent some time in the Hilton's casino and the Club Caribe. The music of the Latin band was spirited and enthusiastic. Everything about the place was plush and expensive.

Lita had told Maria she would not be home until the following afternoon. Although her aunt seemed to disapprove in general, there was no doubt that Cade Thomas was high on the woman's list of acceptable people. Tomorrow, Lita would tell Maria of her plans to leave Puerto Rico.

Happy and carefree, Lita tossed her head as she and Cade entered his room at two o'clock. Giving him a sensuous smile, she turned her back to him so he could unzip the Mediterranean-blue lacy cotton dress that emphasized her breasts and slim waist. It whispered elegantly as it fell to her feet. Cade watched her, a nerve jumping in his cheek.

"Do I get help with the rest?" she asked softly.

"You do," he said, his voice so low, she could barely hear him.

Tenderly he unhooked the lace bra. Watching it tumble from her arms, he stepped up to her, cupping each lovely breast in his large hands.

The familiar throbbing began in her loins and she was lost. No man had ever affected her this way. When the silky panties followed the other garments, he stepped back to shed his own clothes. She sighed softly as he stripped off his shorts, his eyes waiting for her approval.

"You've spoiled me for any other man," she murmured longingly.

Cade moved toward her slowly. "You still surprise me with your candidness. I thought it was up to the man to whisper sweet nothings."

"You asked me once if I could honestly tell you how I feel. I—"

He pressed two fingers to her lips, halting any further confessions. "It isn't time for that yet, love."

Confusion swept over her, but then he erased every conscious thought from her mind with the tenderness of his lovemaking. If Cade had not expressed his feelings for her before, he did so now with every stroke and caress, each movement of his magnificent body. For the rest of their wonderful night together she questioned nothing more.

Lita awakened to the sound of Cade's low voice speaking on the telephone. "I'm leaving tomorrow morning," he said. "If there's any change, call Tony. I'll stop by."

Covertly, she observed him: the frown that marred his high classic forehead; the narrowed "made in heaven" eyes. When he replaced the receiver, he stood for several minutes staring down at her. There was nothing loving in that glare. What had she done to him to deserve it?

It must be his normal morning look, she decided as he walked toward the bathroom. He was probably thinking of something—someone? She had a sudden urgent need to know more about him, what made him tick, what his family was like.

Shrugging, she slipped from the bed and pulled a velour robe from the closet. The label caught her eye—Hamilton Exclusive. Lord. She almost hated that name. In recent days she had completely forgotten Jeremy. What she had felt for him was like a drop in a bucket compared with her ocean of love for Cade. Now there was no doubt in her mind of the depth of her emotions.

Pulling on the robe, she tiptoed to the open bathroom door and peeked around the corner of the jamb. "Hi," she said throatily.

"Morning, love." He gazed at her reflection in the mirror. "I thought you would sleep for a while."

"I'll have lots of time for that in a few days," she said.

His eyes lit up with mischief. "Don't be so sure of that. I plan to keep you *very* busy."

One eyebrow arched upward. "Are we staying in your room today?"

He grinned and turned toward her. "If that's what you want to do."

"I have to see Maria." She hesitated. "To tell her I'm going with you."

He frowned. "How do you think she'll take it?"

Lita shrugged. "She won't approve, but she realizes that I have to live my own life, make my own decisions."

Cade nodded. "While I'm here, I would like to see El Yunque, the rain forest." His eyes were soft and warm as he looked down at her. "I want you to come with me."

Lita had hoped to see more of the island, but a lack of money had prevented it. "I hear it's very beautiful, with hundreds of different kinds of trees—most of them never seen in the States."

Several hours later, they were exploring the forest together. "Look at the wild orchids," she said excitedly. "And the parrots." It was a cool, magical world of splashing mountain waterfalls, luxuriant ferns and vines.

" 'Two hundred inches of rainfall make it a tropical fairyland,' " Cade read from a booklet they had been given. His arm around her increased in pressure.

Awed by the splendor of the panorama, she murmured, "Maybe we'll hear the little tree frogs."

They looked down from the observation tower, astonished to find that the verdant forest was surrounded by palm-covered plains.

"It's a different world." He smiled down at her. "If it were only possible to stay forever in a beautiful place like this—forget the problems of business, the pressures, the bad feelings we have toward other human beings."

She swallowed hard at the unnatural glitter in his eyes. What was he telling her? More important, why?

"Do you have bad feelings toward your fellow men?"

He seemed to watch the flight of a brilliantly colored bird. "And women."

Her mouth opened to ask why he had added that, but something in the rigid profile warned her off. Was he referring to *all* women—or to one specifically?

He turned his gaze to her. "There's a restaurant up ahead. Shall we try it?"

Had he seen the puzzlement that must have been evident on her face? He was such an enigmatic, secretive type of person. She was open . . . perhaps too much so.

While they sipped cool drinks, Lita studied Cade surreptitiously. She asked herself time and again why she had agreed to go to Florida with him. You must be crazy, her rational side asserted. What do you know about him? *You* haven't been in his arms, the romantic side argued.

She was silent on the trip back to San Juan and he welcomed it. She seemed to sense his moods, adjusting her conversation to fit his. An unusual woman, he mused. Most of the others he knew chattered like magpies, as though they were afraid of silence.

Lita was a thinker. He appreciated her intelligence, her softness when he needed it, the fieriness when he most welcomed it. He would probably end up hurting her—emotionally. But hadn't she hurt Jeremy physically?

When they reached her apartment, he eased the car into a parking space, then reached over to kiss her. "Would you like me to come with you?"

"No." She grimaced. "I prefer telling Maria myself."

He nodded, grasping the handle of her door. "I'll stop by at seven to pick you up for work."

"Thank you for a very special day," she said, and stepped onto the sidewalk.

"It was all my pleasure. I'm glad I saw it with you." His voice softened. "A very special day."

She smiled, her eyes vivid with memories, color high on her cheeks. Her feet barely touched the pavement as she entered the courtyard.

Maria was speaking to several neighbors. Lita waved and minutes later her aunt joined her in the kitchen. Lita forced herself to say the words.

The woman nodded. "I could see it coming. His persistence and the glow of love shining in your eyes."

"You're not angry?"

"Of course not, child." She reached for Lita's hand. "We all have to make our own mistakes. I would have preferred it to be a marriage ceremony. But I realize that young people today look at things differently. Who is to say which generation is right?"

"I would much prefer telling you that it was a permanent commitment. But . . ." She let her voice trail off. "If it doesn't work out, may I come back?"

Tears sprang to Maria's eyes. "You are like my own. I would be delighted to have you." She paused. "Make the best of this relationship. Cade is a good man."

Lita nodded and looked away, aware of pressure behind her eyelids.

"It is time for you to get dressed," Maria said, rising from the table.

Lita stood up and grasped the tiny woman in a warm hug. "Thank you for everything."

"*De nada*," the older woman said, blinking rapidly.

"Did you forget something on the yacht?" Lita asked

Cade the next day. She met his vibrant gaze, then looked away in puzzlement.

"No."

"The airport is *that* way." She pointed.

"We're not going to fly."

She peered at him out of the corners of her eyes. "I wasn't aware that Rolls-Royce had made a car that could ride the waves."

"The last I knew they hadn't."

Her mouth twitched while she pondered the alternatives. She tried again. "A cruise ship?"

"Three times and you struck out."

She didn't really know him, she thought. Maybe she was wrong to place her trust in him. She'd just have to wait and see.

The white paint of the yacht glistened in the morning sun. It was trim and polished and seaworthy. That was it! The *Sea Sprite*. They were going to Florida on the yacht! Now she realized why he had questioned her about having a valid passport. But that had been the first night they were together. How could he have known then that he'd want her to join him?

"Were you concerned that I might back out?" she asked.

He chuckled. "It entered my mind. You know what I'm like as a lover and an escort. Perhaps it's too much to ask you to have faith in me as a skipper?"

She caught her bottom lip with her teeth. "I've seen you handle the craft. But a thousand-mile ocean voyage?"

"We're never far from land with all the islands between here and Miami."

Her eyes widened with concern. "Are you lucky?"

He frowned. "I always thought so."

"But now you're not so sure?"

He shrugged. "I made the trip down here alone. I'm certain I can get you to our destination safely."

She pondered that for a minute. "Old-time mariners didn't think it was safe to sail with a woman aboard."

"You're not the first."

Or the last? She smiled sickly. "Can I back out now?"

She heard his swift indrawn breath. "I never forced a woman to do anything she didn't want to do."

"This is just a bit different," she said softly. "I've burned my bridges."

He grinned mischievously. "Then I guess you'll just have to swim with the tide. You do that well, you know."

"I never attempted an ocean."

"Consider it a new experience."

She tossed her hair lightly. "Oh, that it is." Her nostrils picked up the scent of his after-shave and she studied his slender, tapered fingers on the steering wheel, the thigh muscles straining against the fabric of his slacks.

He drove into a parking space, got out of the car, and opened the trunk. He removed her suitcases. When he opened her door and assisted her out, his mouth brushed hers in a soft, lingering kiss.

Should I travel a thousand miles with this man? she wondered. Then she grinned, shook her head, and followed him along the dock. He boarded the *Sea Sprite*, then turned to extend his hand.

"Thanks," she murmured as he lifted her aboard and held her close.

He made a low growling sound deep in his throat. A ripple of excitement scampered up her spine. "Make yourself comfortable," he said. "I have to arrange for the car to be picked up."

She nodded and headed for a chair. Cade loped along the dock and returned minutes later, his feet thudding on the deck. She smiled. He paused to lower his mouth, to gently nibble on her lips. Something intense flared within her as all of her feelings for him welled up in her throat.

When he lifted his head, she felt the cool ocean breeze on her moist mouth. He backed away from her, his gaze like a whispered caress. Only as he started to climb the ladder to the fly bridge did she release her breath.

The engine roared to life. He steered the craft slowly away from the dock. As the *Sea Sprite* picked up speed, Lita lifted her eyes to bid farewell to San Juan. A long voyage lay ahead of them and they would only have each other to depend on.

Later, as the sun cast shimmering gold highlights on the waves, she staggered across the rear deck and managed to grip the ladder leading to the cockpit.

Coming up behind Cade, she saw that he had shed his outer clothes and was clad only in brief swim trunks. The muscles of his broad shoulders rippled as he maneuvered the controls. She placed her arms around his neck and blew softly in his ear. "Want something for lunch?" she purred.

"Mmmm."

"What would you like?"

"You."

"Oh." Her mouth curved into a smile. "I can offer only sandwiches."

"A poor substitute, but they'll have to do for now."

She kissed the back of his head, then slowly descended the ladder.

As the sun sank low in the west, the small cay where Cade planned to refuel came into view. It was much the same as many of the sunbaked Caribbean islands. Lush, unspoiled, it seemed to be a romantic haven. Brilliant purple bougainvillea, yellow hibiscus, and pink oleander dotted the landscape. The perfume of a dozen varieties of trees and bushes mingled in the flower-scented breeze. Undersea coral reefs would keep yachtsmen on their toes. Sea gardens lured scuba divers to the exotic ocean floor.

Lita waved to the balding man who tied the yacht to a flimsy dock. He greeted her, his decidedly British accent sounding rather stilted to her ears. Cade leaped over the rail to shake the man's hand. They chatted for a few minutes, obviously pleased to see each other. While the fuel tank was being filled, Lita walked along the palm-lined beach. Just as dusk shadowed the island, she and Cade reboarded the *Sea Sprite* and headed through the shallow waters.

"There's a cove that's perfect for us," he called to her. "Get the barbecue equipment, a blanket, and some towels from the forward locker. Oh, and mosquito repellent too!" Happily, she did as he requested.

He anchored in a magnificent setting. Palm trees swayed, colorful birds cawed and sang in the treetops. Soon they were wading ashore through the clear warm water.

An hour later, Lita's nose began to twitch at the aromatic smell of barbecued beef ribs. Cade tended the meat while she set out potato salad and fresh fruits.

"We'll have a full moon tonight," he said, barely loud enough to be heard over the sound of waves lapping at the shore.

"Hmmm." She sighed. "Shall I get out my hat and broomstick?" She looked at him across the crimson reflection of the coals in the fire.

"You've already bewitched me, Lita." Desire smoldered in his eyes. "We'll make it a time to remember—the warm night, the beauty of this place, and two lonely people who found each other."

"How romantic," she said lightly, but her heart completed a happy somersault at the lovely scene he described.

"Do liberated women still want romance?" he asked.

"Oh, we want it all right."

"Then you shall have it," he promised. "Tonight."

She shivered in anticipation of his burning lips on hers. Relishing each mouthful, she finished eating the delicious food.

He raised a glass of wine. "To us," he said.

"To tonight," she murmured. Who knew what tomorrow would bring?

"As the lady pleases." He sipped the wine, his gaze ceaselessly searching hers.

"I'd forgotten how good potatoes cooked in the coals of a fire could taste," he said. "My mother calls them Mickies. It's been a long time since I've had some."

"I guess I don't have those kind of fond memories, of picnics and gatherings with family."

"What did you do as a child?"

"My parents were too busy to do anything with me. I did the ordinary things most kids do. I tried to win their love and approval." She caught a sob in her throat. "It was a lost cause."

"Are you still looking for love?"

She laughed. "Up to now I haven't chosen the right man."

"It only takes *one* man."

"I know."

She relaxed against a tree trunk. He studied the way she lifted her head, pride and stubbornness apparent in that simple gesture. Without makeup of any kind, she had an innocent beauty. If Jeremy's blood was not staining her hands, he felt that for the first time in his life he could happily choose her as the one woman to be his wife. Eventually, there might be a little girl with auburn hair to cherish, a son to carry on his share of the Hamilton fortune.

Why? he asked himself. Why did it have to be Lita who'd been involved with his brother? Could a sweet, caring woman like her be guilty? If it was not Lita, then *who* had attempted to take the life's breath from fun-loving Jeremy?

Cade put the disturbing thoughts aside. Tonight was made for love, and love they would share. His mouth curved up in expectation.

Crickets chirped their sensual serenade. When Lita stood up, he leaned back lazily, watching her walk with rhythmic grace along the edge of the surf, the lush curves of her breasts beneath the scanty bikini causing his mouth to water.

"I'll love her tonight," he said softly. "Maybe tomorrow will bring a solution."

He stood up, dusted sand from his legs, and followed her along the beach. Catching up to her, he slipped his arm around her waist. They walked for a while, and when they turned back to the yacht she stopped, an unanswerable question in her eyes.

His head descended. The warm, velvet tongue glided between her lips, mingling with the soft flesh of her mouth. Lita felt the coolness of the evening disappear, a mindless need surfacing. Her hands slid down Cade's muscled thighs to grip his firm buttocks. Excitement threaded through her, heat flaring in her stomach.

The bikini top fell to the sand. Seconds later the bottoms lay around her ankles. Lita took in huge gulps of air as Cade lowered his head to stroke her breast with his tongue. A storm of passion rose within her.

She gasped his name, her hands flying to his head, fingers combing the crisp dark hair. The sucking action of his lips on one firm peak sent her into a frenzy of torment.

His hands seemed to roam without direction, sending waves of pleasure to each silky inch of bare flesh. He eased her to the sand, his sweet, hot breath once again absorbing her mouth. She felt her hip dig into the sand as they lay facing each other.

Reaching down to press one hand between their steaming bodies, she grasped the firm flesh swelling his swim trunks. She heard his groan and he shifted his body toward hers. Peeling off the trunks, she pushed them down his legs as the sound of his staccato breathing beat a vibrant tattoo.

His eyes, like brilliant pinpoints of silver, were spellbinding. She felt a fiery flow of liquid in her veins, a wild pulse rate throb in her temples. Then his mouth claimed hers in a drugging kiss that sent her lashes fluttering to her cheeks.

"Lita," he murmured. "You feel so good, so perfect in my arms." He kissed her quivering lids. When her eyes slowly opened, he lifted his gaze to search them.

She moaned, hot surges of passion lashing her body. Electrical charges stimulated her sensitive nerve endings. She pulled his mouth to hers, seeking its moistness, exploring its heated contours, weaving a sense of oneness as their tongues became entwined.

Never in her wildest dreams had she imagined the pleasure she now found in her own aggressiveness, the floating, soaring joy she could elicit by actively pursuing him. *I love you*, she wanted to cry out, but in spite of the dizzying explosion of her senses, some semblance of reason remained.

"Love me," she gasped, caught up in a whirlwind of chaotic passion. His limbs moved to cover hers, then he was above her.

"Oh," she cried softly as he entered her. Savage hunger forged them together, his plundering kiss robbing her of sanity, the stroking motions lifting her to mind-less heights.

Together, they rode a swell of surging rapture, billowing and ebbing, their reeling senses overwhelmed and unresisting against a tidal wave of emotion which finally burst and skyrocketed them both to ecstasy. With a gentle swaying rhythm, Cade rocked her in his arms. In the magic of their embrace, they kissed with exquisite sweetness. Gradually, their breathing slowed and evened.

She couldn't have said whether it was minutes or hours later that the moon once again appeared above them, the surf swelled and receded around their feet, the poignant scent of flowers filled her nostrils.

"It was glorious," she whispered, nibbling the skin of his shoulders, holding back from biting into his musky flesh.

"Magnificent," he murmured.

"Intoxicating."

"Divine."

She giggled. "We could go on endlessly."

He grinned. "Why don't we? We have all night."

A phosphorescent wave washed up to their waists as they lay encircled in each other's arms.

"Remember"—she brushed her lips against his neck—"the scene in *From Here to Eternity*?"

"Where Deborah Kerr and Burt Lancaster make love on the Hawaiian shore?"

"Ummm. You do remember."

"You're more beautiful than Deborah."

"And you're more handsome and virile than Burt."

"I don't think their love scene has the faintest resemblance to ours," he murmured.

"They were amateurs," she said huskily.

"Mmmm." He nuzzled her lips. "After all that activity, we should go for a swim."

She'd rather stay right there in his arms, she thought. Forever.

Cade helped her up, bestowing a kiss on her upturned face. The full moon carved his features in silver. Together they splashed in the shallow surf to refresh themselves.

Until the early hours of the morning, they caught snatches of sleep between movingly emotional bouts of lovemaking. The moon kept watch over them, renewing their passion as it lifted and pulled the water in the never-ending movement of the tides. They whispered and touched in a blissful transfer of affection. All of the soul-stirring emotions Lita felt for Cade had surfaced.

Just before dawn, they gathered the remnants of their dinner from the beach and returned to the yacht. When Cade left a butterfly kiss on her lips and told her he was heading for the other side of the island to make a telephone call, Lita nodded wearily. Entering the cabin, she closed the drapes and crawled beneath the covers of the bunk.

Although aware of the roar of the engine and the steady splash of water against the hull, all she really heard in her tired brain were the important words of love Cade had never spoken.

Seven

The sun was high overhead when Lita awoke and stretched. She glanced at Cade's bunk. It hadn't been disturbed. She heard the steady hum of the engine and the easy rolling motion of the *Sea Sprite*.

She smiled to herself, cherishing the moments of lazy contentment in the aftermath of their intoxicating night of love. Feeling luxuriously wicked in her nakedness, she slipped off the bunk and went into the tiny bathroom. Cade called it by its nautical name, the "head." She washed and rolled on lip gloss, a mischievous gleam in her eyes.

Walking through the saloon minutes later, she stepped to the deck and peered around. They were alone on the ocean. Lita climbed the ladder and paused at the top to admire Cade's wide coppery shoulders and steady hands on the controls. Tiptoeing to stand behind him, she lightly nipped his earlobe, then stepped back to observe his reaction.

Puzzled when he said nothing, she had a sinking sensation that something was wrong. "Cade?" she whispered uncertainly.

"Yes?" He glanced around at her, his tone low and slightly irritated. There was no welcoming smile, no softening of the look in his eyes.

Lita's teeth dug hard into her trembling lower lip. "What is it?" she asked.

"What is what?"

"Something is bothering you."

"Perhaps."

"I'd like to know what it is." She heard the quiver in her voice.

He shook his head, lifting his chin slightly and staring at the open sea.

She gave it one more try. "Will you tell me later?"

"I doubt it."

She felt her throat tightening, nausea churning in her stomach.

"I think you'd better get some clothes on," he said.

Who was out in this wide expanse of ocean to see her nakedness? She looked down at her nude body and felt a sudden sense of shame. She had done something, said something that had caused his brooding mood. But what?

Quickly descending the ladder, she walked to the bow and opened the drawer in which she had placed some of her clothes. She pulled out a bikini and slipped on the small scraps of fabric. Her actions were automatic, her mind a maze of confusion.

The telephone call he had planned to make . . . Could he have received some disturbing news? But why wouldn't he tell her?

Cade swept a hand through his thick hair, then rested it again on the wheel. He felt thoroughly thrashed, as though whipped by waves in a raging sea. Jeremy's condition had steadily worsened. Bitterness welled up in his throat. It was quite possible that the Hamilton family would lose its youngest member soon. And all because of Lita Jamison.

He turned on the autopilot and bolted out of the seat. At the top of the ladder he halted. Below him was the woman who was the cause of his grief . . . and his joy, a small voice of conscience reminded him. Reclining on the pillows—their bed of love—she seemed to be asleep.

"Lita!" he barked.

She jolted to a sitting position. "Yes?"

"Don't get too much sun at one time. We're far from medical aid." His eyes narrowed.

She squinted up at him. "I don't burn."

"Too much of anything is no good for you."

Lita hated that tone of voice, that I-know-best attitude. "Really?" She saw him clench his fists. Anger shot through her.

He ignored her challenge to argue. "Would you make a couple of sandwiches and bring them up to me?"

"Aye, aye." She saluted smartly and leaped to her feet. He watched her as she walked across the deck.

Once in the galley, pure fury drove her to slap sliced roast beef and mustard on four pieces of bread. She wielded the knife dangerously as she halved the sandwiches, metal clattering on the dish. With a half-quart of milk tucked under her arm, she carried the food up the ladder and silently left it on the instrument panel. As she turned to leave, he called her name.

"Yes?"

"Thanks," he said.

She nodded, tossed her head, and briskly departed.

Anger rose and ebbed within her throughout the rest of the day. Several times Cade went through the saloon to the head. She never looked up.

As the sun dipped beyond the horizon, she put the final touches on their evening meal. She called up to Cade, but didn't wait for him to come down. At the table, he sat across from her, but she refused to meet his eyes.

Far into the night, Cade kept the *Sea Sprite* on a steady course. High on his perch in the fly bridge, he might as well have been a thousand miles away. She lay on the bunk, listening to the endless droning sound. Only when her long lashes rested on her cheek and she finally slept did the heartsick man cut the engine and climb down the ladder.

*　　*　　*

Lita and Cade were in a state of limbo. Beyond the few words he had said the previous day, he made no attempt to repair the damage to their relationship. Lita prepared the meals and made up the bunks while he kept watch on their progress.

Except for a few sailboats and yachts, there was nothing on the horizon. Although she loved the sea, the heavy atmosphere between her and Cade was getting on Lita's nerves.

Slipping off the lounge chair on the rear deck, she made her way to the cockpit. She stood quietly beside him, watching the ripple of muscles in his bare shoulders. "Look, uh, can't we talk?" she said finally, her bottom lip in a vulnerable curve.

"What would you like to talk about?"

"You, me, us, your family . . . anything."

"I've missed you, Lita."

She cursed the tears that stung her lids. "I've missed you too," she choked.

For the first time since their last night of love, the shadow of a grin crossed his lips. "Can we work this out?"

"It's a must." A ghost of a smile lit up her features. "I lay on the bunk last night fighting my wounded pride, but I can't stand this—this void between us."

"How do you think I felt knowing that you were only a few feet away, although mentally you could have been hundreds of miles from me."

"We could have communicated—"

"I do much better communicating physically." He moved off the seat and pulled her toward him, his granite-hard chest pressing against her soft breasts. She felt him shudder.

"Please don't ignore me anymore," he said. His mouth was warm and possessive against her hair.

"If you promise not to ignore me."

He gave a short, harsh laugh. "I was so aware of you, I barely slept two hours last night. Do you know you make funny little noises in your sleep, like you're laughing and crying at the same time?"

"I had a bad dream—about you."

His hands slipped down to cup her buttocks, drawing

her closer to his firm thighs. "I ache for you, Lita." He gently persuaded her to allow his tongue to enter her mouth.

A moan escaped her lips and she clung to him, her head falling back as he pursued the silken skin of her neck. Brushing aside the bikini top, his tongue fastened on a nipple, stroking it, sweetly tormenting her.

"I don't know if I can stop," he murmured before tenderly absorbing the other button-hard tip. She flung her head from side to side.

"Please . . . stop," she gasped.

One hand left her to reach behind him. The next instant the engine was silent and the *Sea Sprite* bobbed and dipped idly. The splash of water was the only sound that mingled with their quickened breathing.

"Come, love." The sheen of his eyes rivaled the vibrant blue of the Atlantic.

"Cade, no," she whispered.

The arms that held her tensed. "What's wrong?"

She took a deep breath. "I have to know where I stand with you."

His eyes darkened. "Meaning?"

She tried to pull away, but he held her tightly to his chest. "What do you want from me?" she asked.

He drew a harsh breath. "You're asking for a commitment?"

She shook her head. "An explanation. You've been angry and uncommunicative for a day and a half. I want to know what the problem is, what *I* have to do with it, and what your purpose was in bringing me on this trip to Florida."

His hands dropped to his sides. A flurry of emotions crossed his face. "I'm afraid I can't tell you that yet," he said stiffly.

"I don't understand." Her tone rose. "Why can't you tell me?"

"I will when we reach Florida."

She stepped back, anger and disappointment clouding her eyes. Her quiet voice belied the smoldering temper within her. "All right." She suddenly felt resigned to the situation between them. "Until I know what's bothering you . . . I'm afraid I won't be comfortable being your lover."

"Lita." His hand reached out in a gesture of appeal.

She swallowed hard. "No."

There was a visible slump to his shoulders, a vulnerable glaze to his eyes that he quickly shuttered. "You'll change your mind," he said.

"No." Wistfully, she turned away from him.

Cade watched as she walked across the fly bridge and descended to the cabin. She didn't look back. He ran his hand through his hair and sat down heavily. Automatically, he started the engine. How could he tell her about Jeremy? There were two fuel stops before they reached their destination. She could easily leave the yacht and then he would never know the truth.

He wanted her with a desperate need that made him ache from the tips of his hair to the nails on his toes. He looked at his watch. The storm that had been forecast was due to strike soon. Sucking in his breath, he awaited the challenge of the sea. It was what he needed to overcome the driving passion that tore at his loins.

Clouds covered the sun and a gloomy haze settled over the Atlantic Ocean. A gale wind rushed over the yacht, which suddenly seemed overwhelmed by giant waves. The squall had come up fast, transforming the tranquil sea into an eerie, frightening, tumultuous monster. Lita almost lost her footing and her lunch several times as she helped Cade drag in the cushions and secure everything movable.

"I can't stay in the cockpit. I'll be using the controls here in the cabin," he said in an even tone.

"You can't see as well, can you?" she said, holding onto the table.

"No, but I can't stay in a half-open cockpit, either." He steadied himself against a wall.

Somehow, in spite of all the turbulence, Lita felt safe because he was there with her. She swayed, losing what little balance she had been able to maintain. When she brushed against him, he caught her to his chest. His kiss was explosive, as always, sending shock waves of passion through her.

A sudden sharp lurch sent her stomach into a tailspin. He looked down at her and smiled, then grimaced as he saw her pallor.

"Your skin is changing to a pale green. Almost matches your eyes. I'll get you some medication and saltines." Helping her to the couch, he gently pressed her back on the cushions.

She nodded and lowered her lashes, but the motion of the craft seemed to worsen with her eyes closed.

"Take these." He handed her some pills and a glass of water. "Chew the crackers slowly."

"Thanks," she managed to say.

Rain pelted the window. The violent rage of the sea was unleashed upon them. "If you think this is a bad storm," he yelled above the roar of the wind, "you should see what it's like in a hurricane."

"How do you know this isn't one?" she yelled back.

"The weather report said this was just a squall. It should be over in a couple of hours."

"You mean you knew this was coming?" She bit into a cracker, chomping on it as she felt anger rise in her. He had placed her life in danger without her knowledge or consent.

At the tone of her voice, Cade glanced her way. "Sailors don't allow a little storm to keep them from the sea."

"I don't happen to be a sailor," she muttered. "If only I could sleep."

Twenty minutes later, the medication seemed to take effect and drowsiness crept over her. The last thing she remembered seeing were Cade's broad bronzed shoulders and mountainous waves sweeping over the yacht.

The *Sea Sprite* was still rocking when she opened her eyes later. The skipper was now at the table consuming a triple-decker sandwich and a tall glass of milk. He looked up at her movement and gave her a half smile.

"Feeling better?" he asked.

"Much." She sat up slowly, expecting a wave of nausea. Nothing happened. "I must be okay. My stomach isn't acting up."

"You'll get used to it," he said soothingly. "I take the

yacht out whenever I get a chance, so I'm accustomed to this kind of weather."

"Alone?" She could have bit her tongue for asking.

"Most of the time." He finished the milk and rummaged in the refrigerator for something more to eat.

"I hope your other women friends have less squeamish constitutions than I have."

"I wouldn't know." He gave her his full attention as he bit into an apple. "I've never taken a woman into a storm before."

"Is the squall over?" She was certain he couldn't miss the spark of hope in her tone.

"Relax, Lita." He came to stand in front of her. "We should have smooth sailing from now on."

Somehow, she had her doubts about that.

An hour later, they were in the cockpit, the *Sea Sprite* lifting her bow proudly as she cut sleekly through the water. There was no sign of the vicious waves. Their world had calmed again.

Cade pointed ahead. "We should see Ragged Island on the horizon soon." He lifted the binoculars. "My friend, Tony, has a small general store there. We'll fill the fuel tanks and replenish our stock of food." He looked at Lita and pulled her close. "You have a good appetite, lady."

She slipped away from his grasp to check on a casserole in the oven. It would be ready in minutes. She placed garlic bread in the oven just as she heard him call to her. At the excitement in his voice, she scampered up the ladder.

He handed her the binoculars and she peered through them, feeling the quickening of her heart as she spied the faint outline of the island. "How long are you planning to stay?"

"It depends on what kind of messages are waiting for us."

She caught the harshness in his tone. Would their relationship change once they reached civilization? Uncertainty clouded her mind as she handed the binoculars back to him.

"Dinner is ready," she said.

"Bad timing," he grumbled.

Her brow furrowed as she moved away from him.

"How unfortunate," she said, refusing to let his comment disturb her.

"I should have told you earlier," he said, obviously trying to lighten the situation.

"Yes, you should have."

"Lord! We sound like a bickering couple who've been together for fifty years."

"Well," she said, feeling a sharp pain cut into her chest, "we don't have to worry about any arrangement like that."

There was chilly accusation in the veiled gaze he turned on her. "No, we don't, do we?"

Was there hurt in his tone? Despair? She shook her head. Even after fifty years with Cade, she doubted she would fully understand him.

He cut the engine and followed her down the ladder to the cabin. As she placed the food before him, she was aware of a nervous silence enveloping them. She filled his coffee cup a second time, noticing how he gulped the liquid down. His attention was focused on the land beyond, which seemed to be rising out of the sea.

When he returned to the cockpit, Lita changed out of her bikini into a mint-green sleeveless blouse and skirt. Her freshly washed hair blew around her face, drying quickly in the brisk breeze. She sighed. So much had changed since their first day on the yacht that had been so heavenly. She had felt so wonderful sharing lovemaking and the sailing life with Cade.

Now she wondered about everything, especially this stop. What would Tony be like? Cade hadn't said much about him, only that the man had come to the island after a devastating divorce. Lita visualized his friend as whiskered and sullen.

She couldn't have been more wrong. An hour later, Cade and Tony were wrapped in a warm bear hug. Over Cade's shoulder, Tony winked at Lita. In his mid-thirties, good-looking in a rugged sort of way, he was absolutely clean shaven.

"Hello, pretty lady." Tony grasped her hand, pumping it vigorously. "You sure bring a touch of class to these quiet islands." His grin was infectious.

Lita smiled warmly. "I'm delighted to be here."

"Boy," he said, turning to Cade, "you sure picked a winner this time. Say, buddy, someone's been trying to reach you since early morning." He glanced at his watch. "They've been calling every hour. Why don't we get back to the house? It's about time for them to try again."

When Lita looked at Cade, she was shocked by the pallor beneath his burnished skin. He seemed to be barely breathing as his friend kept up a running conversation.

"Do you know where the call was from?" he asked hollowly.

"I kept asking if I could have you return the call, but they didn't say where it was from and they said they preferred to keep trying."

Cade nodded and strode purposefully toward the weathered cottage. Just as the three of them entered the tiny living room, the telephone rang. Cade leaped toward it.

"Yes?" He swallowed hard. "Debbie?" His jaw tightened as he listened. "When?" His voice was hoarse. He pivoted to face them, his eyes stark and forbidding as they slowly, calculatedly, swept over Lita. "I could make it if I fly back." He paused, listening. "That would be better. I'll see you Thursday. Is Mother all right?" He nodded, mumbled something, and replaced the receiver.

"Bad news?" Tony asked.

Cade nodded. "We'll have to load those groceries and fuel up as quickly as possible. We're leaving as soon as it's all done."

"I was hoping you could spend a few days, do some fishing," Tony said. "Visit awhile."

Cade shook his head. "I'd sure like to. But it's urgent. I'll have to get back as soon as possible."

The islander placed an arm around Lita's shoulder. "I was hoping to get to know you. Maybe some other time." At Cade's glare, Tony released her, his ears turning lobster red. "You're lovely," he whispered, and winked.

Lita pitched in as they loaded several boxes of food into the galley. Her brow was creased, eyes narrowed as she tried to figure out what had caused the sudden change in Cade. What was the message he'd received? He had a morose, almost sullen look as he silently left the cabin.

A short time later, Tony pumped his friend's hand, and Cade climbed to the cockpit and started the engine. He reversed the *Sea Sprite*. Lita hurried from the galley to the deck. Tony, standing with his hands in his pockets, and looking disappointed and forlorn, watched the yacht pull away.

Lita yelled and waved. Cade hadn't even given her time to say good-bye properly to the friendly man who was waving back and blowing kisses.

A chill wind caused her spine to tingle. She looked up at Cade's rigid back as he sat at the controls. At first he had greeted Tony so warmly. Now it was as though a chilly Arctic wind had cooled his personality. What kind of man was he? She had a strange, unsettling feeling that she would find out more than she cared to in the final phase of their trip to Miami.

Cade was barely civil to her the next day. They ate their meals in silence and there was no communication, either verbal or physical. It was as though someone had wound him up and at the slightest offbeat action he would be released like a well-oiled spring. And if his expression was any indication, she didn't want to be the recipient of his anger.

The engine droned on long after she had bid him good night and slipped between the sheets. It was a cool evening—but maybe that was because of the icy atmosphere that hung between them. She pulled the drapes closed, shutting out the moon's rays.

Sometime during the night, she awoke to a sound. The throb of the engine had ceased and the running light was on. She raised herself up on an elbow to check the other bunk. Cade's lean body was tossing and turning beneath a blanket. Over and over she heard him mumble the same words. Slipping her feet over the side of the bunk, she crept slowly toward him.

"He's dead."

She heard him plainly now—the low, moaning cry. When she touched his arm, he shuddered. Should she wake him? she wondered.

"Cade?" she whispered. "You're having a nightmare. Cade?"

He bolted upright, grabbing her, his fingers biting into the flesh of her arms.

"Cade," she cried out. "It's me, Lita." She gasped. "You're hurting me."

He released her and slumped back on the bunk, his breathing harsh and unsteady. "Oh, God, why can't I really hurt you?"

She stepped back, stung by his statement. "Why?" she whispered.

"You'll know soon enough."

"No. I want to know now." The hair on the nape of her neck was damp with perspiration. Was she safe with him?

"Go to sleep, Lita," he ordered. "It will soon be dawn."

She slipped back into her bunk. An hour passed and she was still wide-awake, aware of the rolling motion of the yacht and Cade's steady breathing. Who had died? And why had he given her that almost violent glare as he was speaking on the telephone at Tony's place?

There were two possibilities: either he was attached in some way to the woman he had spoken with and Lita's presence had reminded him of his philandering, or he was having second thoughts about taking her along. She shook her head in total confusion . . . *and fear.* Sighing, she willed her mind to blankness and gradually slipped into a fitful slumber.

The next morning Cade seemed in better humor. He told her they had made good progress and would stop that evening for diesel fuel and a few items of fresh food.

Over lunch, he mentioned a young man he had known who had died recently. "He was young and carefree, happy, with a touch of wildness."

"What happened?"

That strained, detached expression changed his features. "He had . . . an accident."

"And lingered?"

He nodded. "Seven months."

"I'm sorry," she said.

She thought she heard him say "Are you?" Then his hand clenched into a fist. "He had everything to live for. Money, family. Then he met a woman—a rather exotic woman." He scrutinized her face.

"She was the cause of this . . . accident?"

His eyes were shadowed and unreadable. "That's what I believe."

Seeing the pain in his face, she asked, "Do you want to talk about it?"

"I'm not sure," he said softly. "Do you?"

"Well . . ." She squirmed in her seat. "If you do. Most of the time it's better to air a problem than to keep it bottled up."

"Have you ever done anything that totally devastated you?"

She paused before answering. She had thought they were talking about the young man and the woman. She shrugged. "I suppose."

"Have you had any sleepless nights because of whatever it was you did?"

She would have to admit that loving Jeremy had had a devastating effect. Many nights had been devoted to wondering how she could have let herself be so misled. "Yes."

"Want to tell me about it?"

A tiny sigh escaped her lips. "It was over a man. He took everything and gave back nothing. He was too youthful, too wild." She laughed nervously. "The description of your young man could easily fit him."

He drew in a long, steadying breath. "I'm curious, Lita." He paused. "Did you grow to hate him? Would you have done him bodily harm if you'd had an opportunity?"

She traced a circle on the table, considering his question. It was certainly a most intriguing subject. "I suppose anyone who is jilted considers physical retribution. But most rational people don't give in to their emotions. They somehow work it out mentally. It passes."

"Did your feelings pass?"

Her brow creased. "Yes, eventually."

"You didn't give in to those initial feelings?"

Lita felt uncomfortable, as though she were on trial and he were the prosecutor. "Why are you asking me all these questions? I thought you wanted to discuss your friend and that woman."

He placed a hand on his chest. "I doubt that you would feel comfortable if I told you the story."

She wanted to say "Try me," but there was something in the rigid features, the taut muscles that spanned his bare shoulders, that prevented the words from being said. "Perhaps some other time," she suggested.

"You can be sure of it," he said, rising from his chair.

She watched him move across the cabin. She couldn't shake the feeling that a shroud hovered over them. What did he mean? What did she have to do with the woman and the young man he had mentioned? What was the connection?

A multitude of questions flashed through her mind, but there were no logical answers. Cade was an enigma. She began to wonder about her love for him.

By early evening, Lita felt thrashed and beaten. She didn't know what she was going to do, but one thing was certain. When they reached Miami, she was going to make some plans of her own. She had a definite sensation of impending doom, and her plans would not include Cade Thomas.

She watched him furtively. On the surface, their behavior toward each other was cordial. But something evil seemed to be bubbling beneath Cade's cool facade. They were scheduled to reach Miami the next morning. It would only take a few minutes for her to pack her bags and slip away.

Lita felt a wrenching sensation at the thought of leaving Cade. He had become her universe, the sphere in which she seemed to glow. Another mistake. She pressed her fingers hard into the flesh beneath her breast. He had given her pleasure—but nothing of himself. Was he capable of sincere emotions? Should she try to dig beneath the burnished skin, question him again as to what he wanted from her? Or was she asking for a rebuff, a rejection she should avoid? Wouldn't such a confrontation shatter the thin veneer covering her heart?

She brought two cups of coffee to the fly bridge. Pushing aside her inclination to hold back her questions, she plowed right in. "What's going to happen tomorrow?"

He was slow to reply. "What would you like to see happen?"

She wouldn't allow him to sidetrack her with evasive answers. "Cade, let's be honest with each other. I'm quite certain that my feelings play no part in your plans. So now I'd like a sincere answer."

He shook his head slowly from side to side. "Still the outspoken, square-shooting female, hmmm? Why can't you be like that in *every* way?"

Lita sighed. "I'm tired of your speaking in riddles. I'd like to know where I stand, what you want of me."

He looked at her, his eyes studying the rise and fall of her breasts, her navel, the tiny bikini pants that were little more than postage-stamp size.

"I have a funeral to go to in the afternoon," he said, his voice choked.

She wouldn't say she was sorry. Was it the same person he had left Puerto Rico to see? "Do I stay on the *Sea Sprite*?"

He hadn't really thought about what to do with her now. He hadn't counted on Jeremy's death. The plan to confront his brother with Lita was a thing of the past. If he could only get her to admit that she had tried to—poor Jeremy.

"Let's play it by ear," he suggested.

"Do you have a house or an apartment?"

"A house."

"Do you live alone?"

"Sometimes my mother comes to visit."

"What's her name?"

"Vivian."

When she was quiet for several minutes, he watched the expressions flit across her face. He had the distinct impression that she would flee as soon as they touched land. He would have to thwart such an attempt until he could think more clearly.

No other woman had ever tied his emotions into knots, claimed his body for her own. Lita Jamison was like a siren luring him, seducing him.

Jeremy never had a chance. Yet, he had rejected *her*. How was that possible?

"No more questions?" he asked mockingly.

A pair of light green, piercing eyes whipped over him. There was pain in them, but his need for revenge overshadowed his concern for her.

Her chin lifted fractionally. "No."

The outline of a passing ship caught his attention. They were now in more congested waters. "We'll anchor off one of the cays tonight. Wouldn't you like a chance to swim and barbecue on the shore?"

"Okay," she said stiffly.

"You don't sound enthused."

"Perhaps I would be"—she paused—"if I thought you were."

"Who wouldn't be enthused about a delightful swim and a meal with one of the most beautiful women I've ever known?"

When she didn't answer, he allowed his thoughts to focus on his personal tragedy. Tomorrow he would see his handsome young brother for the last time. Could his mother bear the burden of losing her youngest child? And all because of a woman's fury at being rejected. . . .

The *Sea Sprite* was anchored in a secluded cay, the moon swept beach a perfect oasis for making love. But Lita would have none of it. The ache within her was all-consuming, the beauty of the romantic atmosphere like a leaden weight on her heart.

Cade barbecued in the shadows of a giant palm tree while she sat and stared at the luminous whitecaps splashing against the coral reefs.

Earlier, they had once again stopped to refuel and purchase fresh food. Lita had remained in the saloon, avoiding Cade's friends. She had nothing to say to them—or him. As they had approached the island, she had given him one last chance to tell her what was wrong, what his plans were for her. Since he'd once again refused to reveal his frustrations, she had no recourse but to leave him. Sadness numbed her heart. This would be their last night together, for she had definitely decided to flee as soon as the yacht docked in Miami.

She blinked back her tears as Cade brought her a dish filled with tempting food. He sat cross-legged on the blanket, his gaze resting on her. The tender steak tasted like straw, the butter-drenched corn as flavorful as pebbles.

"Why aren't you eating?" he asked.

She shrugged and shook her head. Who could swallow with a tightened throat? "It's good," she managed to say.

"Lita," he began, "can't we be friends tonight?"

"Friends are fine. Lovers . . . no."

When he didn't reply, she finally met his gaze. "I need you," he said softly. "Not just for sex, but for your warmth and caring."

She set down her dish and clung to the edge of the blanket. "I can't ignore the change in you, not even for one night of love. It would be a total disregard of my basic morals. I can't do that—even for you."

Pain showed clearly in his silvery eyes. He placed the empty dish beside him and lay back on the blanket.

"I can appreciate that. But we've shared something wonderful. Why should we let it slip through our fingers?"

He had almost made up his mind to reveal all to Lita. He would have to do it tomorrow. Why not tonight? But how would she react to an accusation such as he planned to make? If he were in her place and she were innocent— No, he wouldn't tell her now.

The setting—the moon, the secluded beach, the warm Caribbean night—made him yearn to hold her, to kiss those soft, endearing lips, to—

"Okay." He leaped to his feet, unable to prolong the anguish, unable to bear the lust he was feeling for her. "Let's go."

He dug a hole to dump the ashes in. The pan sizzled as he set it in the water to cool. Gathering up the pan and dishes, he waded into the surf, climbed the ladder, and jumped over the rail.

Shattered by his sudden action, Lita pulled the sides of the blanket together and carried it to the craft.

"Farewell, my love," she said softly as minutes later the *Sea Sprite* headed for the open sea.

Eight

It was almost noon when Lita woke, stretched, and snuggled into the covers. The engine was silent. Suddenly feeling uncomfortable, she opened one eye to peer around the cabin.

When she saw the shadowy figure sitting on the opposite bunk, both eyes flew open. Cade, dressed in a dark suit and tie, was staring at her. She lifted herself on her elbows. "Good morning," she said huskily.

"Get dressed, Lita," he ordered.

Her lips pursed to ask a question, but she dutifully pushed aside the blanket and stood up. He frankly appraised her shortie nightgown, his eyes cold and unblinking as she reached for a robe.

"What is it, Cade?" she asked. "Is something wrong?"

"Everything is wrong."

She pulled on the garment and sat down on the bunk. "What do you mean?" Only then did she look through the tinted glass window at the manicured beauty of a perfect lawn and an elegant oceanfront mansion.

Any further questions died in her throat. There was

no mistaking the Hamilton multimillion-dollar family residence that she had visited once with Jeremy.

Her eyes were wide with disbelief as she stared at the man across from her. There was no pain, no anger, only despair. As though completely devoid of feeling, she looked to him for some explanation. Gazing down at the hands now splayed against his thighs, she remembered the sweet magic they had woven in the past and the fiery intensity they could create within her.

"I don't have time to tell you why now," he said, glancing at his watch. "I want you to get dressed and come with me."

She passed a hand across her eyes. "To the funeral?"

"Yes."

"Why?" Her tone was incredulous.

"Because I think it will tell you all you need to know."

"Like what?"

Cade rose from the bunk. He kept his rigid back to her. Lita took in the broad shoulders, the lean length of his muscled frame, the way his clothes fit him flawlessly. Hamilton Exclusive was on the label of all his outer clothing. She could refrain from asking questions no longer.

"Who are you?" she burst out.

He pivoted to face her. "I'm Cade Thomas Hamilton. Jeremy's brother."

"But why—"

"One of the reasons you're here is to see my brother."

"Jeremy?" She saw the pain in his eyes and suddenly knew. "Jeremy's dead?"

"Yes." He hesitated. "We're pressed for time. That dark dress you wore in Puerto Rico will be fine."

A tinge of anger crept into her chest. "I'm sure I'm capable of deciding what to wear." She felt a shiver skid down her spine. Jeremy was dead . . . Cade wasn't who he'd said he was. He was Jeremy's brother! He'd been playing some deep and horrifying game with her. He didn't care for her at all.

She fumbled with underwear and shoes. After splashing water over her face and hands in the bathroom, she mechanically rolled on mascara, brushed her hair, and dabbed her lips with gloss.

Cade was still in the same spot when she sat down on the bunk to put on pantyhose and plain black pumps. Throwing open the locker, she grabbed a simple dark green oxford-cloth shirtdress with a stand-up collar and obi-style belt and yanked it over her head. In less than ten minutes she was ready.

She swallowed, aware that her teeth had begun to chatter. She felt sick. With a last baleful glare, she walked past Cade and out the door. At the rail, she gestured for him not to touch her as she climbed over it and onto the dock. Her heels clicked on the wooden planks.

Stopping at the V that marked two paths, she waited until he chose one, then followed him. She scanned the two-story Mediterranean-style mansion, with its contrasts of brick, masonry, and wood trim. She remembered the elegance of the interior, the spacious drawing room and loggia, a terraced affair that had an ocean as well as a colorful garden view.

In the driveway stood a low-slung black Maserati. When he opened the passenger door, she slid inside, her face a hostile mask. They were going to see Jeremy . . . for the last time. She vowed there would be no tears. Not for Cade's brother. Perhaps she would shed some for herself.

Twice in one year she had fallen for an unfeeling, treacherous Hamilton. *I'd like to pay them back—both of them.*

"Comfortable?" he asked. She felt his gaze on her and lifted her chin.

"I suppose you've been in a Maserati before?" he went on. There was a slight jealous, nagging quality to his tone that added to her irritation.

"What if I have?" she snapped.

Twenty minutes passed before Cade brought the car to a halt in a parking lot. She glanced up at the sign. A mortuary. Goose bumps roughened her skin.

At the entry, they were greeted by a small, pale-faced man who spoke in gentle tones. Cade nodded to him, grasped Lita's arm, and led her swiftly into a viewing room. Her steps slowed. Cade urged her on.

"This is the last time you'll ever see him."

"No," she whispered.

He drew her toward the casket. Lita stared down, something in her head making popping noises, her ears throbbing with thunderous sounds.

"Jeremy," she gasped, and swayed toward Cade. A feeling of nausea swept over her.

He placed his arm around her for support. "Can you stand?" he asked.

Oh, I can stand all right. I can stand anyone except you and your brother. "Yes," she murmured.

Jeremy was dead. Lively, wild, carefree Jeremy would no longer break women's hearts. But he hadn't broken hers, had only scratched the surface a bit. His brother was the one for whom she was feeling the shattering force of pain at the utter betrayal of Cade Hamilton.

Cade led her to a chair in the first row. The overpowering smell of massive bouquets added to the queasiness in her stomach. She kept her eyes downcast as silent people filed into the room. After all of them were seated, a low murmur swept the group. Glancing at the casket, she saw that it had been closed.

A dark-haired young woman who seemed vaguely familiar to Lita, and an older, silver-haired woman were seated on the middle aisle. A tall, suntanned man in his late thirties sat down beside the younger woman. His profile was an older edition of Cade. His brother?

Cade had left her to speak softly with those people. Now he returned and sat down beside her as a young man of Jeremy's age stood before the mourners to deliver the eulogy. Lita was aware of Cade's frequent glances, but she kept her stony gaze forward.

As the young man ended his speech, there were tears in his eyes. Lita, still reeling from all that had happened, felt no emotion. At the end of the service she remained in her seat, as in a dream, watching the casket being removed. Among the bearers were Cade and the man who looked like him.

Lita followed the group to the gravesite. A minister spoke in low tones, but she didn't really hear the message. Her attention was focused solely on the handsome, grim-faced man staring down at the casket. As the crowd slowly dispersed, she remained.

" 'Bye, Jeremy," she murmured softly.

"Any regrets?"

The low, harsh voice from close behind her chased away her lethargy. "None," she replied, her chin rising.

"I wonder if we're talking about the same thing," he muttered.

"Shouldn't you be looking after your mother?"

"My brother, Ray, is doing that. We'll be joining them at the house."

She turned to face him. "I'd rather not, Cade. I don't know her or anyone else. I'll feel out of place . . ."

"Oh, but you knew Jeremy," he said caustically, "and that provides us with a certain relevance."

"You owe your allegiance to your family at a time like this. I'll be all right on the yacht."

"Do you think I brought you here to spend your time on the *Sea Sprite*?" He took her arm and led her across the grass.

She shook her hair away from her face, feeling a slight throb, the beginning of a headache. "I haven't the vaguest idea why you brought me here. I thought we were going to Miami."

He made no comment. "Was it a free ride you wanted?"

She glared at him, her green eyes burning into his. "I think *you* got the free ride." She felt a flush begin at her throat.

"I want you to stay, Lita. In spite of what you may think, it may be possible for us to resolve our problems."

"I doubt it. Until you come clean about your motives and whatever is troubling you, I have no alternative but to consider this a trial run that didn't work out."

He opened the door to the sports car and helped her into it. "I'll reveal all of it when we go out on the *Sea Sprite* this afternoon. Hold your questions. Right now, I have to try to console my mother."

On the way to his home, Lita was dimly aware of the palm trees, the masses of hibiscus in dazzling shades of pink, red, and yellow. So much beauty surrounding them, so much pain in their hearts?

The lavish mansion loomed ahead, its white brick and wood facade gleaming in the sunlight. Cade pulled into the circular driveway behind a number of Rolls-Royces and expensive dark-windowed cars. Wealth seemed to ooze from every corner of the house and grounds.

When Cade sprang from the driver's seat and stalked around the front of the Maserati, she felt herself recoil. "Come, Lita," he said, helping her from the car. He escorted her to the double front doors which opened at their approach. A butler greeted them. Cade led her through the mural-walled entry hall and into the breathtaking loggia, the covered outdoor room with open sides. One side revealed the grandeur of a sculptured pool with statues and tropical greenery. The other looked out on the expanse of ocean. Coral columns supported the exposed roof beams.

Lita halted in the doorway, her heart beating like a hummingbird's wings. Actually, she felt like an impaled butterfly as the conversation among two dozen people stopped. Friendly smiles were cast their way.

"Cade." His mother stepped forward, her aging beauty enhanced by a designer dress the same shade as Lita's. Her welcoming smile was tinged with sorrow; the shadowed skin beneath her eyes told its own story.

"Mother, this is Lita Jamison."

Lita's extended hand was warmly taken by Mrs. Hamilton. "My dear, we're pleased you could join us. You knew Jeremy?"

Lita met the dull blue eyes that must once have been vivid and dramatic like her son's. "Yes, I knew him," she replied softly.

"Cade"—his mother's hand fluttered uncertainly—"please see that Miss Jamison has a drink and some of that excellent caviar. I'd like to chat with you later."

"I'll take care of her," Cade said. He led Lita across the Italian marble floor to the bar and an elegant buffet with a tempting arrangement of food.

"I really don't want anything, Cade," she whispered. "I'm not hungry."

"You haven't eaten anything since last night."

"No—please. I'll have something later."

"How about some ginger ale, just so you'll have a drink to hold in your hand . . . which is shaking, incidentally."

Lita looked down at her purse, seeing the nervous movement.

"You've obviously been here before, so I can't understand why your nerves are so on edge."

"Perhaps it's because of you."

His eyes narrowed. "I hardly think that's the reason."

She inclined her head toward the guests. "Since you wanted me to come, shouldn't you introduce me to the others? Or are you ashamed of my less-than-designer clothes?"

The color of his eyes deepened as he looked down at her. "You're the most beautiful woman in the room," he murmured. "No one will be looking at your clothes."

"Surely the ladies—"

"Come, Lita," he interrupted gently.

She walked with him across the floor, his hand grasping her arm. The guests were all cordial, the women mentally assessing her, the men seemingly bewitched by her. Any questions asked of her were promptly answered by Cade. Lita saw a few puzzled looks, silent signals passing among several guests.

"Now that I've met them, can I go?" she asked him.

"I'd like you to meet my brother and his wife, Debbie. Then, if you like, we can leave."

"You should stay. It's your duty."

"That's all I've ever been, the dutiful son," he said sharply. "Here they are." He lowered his voice as the couple made their entrance into the room.

Debbie! Lita thought. Of course. She remembered her now from high school.

The young woman broke from her husband's grasp. "Lita!" She hugged Cade's companion, tears clinging to her lashes. "It's been years."

"You two know each other?" Cade asked, suspicion and surprise in his tone.

"Of course," Debbie said. "We went to school together. Are you staying in Palm Beach?" she asked Lita excitedly.

Lita met Cade's gaze. "For a few days."

"That's wonderful! We can get together. I want to hear about all our old friends."

"I've only kept in touch with a few."

Debbie wiped a tear from her lashes. "Please say you'll meet me for lunch tomorrow. Can I call you?"

"Well . . ." She paused. "I'm not sure—"

"Of course she'll meet you," Cade broke in. "I know she wouldn't miss it."

Lita's teeth clamped together as Cade kneaded the flesh of her waist. She nodded. But later, she would tell him off.

Debbie had been a mousy girl whom Lita and a couple of her friends had taken under their wings. A dependent soul, gaminelike, she was sincere and honest to a fault. As a teenager she had loved one boy secretly for years, always too timid to say much about him. Lita looked up at the man who stood behind Debbie.

"I'm Ray," he said, his voice so similar in timbre to Cade's.

Lita smiled and shook his warm hand. She liked him instantly. He seemed cordial, open, and friendly. Quite a difference from his moody brother.

The men began to talk about business and about Cade's trip to Puerto Rico. Debbie took Lita aside, obviously so thrilled to see an old friend, she was beaming with happiness. As she chattered, Lita noticed how much she had changed from the shy girl she had once been.

"So that's the man you kept so secretly in your background," Lita teased. "I like him. He's a real man."

"Oh, you mean Ray?" She laughed, but a tiny frown formed on her forehead. "Yes, he's . . . very nice."

"I always wondered if you had landed your one true love." Lita saw Debbie gulp and turn away.

"Yes, I'm . . . lucky. But let's talk about you. What have you been doing?"

Lita told her about attending the University of Miami for several years and that when her parents had died she had turned her back on all that was familiar and pursued a dancing career.

"How exciting! You must have traveled a great deal, met lots of people."

Lita laughed. "My share, I guess."

When Ray joined them and reminded his wife of obligations yet to be fulfilled, Debbie wailed, "Must we leave now?"

"You know we have to," Ray said patiently.

"Oh, all right," she said, childlike.

"It's been a pleasure meeting you, Lita," Ray said warmly. "Try to keep that brother of mine on an even keel." At her questioning look, he added, "You know—yacht—keel."

Lita giggled, the first sincere response she had given anyone that day. "I'm sure he can manage to do that quite well himself."

Cade watched them critically—especially the warm, delighted expression on Lita's face as she gazed up at his brother.

"Will you meet me at one o'clock at Marchand's?" Debbie asked.

Lita nodded, mentally adding up her small horde of money. "I'll be there," she promised. She watched the couple make the rounds. The elder Mrs. Hamilton hugged her son and his wife, wiping away tears as they left the room.

"Can I go now?" Lita begged, wanting desperately to leave all of this behind. Jeremy's family—Lord, she had never thought of meeting them this way.

"We'll see my mother for a minute and then leave," Cade said. With an arm loosely around her waist, he led her toward the elegant lady.

"Oh, must you go so soon?" Vivian Hamilton asked softly.

"Lita and I are going out on the *Sea Sprite*," Cade said.

"But you just got back . . ."

Cade's smile was gentle. "You'll only be here another hour yourself."

"That's true," she said sadly. Then to Lita, "Several friends are taking me to spend a few weeks at their villa in France. It will help smooth over these past terrible months."

Lita nodded. "It was a pleasure meeting you." She met the woman's genial handclasp.

"Jamison," Mrs. Hamilton murmured. "Any relation to Elva Jamison?"

Lita's muscles clenched with tension. "Yes. I'm her daughter."

The woman's eyes seemed to brighten. "She was so beautiful, so brilliant. I was sorry to hear of the accident."

Lita murmured her gracious thanks.

"You knew her mother?" Cade asked.

"And father," Mrs. Hamilton replied. "Don't you recall Matthew Jamison? Their expeditions were written up in all the botany journals. They were part of the Miami social set."

"Yes, of course." He glanced at Lita with puzzlement and a trace of anger. Then Cade hugged his mother and led Lita from the house to the yacht.

Sunlight danced on the foam-flecked waves as Cade unplugged the dockside power cord, removed his jacket and tie, and climbed the ladder to the fly bridge. Moments later, the engine started.

Lita stood on the rear deck welcoming the cool, moist breeze, relief spreading over her as they moved away from the Hamilton family's sorrow. As the *Sea Sprite* sped farther from land, she stepped inside the cabin and swiftly changed into shorts and a haltertop, then went back on deck. When Palm Beach was only a distant haze on the horizon, Cade abruptly cut the engine and climbed down to the deck.

"I could use something to eat," he said, immediately shedding his clothes. Averting her eyes from his lean, sun-drenched body, she walked rapidly into the cabin.

When she turned to place the food and a glass of iced tea on the table, he was already seated, wearing only swim trunks. "This looks good," he said, glancing down at the chicken salad sandwiches. "Much better tasting than that horrid caviar my mother seems to feel is a necessity for any social occasion. I only eat it to please her."

"Oh," she said, sitting down across from him.

He seemed to read something into her noncommittal reply. "I happen to love my mother. I've done a lot of things to please her."

"How nice," she said. "I really didn't think that love was in your emotional makeup."

For endless moments he met her steady gaze. "I'll admit that I haven't offered my everlasting affection to any one of my lovers. But I certainly feel I'm capable of it. Perhaps it would take the right partner."

"Have you ever searched for her?" It pained her, but she had to ask.

"Let's say I've kept an eye open. But I never purposefully canvassed the crowd. I sort of had the feeling that if a relationship was right, I would certainly know it."

Lita sipped her cool drink, ignoring the sandwiches. Cade had brought her out here to discuss what he had been up to all along. "You said we would talk," she reminded him.

He wiped his mouth with a napkin, then peered over the rim of his glass as he took a sip. "I want you to promise one thing." She waited for him to finish. "That you won't try to leave here until I agree to it."

She lowered her gaze. "I don't think I owe you anything." She felt herself reel with excitement, fear. "Why should I make such a promise?"

"Because I feel this is my only chance to clear up a mystery. And I need you in order to do that."

She tried to thrust aside her sense of rejection and foreboding as she faced him. "Are you going to tell me what the mystery is?"

"When I have your word."

"How do you know I'll keep it?"

"I don't. But I've been exposed to what I feel confident is a semblance of honesty."

"Cade," she began, leaning forward, "you don't really want me here. You asked me to accompany you for some unexplained reason. Sex"—she halted his protest with a gesture—"was part of it. Lies and pretense were part of it. Now it is time for you to be honest with me."

He leaned back against the chair, taking in a deep breath. "All right. It was because of Jeremy."

She nodded. That much she had assumed since her arrival in Palm Beach.

"Jeremy let you think he was in love with you. But he wasn't." He paused to rap his fingers on the table. "When he told you his feelings, it left you angry and upset."

"Of course," she whispered.

"Jeremy was wealthy, a playboy who was spoiled by our mother and had a wild streak that was uncontrollable." He stopped the rapping, holding her in suspense. "But I think you have a kind of tamed wildness that could reach out and strike someone who had disappointed you."

Lita was suddenly seized by scattered thoughts of the young man and the exotic woman Cade had spoken of. She searched his face for a clue. "I don't know what you mean."

"I think you do, Lita." His tone was harsh, emotional. "Do I seem to you to be the kind of man who couldn't see through a lie?"

Tears brimmed beneath her lids. "I haven't lied to you. You've lied to me by omission." Her voice rose shrilly. "What are you talking about? What are you driving at in that harsh tone of voice?" She watched his expression, noticing the way a fine white line seemed to encircle his lips.

"Jeremy was in love with someone else. He talked to me on the telephone a few hours before you were due to arrive at his apartment." His hands curled into fists. "Although he was usually very secretive about his women, he mentioned your name, told me that he was going to tell you to get lost."

Suspense built up in her like a living, breathing thing. She would finally learn the truth about Jeremy's desertion.

"Someone shot my brother that evening," Cade said calmly, watching her reactions like a shark watches its prey. "I think that person was you!"

Nine

Lita felt as though a blow had struck her stomach. A wave of dizziness and nausea rocked her body. Cade—what he was saying didn't make sense. He caught her as she swayed on the chair.

"Hurt Jeremy?" she mumbled. "You think I could . . . shoot Jeremy?"

"Tell me the truth, Lita," he said huskily, holding her rigidly by the shoulders.

"No," she cried out softly.

"You didn't do it?"

She swung her head lightly back and forth, eyes wide and tear-filled. "No," she repeated.

He stepped back, standing menacingly over her. "Someone did. I aim to find out who."

"I loved him," she murmured. "At least I thought I did until—"

"Until what?"

She felt the tremor in her body as she tried to swallow a sob. She couldn't reveal her feelings about Cade. It would be like a second rejection. *I don't need that.*

"I had no experience with love. Only after I left Miami

did I realize that it was the excitement he'd created that had made me think I cared for him."

"What was your immediate reaction when he told you he didn't want you? Revenge?"

She took a deep breath. "I would have liked to throw something at his smiling, handsome face. But I didn't. And I didn't do anything else, except take his car and ride crazily for hours on the highway that leads through the Everglades."

"What then?"

"I ran off the road and into a swamp." She shuddered, remembering that evening. "I got out of the car as it started to sink. A family picked me up and took me to their home so I could clean up. Then I got a cab back to Miami, packed, and took the first flight to Puerto Rico."

Cade watched as tears trickled down her cheeks. He wanted to believe her—desperately. She had mocked him earlier about his ability to feel deeply. At this precise moment, he knew that he truly loved her. But he could never live with himself if Lita turned out to be the one who . . .

He pulled her to his chest, cradling her against him until the sobbing stopped.

Reaching for her chin, he guided her lips to his, savoring the moistness of her warm mouth and the heat that radiated within. His hand reached up to cup a breast.

"No," he heard her moan. She couldn't mean that, not when her skin was already hot and damp. "Please don't," she begged.

"Why not?" he whispered, his panting breath fanning her cheek.

"You think I . . . shot Jeremy."

"No."

"Until you find out something definite, you'll never be sure."

"I thought so, but I know better now. The police are convinced the injury was self-inflicted. I'm the one who—"

She shook her head violently. "Don't touch me again . . . until it's proved."

He stepped back, still holding her, seeing the smoky

dullness of her eyes. Had she really said that? "If it's what you want," he said slowly.

"It is."

He swallowed the hard lump in his throat. "Do I have your promise to stay?"

"Yes," she said. He had forced her to agree. "At least for now."

"Good." He wanted to love that beautiful mouth until she came to him willingly. But something in her eyes caused him to subjugate his desires. He would have to consider her wishes. At the moment, he wasn't included in them.

"I want you to stay at the house as my guest. There are servants, so it will be entirely respectable. I need your help, Lita."

"I'll stay."

"Fine," he said, aware of the husky tremor in his voice. He made his way to the fly bridge, flustered by his efforts to make her admit her guilt. He hadn't really thought she could commit a crime and still act so innocent. He now believed that she had been sincerely shocked when he had told her of the shooting. But he couldn't help wondering if he had irreversibly damaged their relationship. How would he have felt if he'd been in Lita's place? Betrayed? Revengeful? That, and much more.

Lita's emotions were churning like violent waves in a stormy ocean. Biting her lower lip, she walked to the deck. Could she ever forgive him for his deception . . . for his vile accusation?

Shoot Jeremy? She was still in shock. She who wouldn't step on an ant, who had even rescued ladybugs fluttering helplessly in a pool of water.

Her gaze focused on the swirling wake behind the yacht. Did his family know what Cade's suspicions were? Embarrassment rose like a red sail on her cheeks. Could anyone successfully mask such suspicions? Cade had.

She had been doubtful of his motives from the beginning. But love was a blinding factor. She couldn't see beyond those broad shoulders and handsome features.

All that had seemed to matter were the lips and hands that caressed her into fiery responsiveness.

He was a great actor and she had fallen for his line. But two could play at his game. With only a partial paycheck in her purse and a few dollars in a bank account in Miami, she would have to accept his accommodations until she had a lead on a job and a place to live. Indirectly, she would be repaid for his treachery.

The motor stopped, and only then did Lita realize they had returned to shore. In the crimson, golden reflection of the sunset, the Hamilton mansion became a study in elegance. The masses of flowers seemed to dip their heads, accepting the coming darkness. Would the somberness of night descend on her life when it became necessary to leave Cade?

She heard the thud of his feet as he leaped over the railing to tie up the yacht. "Dinner should be ready in an hour," he called. "That will give us time to shower and dress."

Brushing her palms down the sides of her shorts, she watched him nervously. "Would you mind if I stayed on board?" She saw his frown and turned away. "I'm afraid my company would be less than stimulating."

"If you prefer." His tone was brusque. "But I would like you to join me."

"Not tonight," she said softly. "I need time to think."

"Okay," he agreed. "The staff will wonder why you chose to stay here." He paused. "Tomorrow I'll have the butler take you to meet Debbie for lunch. I hope it's enjoyable, renewing your friendship with her."

"Thank you."

"I'll see you in the evening." She heard his footsteps retreat. "It's about time I got back in harness and ran Hamilton Industries." The silence between them crackled with unspoken words. "Be sure to lock yourself in."

"I will," she said. "Good night."

Her eyes devoured his tall, imposing body as he walked stiffly along the dock and up the path leading to the house. As dusk swiftly melted into night, a shiver ran across her skin. She realized that she had been clenching her nails into her palms so hard, there were indentations in the flesh.

Raising her head to the darkened skies, she saw only Cade's handsome face. Would she ever be able to get over his pained expression or his accusation? The words were written across her brain.

She turned and fumbled for the knob. Stepping into the darkened saloon, she heard the click of the lock behind her and breathed in relief for the first time since Cade had left. Flipping on the light switch and drawing the drapes, she was enveloped by the stillness of her surroundings.

Lita had a great deal to consider and a few nights of sleep to catch up on. Brushing her teeth, she noticed her vacant stare as she peered into the mirror. This day had taken its toll of her. It had cost her all the underlying hope that somehow, through some miracle, Cade would want her.

She watched television for a brief time, not fully cognizant of the entertainers or the change of programs. Switching off the set, she stepped to the door. Fog had drifted in, like a shade drawn between the mansion and the yacht. "How symbolic," she murmured.

The swirling mist and the occasional haunting sound of a ship's wailful warning added to her sense of abandonment. Any remaining tinges of bitterness toward Jeremy had been wiped clean when his casket had been positioned above its final resting place. That vibrant young man would no longer love or be loved.

It was eleven o'clock the next morning before she crawled from her bunk to shower and dress. Aware of a numbness in the region of her heart, she felt the need to cry, to release her pent-up emotions. But tears would not come.

Standing on the deck, seeing their love nest of pillows through a blur of tears, Lita realized how much she had learned to love the *Sea Sprite*. The balmy days on deck had provided idle moments in which to think about her past and future, for the first time since she had left her parents' home. Any spare hours before had always been spent rushing to and from work, squeezing in the necessary daily chores. This was a new pattern of living. Had she been stupid in being too proud to accept the money left to her by her parents? Had she been too hard on them for pursuing their own interests?

"I'd like to retire to the beautiful ocean for the rest of my life," she said aloud. "It's a wonderful way to live." She turned on the television for company, washed some clothes, and placed them in the dryer. "All the conveniences," she said with a sigh.

There was plenty of food in the refrigerator. With the exception of milk and bread, it held a sufficient supply for one person for a month. Tossing a croissant into the microwave oven, she put on the kettle for instant coffee. What was Cade doing now? Acting the part of a big business executive? She visualized him in a blue suit, conservative tie, and white shirt. That wasn't quite the image she'd had of him lately as he'd spent most days in the briefest of shorts, traversing the rough Atlantic in his trusty boat.

She would have to write Maria, describing their trip but withholding any mention of what had transpired when they reached Palm Beach. Her aunt must be assured that all was well. She would not disillusion Maria in her appraisal of Cade.

The full impact of his accusation only seemed real to her now. A stab of pain entered her chest, shattering the protective cocoon she had woven around her emotions. Cade hadn't really cared about her. All he'd wanted was to return her to the scene of the supposed crime. He'd accepted the entertainment she had offered as a bonus for his trouble.

At ten minutes before one o'clock, Lita entered Marchand's Restaurant. Ignoring the interested glances of the male diners, she waited for the hostess. Debbie was already seated at a corner table.

"For some reason, I was afraid you wouldn't make it," Debbie said.

"If you remember correctly, Cade guaranteed my showing up."

"I noticed," Debbie said, sipping on an Alexander. The waiter took Lita's drink order. "Tell me, is there anything serious between you two?"

Lita smiled. "Not really." She avoided Debbie's eyes by concentrating on the menu. "I met him in San Juan and he asked me to join him. So I did. I'm staying on the yacht."

"Cade doesn't make commitments," Debbie said softly. "I would hate to see you get hurt."

Lita laughed huskily. "Don't worry about that. I'm getting used to it." Changing the subject, she added, "Tell me about that marvelous hunk of man you married."

Debbie's lashes lowered. "He's a good husband. I just don't appreciate him enough."

"He seemed to have such warm, wonderful qualities." Lita glanced away as a stain of pink sped up her friend's cheeks. "Is he involved in the Hamilton enterprises?"

"Yes. We're going to be moving permanently to the West Coast. Ray has taken over that part of the operation. There are seven allied industries: mills, factories, and also a couple of food distribution warehouses."

"You married a rich man." There was no envy in Lita's voice. She thanked the waiter as he placed the margarita before her and took their orders. When he moved away, Debbie released a long, shuddering sigh.

"I grew up next door to the Hamiltons. They weren't always rich. Comfortable, perhaps. I was a little sister to the three of them. Cade was always the leader. Also the one to keep his brothers in line. Jeremy, especially," she added wistfully.

Lita toyed with the rim of her glass. She wondered what Cade had been like as a young boy. Had he also worn braces, hating the mouthful of metal? "What made you choose Ray?"

There were tears in Debbie's eyes when she finally acknowledged Lita's question. "It's a long story. Perhaps I'll tell you all about it one of these days."

Lita smiled warmly at her. "Sure," she said, feeling it wouldn't be a happy tale.

"Now." Debbie brightened. "I want to hear all about you and the friends you've kept in touch with."

All through the seafood salad and pecan pie, Lita brought her up to date. "Karla and Peg still live in Miami. They'll be pleased to hear you married so well. Neither of them have met Mister Right."

"That means all three of you are still bachelorettes."

Debbie's eyes seemed to glitter, remembering their friends.

Lita shrugged. "I suppose you're right. But one of these days, with a little luck . . ."

"You were always the one who protected me," Debbie murmured, "and kept my secrets. You never told your best buddies what I confided to you."

"I never told you their secrets either."

"That's a rare thing, having a discreet, trustworthy friend. I've missed that."

"And I've missed you," Lita said.

"Let's keep in touch this time. I don't want to lose you again."

When it came time to leave, Debbie picked up the check. In spite of Lita's protest, she refused to budge. "I owe you more than a lunch," she said. "You often paid for me. Of course, your parents were wealthy. I still don't understand why you don't use your inheritance."

"It's a matter of pride, I suppose. My parents gave me nothing of themselves. I don't want anything they left. I had to prove to myself that I could be self-sustaining. Well, I can be." She laughed, remembering the degrading job in Puerto Rico. "Sometimes we have to compromise our lofty ideals."

"Independent, huh?" Debbie said. "Much more than I ever was—or will be. Maybe someday you'll find the answer to what to do with your fortune."

"As the years go by, I'm trying to be more understanding of my parents. I'd like to do something for my aunt Maria and maybe donate some to a charity."

Debbie nodded. "Look, if you're going to be staying at Cade's, I'd like to see you again before we leave for California. Can I call or leave a message?"

"Of course." Lita hugged her friend, then watched as the petite woman left the restaurant. She placed a call to the Hamilton butler to pick her up. Rather liking the big black car with the dark windows, she thought that it wouldn't be difficult to get used to wealth again.

At dusk, Cade came to the *Sea Sprite*, suggesting she join him for dinner at the mansion. Tonight she was not reluctant to share a meal with the autocratic man. In fact, she welcomed the invitation.

He listened intently all through dinner as she told him of her luncheon with Debbie. He discussed some of the more humorous aspects of his business. He seemed in fine spirits, although she was certain she detected a watchful, waiting expression in his eyes.

When she excused herself to return to the *Sea Sprite*, he seemed reluctant to allow her to leave. Walking beside her, he suddenly asked, "Why didn't you tell me you were from a wealthy family?"

"Would it have made a difference?" she asked quietly.

"Perhaps, though not because of the money itself. It . . . it would have shown you in a different light." He ran a hand through his thick, dark hair. "Why were you living in such humble circumstances when you could have been at the Hilton?"

She tilted her head to gaze up at him. "I never accepted my inheritance. It's still in trust until I decide what I want to do with it."

"Is that why you took the job at the Mariposa—because you lacked money?"

"Yes, and to help with Maria's financial problems."

"You could do a lot to help her if you took advantage of the money that was left to you."

"I've thought about that. Maria deserves a break." She sighed. "I guess I have to come to terms with my feelings about my father and mother first."

He nodded as she opened the cabin door. "Sleep well," he said gently, running a finger down her cheek.

She stared at the path he had taken long after he had disappeared into the mansion.

Lita spent the better part of the next two days on the yacht. She made some calls from a pay phone, hoping to line up a job, but without success. At Cade's request, she joined him each evening for dinner. He continued to study her, sometimes covertly. In spite of his declaration, she wondered if he still doubted her innocence.

Late one afternoon she emerged from the shower wearing only a large towel. She halted in mid-stride at the sight of Cade, clad in jeans and a T-shirt, reclining on his bunk.

"Hi," he said softly, his eyes lazily taking in the golden skin above and below the towel.

"Hi, yourself." She busied her trembling hands with taking underwear from a drawer and choosing a sundress.

"You don't seem surprised to see me," he murmured.

"This is your yacht. Why shouldn't you be here?"

"I could ask why you didn't lock the door?"

"I didn't think of it." She pulled on a pair of bikini panties.

"I'm concerned about your safety."

She shrugged and turned her back to him while she slipped on the dress.

"Do you give all your men this kind of show?"

She faced him squarely, hands on her hips. "There isn't anything you haven't already seen with dozens of women, including me. As for other men, there really haven't been that many in my life."

"I'd like to keep it that way."

Her eyes widened. "Meaning?"

He lifted himself to a sitting position. "I'd like to keep you for my own."

"I'm really not interested in becoming a possession, Cade. I've been independent for a long time—ever since I was about six. You get that way when your parents don't take the time to care about you."

"Is that what you need—love?"

"Don't we all?"

"I could give you that."

She tossed her head. "Lovemaking, Cade, not love. There's one heck of a big difference."

"You don't believe I'm capable of loving you?"

"Let's just say I haven't seen any evidence." The blood in her temples was throbbing so loudly, she could barely hear.

"Would you like me to demonstrate?"

"No." The word wobbled out.

"Why?" His tone was husky, sensual.

"Because you still believe I'm capable of a horrendous crime. How could I possibly ignore what is so much on your mind?"

"There was another woman in Jeremy's life. I'm going to try to locate her."

"What good will it do to find her? How would she figure in his death?"

"I could narrow the field of suspects. A neighbor who just returned to Florida from an extended stay in Europe gave me a description."

"Probably of me racing out of his apartment." She brushed her hair until it fanned about her face. "It still won't make a difference between us until your phantom killer is found and confesses."

"Why are you so insistent on waiting? We could be beautiful together again."

"Not with a ghost standing between us." She glossed her generous lips.

"I need you, Lita. And believe me, I've never said that to a woman before."

"I need you too," she admitted. "But not like this."

He drew his lean body up slowly from the bunk and stood beside her. "Are you making me beg?" He caught her by the waist and pulled her to him. "I'm suffering enough for the both of us."

"You couldn't know what begging is. And I have no desire to see you suffer."

"Don't do this to us." He buried his face in her hair and his voice was like the roughened purr of a jungle cat. "I really do believe that you have no connection with Jeremy's death. Why can't we take up where we left off that fantastic tropical night beneath the stars? Do you know how I felt loving you with the crickets chirping, the surf lapping at the beach, and the moon looking down on our naked bodies?" He lowered his voice. "And do you know how I missed making love to you since?"

She was aware of her quickened breathing, the blood that was racing hotly in her veins. "Why are you doing this?" she demanded.

"Don't you realize that we found something special? How rare that is. How lucky we are to be unencumbered by other attachments, to have time to get to know each other."

"What you're saying is true, but it doesn't change one very important fact. You once thought I could be capable of—I don't even want to mention it. Nevertheless, it's a barrier between us."

"I'm well aware of that." He sighed wearily. "But I had to get it out in the open, had to voice what was like a lead weight on my heart."

"It will take a while to put it behind me."

"We have time. As long as we're together."

"Not the way you want to be."

Cade stood very still, the muscles of his shoulders taut, a nerve jumping in his throat. Stepping back, he looked down at her. "All right," he said finally. "We'll do it your way. Give me time to erase what I've done—what I suspected."

"Does anyone else know?"

He shook his head. "The driving force to locate you was in me. I couldn't share my suspicions."

"I'm glad of that," she murmured.

He started to move away, then met her gaze once again. "There's a dinner-dance tonight. I'd like you to come with me."

She gave a tiny laugh. "I'm sure I don't have the kind of clothes required for one of your elite gatherings."

He glanced at his watch. "I could have everything you need here in an hour."

"What do you mean?"

"I intended asking you to come with me, so I contacted a boutique earlier."

"You knew what I would say . . . about the clothes?"

He nodded, a slow grin curving his lips. "In some ways, women are predictable."

She softened toward him. "I'd like to go with you."

His smile broadened. Stepping closer, he placed a chaste kiss on her cheek. "I'll be back when the clothes are delivered."

"How did you know my size?"

"I remembered how my arms wrapped around you and demonstrated to the saleslady." He took in her willowy length with one long, sensuous glance. "Actually, I checked your dress and shoe sizes."

"But I've been here—"

He winked. "You'll just have to wonder when I did it,

won't you?" He walked briskly through the cabin and out the door, laughing softly.

Lita sank down on the bunk, vaguely weakened by their conversation, feeling light-headed at the prospect of spending time with Cade. Her love for him welled up in her throat, and an uncontrollable shudder of excitement tore through her carefully guarded heart.

A thin layer of ice had been penetrated by his warm, rakish attitude. Would their shaky relationship hold firm or were there circumstances that would once again shatter their fragile truce?

An aura of uncertainty plagued her as she awaited Cade's return.

Ten

The magnificent crystal and bronze chandelier caught Lita's eye as she and Cade were ushered into the elaborate entry hall. Built in the Art Deco style of the 1930s, the house was another picture-perfect mansion designed for people with unlimited wealth. The fragrant scent of gardenias permeated the air while a five-piece band, in black-tie, played softly in the background.

On their way to a bar set up in a corner of the huge living room, she peeked into the dining area. The elegant mahogany table was set with antique china for twenty people and was enhanced by candelabras and arrangements of orchids, roses, and white lilies.

With a sharp pang, she recalled the elaborate dinner parties her parents had arranged for their fellow botanists on their rare times at home. Mostly they were either planning an expedition into the wilds of Africa or Borneo for new plant specimens, or just returning from a journey. It was a miracle that she had retained her love of flowers. As a child, she had usually been told to run along. After she had waited for them for months, they couldn't seem to find time to spend even ten minutes with her.

If I ever have a child, she thought, *I'll smother it with love.*

Cade handed her a fruit drink mixed with rum and she nodded her thanks. The guests, all "beautiful people," were of varying ages and interests. She silently blessed Cade for the gown of creamy silk and the high-heeled sandals just a shade darker. The V neckline was an open invitation for the thin emerald necklace gracing her swanlike throat. After telling her she looked lovely, Cade had taken it from the family safe and fastened it for her. His fingers had lingered at the nape of her neck and he had gently kissed her earlobe.

He had then stepped back to admire his handiwork, his pupils dilating as his eyes caressed her slender form. "No one at the dinner could hope to look more ravishing than you."

She recalled the shiver that had flowed down her spine at the hypnotic glow of his captivating gaze and how her legs had felt about as sturdy as cooked linguini.

Cade introduced her to his friends, never once mentioning her background or family. She was grateful for that. It wasn't that she didn't feel a sense of pride at her parents' accomplishments. She found it much simpler, though, to be taken at face value.

In spite of the fact that she was virtually penniless, at least for one night she fit into the congenial atmosphere of the Palm Beach set. Cade, in his well-fitting tuxedo, with his dark good looks, was an escort fit for a princess. He was so handsome, she caught her breath when he smiled at her.

After the seven-course dinner the guests milled about on the covered terrace, their conversations stimulating and interesting. People from a dozen diversified walks of life circulated and seemed to be having a fine time, just as envisioned by their vivacious young hostess, who seemed to have planned every detail. Several dozen other guests, who joined them after dinner, greeted Cade and Lita with genuine enthusiasm.

When Cade pressed her to his hard chest for a slow,

languid fox-trot, she melted into him. "Having a good time?" he murmured.

"Delightful," she whispered.

"I knew you would like these people. And they like you."

"Thank you," she said against his chest. "There's no doubt about how much respect and admiration they have for you."

"I've known most of them for years. They always treat the ambitious with deference. One never knows when one might need a rich young man as an escort, to buy into a new project, or become chairman of some worthy cause."

"You mean it's all surface charm?"

"Not really. But one has to be on his toes with this kind of social crowd. Basically, they're a fine group. But there's always at least one manipulator to beware of."

"How often do you go to these affairs?"

"Two, maybe three times a year. I turn down most invitations—you know those beautifully inscribed kind." As the tempo of the music increased, he whirled her in a samba. At the end of the number, he led her to the bar.

"Isn't it important to your business to keep up your social obligations?" she asked as the bartender served her a margarita.

"Since I don't have a wife or hostess, I'm excused from returning any of these posh affairs. Most of my entertaining is done in restaurants."

Would having a mistress change that? she wondered, but refused to comment or ask the obvious question, and he dropped the subject. The chemical attraction between them came alive, became tangible, as he held her in his arms. They swayed to the popular new dances and to the oldies. He had a natural rhythm that seemed to flow through him.

"Will you be ready to leave soon?" he asked during a break in the music.

She smiled. "Whenever you are." His eyes were glowing like brilliant sapphires within the burnished skin. How she wished he could really be with her that night.

"You're the loveliest woman in this entire group," he said, holding her gaze.

"Thanks to this heavenly creation."

"The clothes have nothing to do with it. You'd be just as beautiful without any kind of covering."

"I'd have to join a nudist colony," she teased.

His eyes clouded. "I wouldn't want any other man to see your gorgeous body. I'm selfish enough to want you all to myself."

She glanced at him suspiciously. "Is this conversation leading to anything?"

One side of his mouth curved up. "I'd like it to lead to my bed. But then"—he paused—"you've already told me no on that score."

"Please, Cade." Her eyes began to fill with tears. "Don't talk about that. It's difficult for me to turn you down when—"

"You want the same thing I do." His voice was a husky whisper.

"I'll admit that."

The muscles in his jaw tightened. "I won't pressure you. By far, you've given me more than any man could hope for."

She turned aside and wiped her cheek with the back of her hand. Why did he have to be so persistent, so sweet, so understanding? And why did he accept her decision? If he bulldozed her, giving her no chance to decline, she would accept him with open arms. Then her own sense of abandonment would overshadow the hurt and disappointment that his accusation had caused.

"I'm ready to go," she said.

With his palm beneath her elbow, he guided her toward their hosts. Ten minutes later the Hamilton mansion, aglow with lights, was directly before them. Could she possibly live with Cade in that magnificent house? She shook her head as he turned into the driveway. In the silence that followed, she wondered what he was thinking, feeling.

"I'm in love with you," he said.

Her head spun toward him. "What?" she whispered. Blood pounded through her temples; her hands were hot and moist.

"I am, you know." He drew in a steadying breath. "I didn't plan to say that now. It sort of . . . burst out."

"Love?" she echoed. "That's a little hard to believe."

"Because of Jeremy?" he asked thickly.

"It's natural that I should question such a declaration." She paused, swallowing hard. "Jeremy spouted those words all the time—obviously to every woman he met."

"I'm not Jeremy," he said firmly. "I'm not a wild, capricious kid. Jeremy never grew up." He moved toward her. "I'm a man, Lita. A caring, sensual being who knows what he wants, but hasn't quite figured out how to get it. Tell me"—his voice was husky—"if it hadn't been for all those unhappy circumstances surrounding my brother, could you have fallen in love with me?"

"Yes," she replied truthfully. *Oh, yes, my darling.*

"I love your honesty. Don't change, Lita. It's such an endearing quality."

"I believe in sincerity. Perhaps it's because I saw so little of it in my formative years." She put her hand on the door handle. "I'm a little tired, so if you don't mind I'd like to go in now."

"I'll walk you to the *Sea Sprite*." There was resignation in his voice. "And then, I'll bid you good night. It's not what I want, but . . ."

"Thank you for the lovely dress and accessories," she said as he extended his hand to assist her. "Please help me remove the necklace." She turned her back to him.

He seemed to pause before she felt the jewelry slip away. "You could have kept it until morning." His voice throbbed.

She laughed. "And have someone come to the yacht and steal it?"

"I worry more about someone stealing *you*," he murmured.

"No fear of that," she assured him, turning to face him. His disarming smile almost forced her to admit defeat, so joyfully would she have welcomed his lovemaking.

He walked beside her along the deck to the cabin door. Their hands reached for the lock simultaneously. When he touched her, she felt a flame burst within her, sky-rockets exploding in her brain.

Cade gently eased her to his chest, his lips moving across her temple. She lifted her arms to his neck.

"It feels so good, so right, holding you like this." His mouth caressed her ear slowly, enticingly. His hands brushed down her back, lightly probing her spine. "It's driving me slightly wild knowing what's beneath that creamy silk. Do you know how much I want to touch you, taste you, smell the fragrance of each erotic spot?" He pulled her closer.

"Please," she said weakly. "Don't make it more diffi-cult to tell you that I can't." She trembled, uncon-sciously pressing more tightly to his frame.

"Will you come visit me in the mental institution?" he teased.

"It won't be necessary. I'll be in the adjoining cell."

"Good." He laughed. "At least you'll be close enough for me to whisper through the walls."

"Oh, Cade." Her throat tightened, making it impossi-ble to say more. Driven by the physical need to have the evening culminate in tender lovemaking, she pressed her curves into the hardness of him.

He lifted away the arms that clutched his neck tightly. "If I don't leave now, I won't leave at all." He put her away from him. "Think about us and how I feel about you," he murmured huskily.

His words echoed as she watched him walk toward the mansion.

Lita's shoulders slumped as she left the telephone booth. She couldn't blame her agent for being irritated with her. In the decade of study and over five years of dancing in Broadway shows and in nightclubs in Los Angeles, London, and Miami, she had never terminated an engagement without giving notice.

But seven months ago, when Jeremy admitted that he hadn't loved her and laughed at her obvious distress, her only rational thought was escape. The commitment to the club where she had been working, to her life in Miami, and to her future plans to choreograph stage dancing were abandoned in her haste to reach Puerto Rico and the haven offered by Aunt Maria.

She could understand her agent's reluctance to send her on a job now. He was interested in dealing with reliable clients because of the keen competition in the entertainment industry. She had to be content with his promise to keep her in mind for future bookings.

She'd be at the bottom of his list, she mused, but with a little luck . . . Damn. In a way, she was relieved that it wasn't necessary to make a decision now. If he had offered her a job, she would have had to leave Cade. Feeling as strongly as she did about him, the mere thought of leaving was heartwrenching.

In his presence, she was more alive, more sensitive, more excited, than she had ever been before. If this wasn't love, then what was it? A persistent thought kept needling her. Was it really so important that the criminal be found before she agreed to become Cade's mistress? He loved her. She loved him. What more could she ask?

Debbie had said that he didn't make commitments. Was asking her to become his mistress a first? Could it lead to something more—a permanent arrangement? Marriage?

Lita shook her head. Since the beginning of time, women had looked for enduring relationships, all sisters in the everlasting struggle to tame men.

As she strolled along the palm-lined street to Cade's home, images formed in her mind: the wonder of her lover's hands stroking her eager flesh; the torrid mouth that tasted and caressed; the contrast between suntanned skin and milk-white skin; his moans of pleasure; the knowing grin when she responded to him in deep, intimate frenzy. She recalled with ecstasy the pleasure he gave, the way he gently manipulated her so that their passion was shared, the bliss when their bodies joined.

The late afternoon sun beat down on her, heating skin that was already hot with desire. A car eased to the curb beside her.

"Hi," a deep, familiar voice called to her.

"Ray!" Lita was surprised at his unexpected appearance and her own delight in seeing him again. The red Porsche suited his dark, suntanned complexion. In looks he favored Cade, except for the earth-brown eyes.

"Hop in," he said as she walked toward the car.

"Well . . . I was out for a walk."

"Please, Lita," he said. "I need to talk to you." He must have seen the puzzled expression flit across her face, for he emerged and led her to the passenger side. "It's rather important."

Her mind raced ahead, fearful that something had happened to Cade. What could Ray possibly want to talk to her about? He didn't seem the philandering type of husband, but she couldn't help being suspicious.

He gunned the motor. The Porsche zipped along the street, finally skidding to a halt in front of the house.

"Can we go to the yacht?" he asked, glancing at Cade's fashionable home.

She nodded, preceding him. Unlocking the door, she gestured for him to enter the cabin. "Coffee?" she offered.

"Booze, if you have it."

"Cade has some Scotch."

"Fine."

She poured the liquid into a glass and set the bottle on the table. From his agitated movements, she strongly suspected he would require a refill. She watched as he tossed the contents down and placed the glass on the table.

Heaving a mighty sigh, he said, "Lord, I needed that."

She sat down opposite him and waited. She wouldn't urge him to talk. Glancing at the wall clock, she realized that Cade would be home soon. What significance would he place on Ray's visit?

"I need your help," Ray said bluntly. "It's Debbie."

"What's wrong?"

"Oh, come on, Lita, you can level with me. I know that she thinks of you as a friend—the one who can keep secrets, who is honest, sincere . . ." His voice trailed off. He poured himself another Scotch and nervously whirled the liquid in the glass.

"I don't understand."

"You had lunch together. Didn't she tell you what was wrong? Why she can't sleep? Why she has the shakes?"

"No. Debbie didn't tell me anything." She leaned back in the chair, straining away from him.

"Look." He ran a hand through his curly black hair. "I don't want to put you on the spot. But I have to find out what's wrong with her." His voice softened. "I love her an awful lot. She's my life. I want to help, but she won't let me ask her any questions. Clams up. Cries. I've never seen her like this and it scares me."

"She hasn't said anything, Ray. I noticed that she was nervous. Maybe she should see a doctor."

"I've suggested it," he said wearily.

"Perhaps you'll have to *insist* on it," she said quietly.

He searched her face, his expression sad, bewildered, defeated. "You're sure she didn't confide in you? Knowing what's wrong could save our marriage."

Lita shook her head, eyes wide with concern. "What makes you think your marriage is in jeopardy?"

His smile didn't reach his eyes. "I'm afraid it's another man. I think she cares for someone else and is afraid to tell me."

Lita frowned and stood up. "I hardly think so, Ray. Debbie never cared much for running around. She rarely dated when I knew her."

"Something's wrong and I'm going to find out what it is," he said, his face hardening. "Will you tell me if you find out?"

Lita's mouth opened and snapped shut. "I couldn't betray a confidence," she said.

His eyes pleaded with her. "Please."

She began to pace the floor nervously. "You're asking me to do something that is totally reprehensible. Debbie is my friend. I could never betray a trust."

"About seven months ago," he said, "I came home one afternoon and found a note from Debbie on the kitchen table." He grimaced in pain. "It said she wasn't coming back. That she was going away with someone."

Lita could only stare at him.

"I went out, not sure what to do, and when I got home later that night she was there—upset, crying, *but she was there.* The note was gone. I never questioned her."

He dropped his face into his hands. "Ever since then I've held my breath, wondering if she would change her mind."

He looked up and studied Lita for several minutes. Rising, he downed the rest of the drink. "Will you do one thing for me?"

"What?"

"If Debbie tells you, will you let me know if I've guessed right? I'd rather be prepared before she runs off."

Lita bit into her lower lip, shaking her head in confusion. "What would you do if she wanted to go?"

His shoulders drooped and a mask of pain covered his handsome features. "I'd let her go," he said, almost inaudibly. "I love her too much to have her unhappy, even though I'd give my right arm to keep her."

Tears stung the back of her eyes. She felt herself propelled forward, her arms closing about his waist. "Oh, Ray," she cried softly.

He drew her close. They stood together in the dusk-filled cabin for many minutes. "I'll do whatever I can for you," she promised, "without revealing any secrets she may tell me."

"Thanks, Lita. You're very special."

"So are you," she murmured.

She felt a cold chill on her back and slowly drew away from Ray. Her gaze searched the area beyond his shoulder and came to rest on a pair of darkened blue eyes.

At her tiny cry, Ray spun around to face Cade. The brothers stared at each other for an endless minute. Lita was mute, unable to utter a single sound.

"What's going on?" Cade asked quietly. Too quietly.

"I came to ask for Lita's help with Debbie," Ray said.

Cade sought Lita's eyes for confirmation. She nodded slowly. "What did you think Lita could do?" he asked calmly.

"I thought Debbie might have said something. Women do confide in other women."

"Women also keep secrets for other women," Cade said huskily. "Did you actually think she would betray Debbie?"

"I hoped . . . when I explained our situation." Color

rose in Ray's face. "Did you think I'd come here to pursue your woman?" he asked bluntly.

"You never have before," Cade said. "Why should I think so now?"

"Maybe"—Ray smiled weakly—"because this lady means more to you than the others did."

Lita nervously brushed the back of her hand over her cheek. She felt like screaming. The tension was so thick, it was overwhelming. She had to do something.

"Cade." She edged closer to him. "Ray is telling you exactly what happened here." She tried to sound unconcerned, but was sure it was a rather feeble attempt. "Ray wants to save his marriage. If there was anything between us, I strongly doubt that we would have sullied your territory by coming here, to your yacht."

Cade seemed to relax. "You'll have to admit the evidence appeared damaging." He faced his brother and extended his hand.

Ray gripped it hard. "You've hugged Debbie lots of times and I never thought anything of it."

"She's like my sister," Cade said.

Ray gave Lita a lingering look. "I wish Lita was my sister. She'd make a nice addition to the family."

Cade ignored the remark. "Hadn't you better get home to that wife of yours?" he suggested.

"Thank you, Lita, for whatever you feel you can do."

She touched Ray's cheek. "Okay," she murmured. "Give Debbie my love."

Ray ducked out the door, leaving Cade and Lita alone. "You don't trust me, do you?" she said, a feeling of heaviness in her chest.

"Sometimes jealousy rears its ugly head and man becomes uncivilized once again." He pulled her into his arms. "I should believe in both of you more. I'll try to do better in the future."

She snuggled closer. If there really was a future for them . . .

Debbie arrived unannounced the next day, carrying her bathing suit and a towel tucked under her arm. "I had to get out of that hotel suite," she said.

Lita noticed her trembling hands. "Why don't you and Ray stay at the mansion?"

She shook her head. "The men see enough of each other at the office all day. Ray thinks it's better this way."

They swam for a while, then lay sunning themselves on the sand. Debbie couldn't seem to keep her hands still.

"What is it?" Lita asked softly.

Debbie released a troubled sigh. "My agitation is obvious, isn't it? I have a big problem. I don't know how to resolve it."

"Would talking about it help?"

"Probably," she murmured, rubbing the back of her neck. "I'm just not sure I want to saddle you with this."

"That's what friends are for."

"I know."

Silence stretched between them, and Lita allowed her mind to wander to Cade.

"It's awful," Debbie said suddenly. She seemed to be thinking out loud. "You wouldn't believe a mousy little thing like me could . . ."

"Is it something to do with your husband?"

"Yes . . . some of it."

Lita heard her friend's teeth chattering. When Debbie was young, every little thing had seemed like a mammoth problem. Perhaps she hadn't outgrown that. "If I can help," Lita said. "Whenever you're ready. Take some time to think it over. You may be able to resolve it yourself."

"You wouldn't understand something like this. No one would."

Not quite knowing how to handle the situation, Lita said, "I'm thirsty. Let's go aboard the *Sea Sprite* and get something cold to drink."

Debbie followed her meekly to the dock and aboard the yacht. "It's a long time since I've been here. I remember the day all three Hamiltons and two other girls and myself went for a cruise. We had such fun," she reminisced. "Jeremy and I paired off. We swam and fished. It was so wonderful."

Jeremy was paired off with her? Lita thought, surprised. "How long ago was that?" She filled two glasses with lemonade and sat down across from Debbie.

"Before he went off on another backpacking trip to New Zealand and Australia. Exactly three years and two months ago."

Lita had the uncomfortable idea that Debbie could come up with the day and the hour as well. "How long have you been married?"

"It will be three years next month."

Three months after Jeremy left. Why did that seem significant? "What made you decide to marry Ray?"

"He's loved me since I was a little girl. It seemed . . . the only thing to do."

"But, Debbie"—Lita sat forward—"didn't you love him? Wasn't he the one you were always so secretive about?"

Debbie's face whitened. "No, Lita, he wasn't." Her voice was so soft, it was barely audible.

Lita frowned. She realized it wasn't right to ask questions. Could Cade have been the one she was in love with? Debbie was so disturbed, her body seemed to jerk. Lita felt her heart beat erratically, as though she were sitting on the edge of a precipice and one more question would push her over.

Something deep inside warned her of impending danger. She was too much of a coward, at this moment, to pursue it. When she glanced at her watch, Debbie followed her action.

"I'll have to get home. We have a big dinner party to attend tonight." She stood up and moved briskly toward the door.

"Stop by again if you have time," Lita said. "I'll be staying at least another few days."

Debbie hugged her. "I feel a little better just knowing you're here. You always were a friend to depend on."

Lita watched the dark-haired woman walk slowly along the dock, across grass each blade of which was meticulously cut, to a cream-colored Ferrari. Seconds later the car took off in a flurry of pebbles.

Feeling strangely depressed, Lita took a shower, hoping to wash away the gloom Debbie had brought with her. In the back of her mind the thought persisted that Debbie wanted to tell her something that might change her own life dramatically. How long would she have to wait?

Two mornings later a delivery man brought one exquisite, long-stemmed yellow rose to the yacht. Lita breathed in its fragrance and hugged it to her breast. Cade was subtly eroding the delicate filament she had woven around her heart as protection from him.

His words at dinner that evening were a caress to her ears, and the moments when their hands met accidentally reacted on her nerves like the explosion of a bomb. She knew she was hanging on to her resolution with strained fibers that would soon weaken and snap.

As he walked her back to the yacht, one arm lightly encircling her shoulders, Lita asked if Cade had any news. He calmly told her that whoever had pulled the trigger that day must have cared a great deal for Jeremy. "He was lying on the floor with a pillow beneath his head when the ambulance arrived. No one who really wanted to destroy him would have taken time to do that or to call for help. The more I think about it, the more I feel it could have been an accident."

"Then why would that person leave?"

"It might have been someone prominent, a married woman. . . . Lord knows!" He brushed his hand over his hair. "Jeremy could pick up women more easily than a rock star."

She didn't reply and averted her eyes. A wave of warmth crept up her cheeks. Cade's brother had been an enchanting boy. *A boy.* She hadn't thought of him in quite that way before. At twenty-eight, he had been childlike and rebellious. Comparing the brothers, Jeremy was more like Peter Pan to Cade's Don Juan. If it weren't so tragic, she could almost laugh now at how she had fallen for the younger Hamilton.

"Why hasn't someone come forward?" she asked. Surely, Lita thought, her own conscience would have bothered her. "How can anyone live a normal life with such a tragedy in his past?"

Cade slowly shook his head. "I don't know. But it's driving me. I can't let up on it."

"I wish I could help."

His gaze rested on her, his arms tightening about her. "You are helping—just by being here. Close. Warm. Giving me affection. Tell me." He cupped her chin in his hand. "Would it be so difficult to love me?"

She drew a deep breath. "It would be pure joy."

"My love," he whispered. His lips devoured hers as his hands wove a spell of madness over her skin. "I think I'll go insane unless I can have you again." His body shuddered for physical release. "Couldn't you— No. I won't ask."

She snuggled closer to him, loving him all the more because he accepted her decision. There was nothing spoiled about Cade Thomas Hamilton. She ran her fingers over the fabric of his Hamilton Exclusive jacket, feeling the muscles ripple beneath her touch. He wore his clothes with the panache of an aristocrat.

After he left her an intuitive shiver crept through her body. It was as though the fine thread that kept them together was doomed to break. "I love you, Cade," she whispered in the quiet cabin. "I always will."

Cloud cover stretched over the coast the following morning. Even the gulls complained as they swooped and wheeled, looking for food through the gloomy mist. The maximum visibility was only a hundred feet in any direction. Lita hoped a hot shower would wash away the foreboding, but she was more convinced than ever that time was running out.

"Maybe I should do something," she murmured to herself. "Go to Miami and see my agent. Buy a dress. Take in a movie. Something."

Before the dreariness burned off and sunshine graced the royal palms, a maid came from the main house to give her a message. Debbie was coming to pick her up for a ride up the coast.

Well, Lita thought, that was one way to escape for a while. Good old Debbie. She'd saved the day.

When Lita heard a car roar into the driveway and a

swish of pebbles, she knew her friend had arrived. With a steady click of heels on the dock, Debbie made her way toward the yacht. Oh, oh, Lita thought when she saw that Debbie was wearing an expensive silk dress. She reached into the closet for a navy cotton dress and pulled off her jeans. "Come on in," she called.

Nothing could have prepared her for the devastation that marked Debbie's face. "What happened?" Lita gasped.

"I haven't slept at all and I'm a nervous wreck," Debbie wailed.

"But why? What is it?"

Debbie watched as Lita whipped off her shirt, pulled on the dress, and stepped into pumps. She had a numbed, pinched look to her lips and deep, dark shadows beneath her puffy eyes.

"I just need to talk, Lita. You're the only one who cares about me. I feel as though I can't trust another soul."

"Not even Ray?" Lita asked in a choked whisper.

"Especially not him."

As Lita wriggled into a half slip and brushed her auburn hair with quick strokes, she wondered how to draw Debbie's attention away from her problems. "Old trusty Lita. That's me," she quipped. "Come on." She tugged on her unhappy friend's sleeve. "Let's go."

A half hour later they had passed Juno Beach and Jupiter, heading north toward Fort Pierce on Interstate 95. Debbie drove as though Satan had attached wings to the Ferrari. Lita kept looking behind to see if there were any police in sight, wishing she could tell Debbie to slow down. There was fierce determination on the swollen features; not a sound passed her lips.

"We'll stop here and have some lunch, okay?" Debbie said sometime later.

"Great." Lita would have agreed to anything to get her away from that gas pedal.

Debbie parked the car, then leaned back against the seat with a sigh. "Brings back old memories," she said.

Lita's clothes felt damp and sticky when she emerged from the car. Inhaling a lungful of moist, hot air, she looked around to see her friend walking briskly toward the restaurant.

"Hey, wait," she called. "You're going to have to slow down, buddy." Panting to catch up with her, she added, "I'm wilting in this heat."

"Sorry," Debbie mumbled. "My air-conditioning has to be fixed. I didn't have time this morning." A shadow seemed to cross her face. "This place will be comfortable."

The noon crowd was just leaving as the hostess seated them near a window with an ocean view. "Don't I remember you?" she said to Debbie. "Oh, quite some time back? You used to come in with a blond young man, good-looking?"

Debbie nodded. "You have a good memory."

The girl laughed. "It's just that I never forget a handsome man." She gave them menus, then hurried off.

"Now," Lita said soothingly, "let's have a drink and talk this out. Whatever it is, it seems to be too much for you to handle. So unload, girl."

Debbie took her lower lip between fine white teeth. "I don't really know where to begin," she said, pouting.

"It's usually easier when you start at the beginning. What will you have to drink?"

"A Manhattan, I think."

"That's pretty potent stuff. You *are* driving," Lita reminded her.

"You're in no hurry to get back, are you?"

Lita's laughter was slightly nervous. "No." She signaled the waitress and ordered. Debbie sighed and clutched her napkin.

"Well, I told you that the Hamiltons and I grew up together. Where one was, the other could usually be found. Even when Ray and Cade went to high school and college, they always paid attention to Jeremy and me. I've always had a special place in my heart for all of them."

The waitress served the Manhattans and took their lunch orders. Lita sat forward expectantly when she left.

"Jeremy and I were just a year apart, so naturally we walked to school together and spent a lot of time with one another."

Lita nodded. "You were good friends."

"Yes. When I was thirteen, my family had 'financial

reverses' and we had to move to Miami to a much smaller home. That's where I met you, one of the Triple Terrors."

Lita grimaced. "You're bringing back some memories I'd rather forget. I guess," she said musingly, "I was trying to draw my parents' attention by getting into minor scrapes."

For the first time since her arrival earlier on the yacht, Debbie grinned. "We became the Terrors Four when I joined you." Suddenly, recalling their youthful days, her shoulders drooped. She seemed remote, abandoned.

"You were so sweet, Lita. So gentle. I needed a good friend and I found one in you."

"We all need someone."

"Oh, God, yes," Debbie blurted out, and seemed to swallow a sob. Her shoulders straightened as she continued. "I kept in touch with the Hamiltons. After graduating from college with high honors, Cade took over his father's failing business. Overnight, he made it into a gigantic success. They moved to the mansion in Palm Beach. But they didn't let their sudden wealth go to their heads. Well, Jeremy did, I guess. He was always my favorite."

Lita took a sip of the Manhattan. It was delicious, but on an empty stomach it felt like TNT. Only then did she notice that most of her companion's drink was already gone.

Debbie's words seemed to slur a bit as she continued. "At eighteen I fell in love with Jeremy."

Lita bolted upright!

"I knew there were other girls—tons of them. But it didn't matter. We . . . uh . . . became intimate the following year and I was hooked for good." She shrugged helplessly. "Jeremy affects women like that."

Lita nodded. She knew the feeling.

"I wanted to marry him, but he said he wasn't ready for a total commitment. So I waited."

Lita took another sip. She wasn't sure she wanted to hear the rest of the story.

"I waited—for five years." Crimson stained the pale cheeks, a flashing glitter appeared in the tired eyes. To Lita's amazement a metamorphosis seemed to occur. With heightened color, the rather plain, mousy girl changed into a lovely young woman. Why, she was pretty—more than that. Was it the memory of Jeremy's lovemaking that had made the difference in her appearance?

"Jeremy kept putting me off, promising that next year we would marry." Her nervous hands rubbed dizzying circles on the tablecloth. "I always wondered what would have happened if I had become pregnant. Would he have married me?"

A wave of nausea enveloped Lita. She had once waited for Jeremy to say those fateful words "Will you marry me?" Lord! How could she have been so foolish? Being his wife would have been calamitous.

"One day he just took off and bummed around the world. His parents only received an occasional postcard. It was the second time he had done this and I stood it for two months. Then one day Ray asked me out. He told me that he had always loved me, that he hoped someday I would wise up to Jeremy and marry him instead." Debbie gulped down the last of the drink and signaled the waitress for a refill.

Lita figured *she* could always drive home. In fact, she'd prefer it.

"Well, to make a long story short, I married Ray."

"That should have been a happy beginning. He's a fine man."

Debbie shook her head. "It was the beginning of disaster."

"Why?"

"I couldn't forget Jeremy. I always wondered if he would have married me if I had waited. When he returned to Palm Beach a year later, he had no qualms about taking me out behind his brother's back. We came here a lot." She stared at Lita. "We became lovers again. He said he'd made a mistake, should never have left me."

The food and Debbie's drink were served, but Lita had lost her appetite for the succulent lobster quiche, green salad, and mouth-watering garlic rolls. She stabbed at a piece of lobster as Debbie continued.

"Jeremy said that he loved only me and asked me to leave Ray and go off with him." She gazed out the window, a faraway look in her eyes. "Then, about a year ago, a new woman came into the picture. She captured his attention more than any of the others he had played with."

My God. That was me! Lita closed her eyes for a moment to steady her nerves.

"Five months later I capitulated. I promised to go off with him if he gave up the other girl." She paused and took a deep, shuddering breath. "My clothes were packed. I had left a note for Ray. As I drove up to his apartment, I saw a woman with auburn hair race off in Jeremy's car." Debbie fanned herself with the napkin in the air-conditioned room.

"Why don't we take a walk along the beach?" Lita suggested. "We'll catch the ocean breeze."

Debbie got up and wove her way unsteadily past the tables. Lita picked up the check and settled with the waitress, then followed Debbie outside. On the beach, they removed their shoes and walked in the sand. Debbie didn't need to be prodded to continue her story.

"I accused Jeremy of leading me on, of not really wanting me. I told him that I thought he got some kind of perverse enjoyment out of keeping me dangling. I told him I didn't think he would ever give up other women. He only laughed at me." A tear trickled down her cheek. "He said, 'I don't really know if I can promise to stay away from those delectable creatures.'

"I must have lost all reasoning then. I screamed, 'If I had a gun, I'd shoot you!' "

Lita's eyes opened wide, her heart beating in double time.

"He—he got his gun from on top of the desk and flipped it to me. I caught it and felt a roar of blood in my ears." She whimpered like a child lost in a storm of emotions.

" 'Do it,' he taunted."

Debbie's hands were clenched together so tightly, the knuckles turned white. "I cocked the gun . . . pointed it. Then he must have realized I might do it. He lunged for the gun." Tears were flowing down her cheeks and her breath was coming in wrenching sobs.

Lita was afraid to urge her on. Her mind went blank,

as though it could not prepare itself for the shock of what Debbie might say next.

Debbie's hands unclasped. She made a gesture of appeal, as though begging for understanding. "As he hit my arm, the gun went off. Lita . . . Are you listening? Are you?"

"Yes," Lita whispered.

"Jeremy fell to the floor." Debbie flung a hand to her chest. "I thought he was dead." There was a long, heartstopping pause. "Do you know what I'm saying, Lita?"

She nodded slowly, painfully.

"I shot Jeremy Hamilton." A sob wracked Debbie's small frame. "He was the only man I ever really loved!"

Eleven

Debbie shot Jeremy!

She flung herself into Lita's arms and a storm of hysterical sobs shook her petite frame. During the grueling minutes that followed, Lita felt shock tremors race through her. As unspoken words tumbled through her mind, life seemed to drain from her body.

The smell of the ocean and the sounds of the gulls vaguely penetrated her dulled senses. If she hadn't been holding tightly to Debbie, her own legs would have buckled beneath her.

It couldn't be true. Lita's mousy friend wouldn't hurt a cockroach. She was sweet and kind and terribly naive. There had to be some mistake. Lita shook her head to clear the voices that tried to hammer sense into her. Finally she heard just one, a mournful sound that brought her back to the present.

"I never meant to hurt him." Debbie gulped for air.

Lita stroked the lustrous black hair and wished she could say something to console her. "It sounds to me as though Jeremy was as much at fault as you were," she murmured. "Perhaps more so. He gave you the gun to taunt you. He was very good at that. If he hadn't lunged, probably nothing would have happened."

"Who would believe that?"

"I do!"

"But you're my friend."

"Yes."

"The police wouldn't. Cade and Ray wouldn't."

Her grip on Lita's arm was so strong that a choking sensation filled her throat. "You'll never know unless you try to convince them."

"No, oh, no!" Debbie cried, her small frame quivering with fear. "You couldn't ask me to do that."

"Honey, I'm not asking you to do anything," Lita said gently. "It's just that I'm wondering if you can live with this on your conscience."

"If the past days are any indication"—she gasped—"I doubt that I can."

"You need time to think, to evaluate."

"I've been doing that for months. I feel . . . I feel as though the only right thing I've done is to tell you."

So now it's my burden too.

Debbie stepped back. "Aren't you horrified that I could have done this?"

Lita's head moved from side to side. "You don't have a mean bone in your body. I'll admit I'm amazed. Yet, I can only guess what you must have been going through." Her heart ached for the young woman.

They started back along the beach. Lita felt a strange numbness, as though her body had joined her mind in shielding her from reality. "I have something to confess."

Debbie halted and reached for Lita's arm. "What?" she whispered.

"I hope you won't hate me too much when I tell you this." She paused, taking a trembling breath. "The auburn-haired woman you saw leaving in Jeremy's car . . . was me."

Debbie's mouth opened, amazement written all over the pixielike features. "You?" Her eyes were wild, incredulous. "*You* were my Jeremy's lover?"

Lita nodded. "The timing seems to fit—from what you and Cade have said. I wish I didn't have to hurt you, but it's best if I tell the truth." She halted at the flare of hatred in Debbie's eyes. "We met at a party and I fell for his slick line. He was a master at seduction. Like all the others—like you—I was drawn to him . . . the golden-haired bronzed macho male. At the time, I guess I needed love and thought I'd found it with him."

"I can't believe . . ." Debbie's voice trailed off.

"The moment you must have seen me was right after he'd told me to get lost. I was startled that he could look so malicious, almost violent. When I first arrived at his apartment, I asked him what the doctor had said about his tests—"

"What tests?"

Lita shrugged. "I'd heard him confirm an appointment on the telephone a few days before and he mentioned something about a doctor."

"He never said a word to me."

"Well, maybe it wasn't particularly important. But there was pain in his face and that's when he became frenzied."

Debbie shook her head, the tears starting to cascade down her cheeks again. "I took his car," Lita continued, "and ran it into a swamp. Maybe that was my way of seeking revenge. I guess my head wasn't on straight."

Debbie pressed her lips together, hiccuping occasionally. She kept looking at Lita as though she were a stranger. The friendship that had blossomed anew was heading for the trash heap.

"In a way," Debbie began, a bitter coolness to her tone, "I'm glad that I know who the woman was. At least I won't have to look at every auburn-haired hussy on the street and wonder if she was his lover."

Hussy. The word reverberated in Lita's brain. *I wasn't married, my friend,* she thought. *You were.* But what good would it do to retaliate with her own personal criticism of Debbie's behavior? She had no desire to hurt a childhood friend who seemed already to have had more than her share of dismal luck. The extent of the problem was much larger than worrying about who had committed what indiscretion.

"I'm not a hussy, Deb. I am sorry." Lita's eyes misted

over. "I wouldn't have hurt you for the world. I just don't think I could have kept it from you."

"You always were exceptionally honest. At this moment I'm not sure whether I feel gratitude or hatred for you."

Lita swallowed hard, her lashes flicking rapidly. "Why don't we head back to Palm Beach?" Not receiving any response, she added, "Would you like me to drive?"

Debbie nodded. Ten minutes later the Ferrari, with Lita at the wheel, was headed south on the coast highway. Her exhausted passenger was soon slumped against the window, getting some much-needed rest.

What did she feel? Lita asked herself. Her thoughts were all mixed up with the Hamilton family. In a way, she wished she had never met any of them. Although she now knew the truth, unless Debbie confessed Cade would never know that his own sister-in-law was responsible. So where did that leave herself? How could she possibly continue a relationship with Cade while there was still a shadow of a doubt in his mind that she might be a suspect?

It wasn't in her nature to reveal what Debbie had told her. So that left her with empty arms—an empty life.

Perhaps it was for the best. Cade wanted her for a mistress, and everything in her moral code rebelled at the thought. *But sometimes we have to compromise our values.* Cade wanted her. He said he loved her. For how long? Wasn't there the possibility that he, too, was a womanizer—like Jeremy?

When Debbie had first blurted out her guilt, she had felt excited that the puzzle had been solved, that she and Cade could start with a clean slate. Then sadness had set in and finally resignation.

In a few minutes they would reach the Palm Beach city limits. Aware of Debbie's confession, could she act natural with Cade? And what of her promise to Ray? She tried to remember exactly what he had requested of her. "Will you let me know if I've guessed right?" he had pleaded.

Debbie wasn't running off with another man. She had planned to, but he *knew* about that. Lita felt a swift stab of conscience. She glanced over at the disturbed young woman who was whimpering in her sleep. She shook her gently. "We're almost home," she said.

Debbie rubbed her eyes and sat up. "Are you going to keep my secret?" she asked, her voice cracking.

"Of course. You told me in confidence. How could I betray you?"

"Thank you," Debbie said stiffly.

Lita drove the car into the driveway and turned off the ignition. "Good-bye, Debbie," she said solemnly. "Perhaps someday you can forget that I was the 'other woman.' "

"I don't know," Debbie said in a bewildered tone. "I've had quite a shock."

Stepping from the vehicle, Lita murmured, "Good luck." With her head held high, she walked toward the yacht, refusing to look back. She had done her share of that. Now, perhaps, it was time to plan for the future.

The conversation was strained that evening when Cade came to request her presence at dinner. He stood in the cabin, dripping water all over the rug from his recent swim in the ocean. Lita felt weary, unresponsive to his light banter.

"What's wrong?" He leaned against the wall of the cabin, cocking his head to one side.

Lita rolled her eyes skyward. "Too much to talk about," she said wearily.

"Anything I can help with?" His quick frown marred the handsome masculine features.

"No."

"Need some loving?"

She stifled a sob. "I'm afraid that might make matters worse."

"What you need is a warm shower and your prettiest clothes. You'll feel better." He edged backward toward the cabin door. "We'll have dinner in an hour. The food will taste much better if you're sharing it with me."

She looked up at his puzzled expression and laughed self-consciously. She might as well enjoy his company. The distinct feeling that they might soon be parted forever jolted her into action. "I'll be there," she promised.

Cade smiled as he left, the same half smile that had twisted her heart with love for him so often lately. He was very special—so refined, so utterly wonderful to love and make love to. *Damn Debbie.* She felt her teeth clench. Why did she have to unload her troubles on her? Didn't she have enough of her own? *You asked her to. You have only yourself to blame,* she thought bitterly.

Slowly, Lita dropped her clothes to the floor. Stepping into the shower, she turned on the water full force, allowing first the cold, then the hot spray to sting her back. *Cade, Cade, Cade,* it seemed to drum into her brain.

If she decided to stay with him, how could she be certain that she wouldn't slip and give away Debbie's secret? And if he found out that she had known, would he forgive her for having withheld the answer to the question that was a daily torture to his mind? What repercussions would such a slip have on Debbie?

Pro and con, she fought with herself, but to no avail. There didn't seem to be an answer.

At exactly seven-thirty she stood before the massive set of doors and rang the chimes. In seconds, the butler welcomed her. Her sling-back shoes thudded softly on the plush rug. Pausing on the threshold of the loggia, she saw Cade pacing before the bar, his eyes searching his drink, deep in thought.

Her clicking heels on the polished marble floor drew his attention. He smiled and extended his hand. "What can I make for you, darling?" he asked.

"Anything potent. I need it tonight."

His gaze took in her slender body in the simple, high-necked white crepe dress and single strand of pearls her mother had sent on her nineteenth birthday. She had never worn them before. The fact that she had removed them from the elegant box and placed them around her neck represented something symbolic. She hadn't taken time to consider it before.

Cade stepped behind the bar and mixed a drink, then handed it to her. "You've heard of boilermakers? Well, I call this a rocket launcher. One drink and you're out in space."

She laughed. "Sounds exactly right. Why don't you

come with me? We can forget everything earthly and concentrate on the moon."

He joined her in front of the bar. "One of us has to keep his feet on the ground."

"Why?" She paused to sip the drink, raising one brow to acknowledge the potency of its contents. "Haven't you done that long enough? Isn't it time you were relieved of the pressures?"

"Someone has been talking."

"Yes." Her chin lifted. "You seem to have carried the burden of this family and business for a number of years. Shouldn't you be freed of responsibility? Ride your own rocket?"

His eyes were glazed with passion as he stared down at her.

"I have—a number of times," he whispered hoarsely. "With you." He reached for her and drew her close. "The greatest joy I've ever known are the days since I met you."

"You never said . . ."

"I told you I'm not the greatest communicator—not in words, that is."

"Ummm," she murmured against him. "You're definitely improving."

"But not resolving the one impossible circumstance that stands between us." His breath stirred the mass of auburn hair.

Lita felt the color drain from her face. "Have you . . . found out anything more?"

His head moved slowly from side to side. "We'll have the results of the autopsy soon."

"I didn't realize—"

"They usually perform one in a case like this."

The butler came to the door and announced dinner. Lita was so high from the effects of Cade's nearness, her feet barely touched the floor. As he pulled out her chair, she thanked him and sat down, aware of a giggle stirring in her throat.

The beautifully bedecked table was set cozily for two. Elegant china vied with sterling silver and mixed flowers on the damask cloth. Across her plate lay a long-stemmed yellow rose. She picked it up and drew in the heavenly scent. When the blossom tickled her nose, she let out the giggle that had been carefully contained.

She looked up to find a pair of eyes lovingly trained on her, eyes glittering like the finest jewels. "I love to hear you laugh," he murmured. "I just wish you would do it more often."

"That bomb you dropped in my drink is about to go off."

"What happens then?"

"Who knows?" She lifted the exquisite wineglass in a toast. "To whatever turns you on." She tipped the glass to her lips.

He chuckled. "I'll drink to that." Then he sobered. "This is to the loveliest lady I've ever known. The one who truly . . . turns me on."

She set the glass down, feeling unwanted tears cloud her vision. "That was the nicest tribute I've ever had."

"You'll have many more of them, darling," he promised. "Just stay with me. Be my love."

"That sounds like a poem I've read."

"You could inspire me to write an 'Ode to Lita.' "

Her voice softened. "I didn't realize there was romance in your soul."

"I never knew I had a soul until you came along."

"Oh, Cade," she breathed. All of the love she felt for him must have been visible in her eyes. She shakily filled her water goblet, her mouth dry and quivery.

When all the courses were removed, Lita could barely recall what she had eaten. She was only aware of the marathon of racing blood in her veins, the swelling throb in her lower abdomen, the light banter that seemed to slip easily from her lips.

As Cade's warm hand reached across the table to cover hers, she knew it was time to admit defeat. Anything was better than denying this torrid desire that overflowed from her body. Her lips parted to acknowledge her love and to ask Cade to join her that night. Just then, the butler hurried into the room carrying a telephone.

"I'm sorry, sir, but there is an urgent call for you."

The cord was connected to a wall plug and Cade

picked up the receiver. "Hamilton," he announced, then listened attentively for several minutes.

Lita noted his facial expression, the clipped, intelligent questions, the rapid-fire decisions he made. Love welled up in her throat. She felt pride in knowing him, in having been selected as his companion.

Something had obviously happened at one of his plants. The concern on his face caused her to sit forward expectantly.

"We've had a fire in our textile mill in Atlanta," he said, replacing the receiver. "I'll have to leave immediately. One of our major operations is a total loss." He called to the butler to pack a bag for him.

His apologies did nothing to satisfy her sexual hunger. She felt dejected and frustrated as he hurriedly saw her to the yacht.

Minutes later, she heard the screech of the Maserati's tires and watched the red lights fade into the distance. The tempest of passion that roared through her body was soon quieted by a series of goose bumps on her cooled flesh.

"Be my love," he had said. She tried to warm herself with that thought. Dropping her clothes to the floor, she didn't bother with her usual neat habits. What was the use? she thought. Who really cared?

The sheets were cold against her skin. As she lay there hour after hour, replaying the mental tape of the time she and Cade had spent together since they had met in Puerto Rico, she became increasingly aware that a permanent relationship was not in the cards for them.

"I love you, love you, love you, Cade," she murmured as the first faint traces of dawn swept across the Florida skies.

"How can I be sure that you won't accept a job and run out again?" Lita's agent grumbled.

She grasped the receiver tightly. "It was a highly emotional situation that prompted me to leave for Puerto Rico so suddenly."

"Yeah," he rasped. "Show folks survive on their emotions."

"It wasn't like that," she protested. "Damn it! You've known me for five years. Have I ever failed you before?"

"Well." He paused. "I guess everyone's entitled to one mistake. Tell you what. You get yourself down to Miami and we'll talk about it."

"Okay," she said. "I'll get the first transportation available." Lita hung up, feeling more enthusiastic than she had felt in days.

An hour later, standing in the entry hall of Cade's mansion with the butler, she was surprised to hear him say, "My orders are to take you wherever you wish. I would be negligent in my duty to Mister Cade if I allowed you to take a public conveyance when the car is available."

"Well, I really didn't want to be a bother."

"No one"—he lowered his voice—"who is important to my employer could ever be a bother."

She smiled her thanks and handed him a note for Cade. "I'll just advise the housekeeper and be right with you," he said.

The hour and forty minutes spent in the car passed serenely as Lita relaxed and caught a nap on the plush seat. As they neared Miami, the traffic became fairly heavy, and soon the car stopped in front of the familiar complex where her agent's office was. When she stepped from the air-conditioned car, the moisture-laden air seemed to close in on her.

"I'll be fine," she assured the butler, who hovered beside her, carrying her suitcase. He moved away reluctantly, only leaving when she walked into the lobby. She waved to him and watched the elegant car sweep back into the traffic.

For the next hour Lita tried to convince her agent that she was worthy of a second chance. He finally agreed to keep her in mind for an opening in about two weeks. She rented an inexpensive motel room, then called Cade's butler to tell him where she could be reached and that she planned to return to Palm Beach at the end of the week.

Early the following morning, Lita borrowed a friend's car and slowly cruised by the lovely home that still belonged to her. It was now rented to an airline executive, and the rent money went to the Jamison estate.

It had been two years since she had seen the house, and for some reason she no longer felt the bitterness associated with her life there. At a nearby florist shop she ordered several hardy potted plants and smiled at the lovely blossoms on the way to the cemetery.

In the quiet shadow of her parents' tombstone, she set the plants on the grass. Tracing the inscription with her fingers, she realized, perhaps for the first time, that Elva and Matthew Jamison's love for each other had been the motivating force of their relationship.

She didn't hear the mammoth jet taking off from Miami International Airport or notice the giant shadow it cast on the ground. She was totally immersed in a sudden understanding of her parents and their feverish lives that had left no time for one small, dependent child.

Because of her love for Cade, she thought, she had finally grown up, found a perspective that was long overdue. Smiling through her tears, she looked back several times as she returned to her car. Today had been one more step in the direction of looking toward the future.

During the next two days, which Lita spent on the beach and shopping in favorite stores, she often wondered why Cade had not called her at the number she had left for him. Did he believe she would return? Or was he so involved with the problems at the plant that he had no time to think of her?

On Friday night she called Cade's home. The butler answered and insisted that he come for her in the morning.

"Mister Cade will be informed," he said.

Lita laughed softly as she hung up. Cade's employee seemed to bend over backward to please her.

The next afternoon Lita was barely resettled in the yacht when Debbie was at her door. "I'm so happy that you're back!"

What now? Lita thought. She couldn't help feeling annoyed with Debbie since her actions had interfered with her love affair with Cade. If it weren't for her . . .

But then, Lita would never have met Cade under normal circumstances.

"I'm not really sure I'm glad to be back," she said, placing a kettle of water on the range.

"Why not? Aren't you and Cade . . ."

"That's just it, Deb." Lita set cups, tea bags, and the sugar bowl on the table. "You've been honest with me. I can only be the same with you." She drew a deep breath. "I'm going to leave soon."

Debbie gasped. "But why?"

"Because I'm in love with Cade," she said simply.

"And he's in love with you," Debbie said, her voice rising. "I saw him at the office while you were gone. We spoke about you. I've never seen him react to another woman in the same way. There's a positive glow in those beautiful eyes."

"I know," Lita murmured, her throat tightening. "He thought I'd shot Jeremy. That's why he tracked me down in Puerto Rico and then brought me back here."

Debbie's face paled. "No."

Lita nodded, pain welling up in her chest. "Although he says he now believes me and wants me to live with him, the doubt would always be between us. I'm afraid I couldn't accept that."

Tears brimmed over in Debbie's eyes. "But you just can't walk out on something as beautiful as your feelings for each other."

"Don't you understand?" Lita's voice rose. "I might give away your secret without meaning to. What then? Cade would lose faith in me. I couldn't take that. Sharing his life means complete honesty." She poured water over the tea bags and sat down. "And what would Cade do about you? Your entire life would be disrupted. I don't even want to think about it."

Debbie seemed to shrink into the seat. Her shadowed eyes became enormous. "It's all my fault. I've already shattered three lives. Now I've added two more. Maybe," she sobbed, "I should do what I've thought about for a long time."

Lita looked at her sharply. The ravaged features and vacant, almost staring eyes disturbed her. What did she mean? "It will all work out somehow," she said soothingly, placing her hand over Debbie's quivering one. "You must have faith in yourself."

Debbie shook her head slowly. "If I wasn't here things might work out for you, Cade, and Ray."

"You're wrong. Ray loves you. I suppose if Cade and I care enough about each other, we should be able to live with his suspicion." Lita frowned at the determined set of Debbie's lips. It was as though she had made up her mind about something. To do what? Kill herself? Good God!

"There's something else . . ."

"Tell me," Lita whispered.

"I'm pregnant."

Lita sat there, cold, mute, as though she had been turned to stone. Slowly, feeling returned. Pain stabbed at her chest.

"It's Ray's." Debbie tried to smile. "He always wanted a son. What do they do with women who have babies in jail? Do they take the child away? What would Ray do? How could he raise it?"

Lita closed her eyes, feeling so weary, she almost toppled off the chair. "Don't worry about that. Nothing is going to happen to you." She opened her eyes slowly. "No one will ever know—just the two of us. It isn't important anymore. You and the baby are all that matter now."

Debbie looked at her with large, appealing eyes. "I love you."

Lita smiled. "I love you too." She patted Debbie's cold hand reassuringly. "You need some rest. And I need some time to think. Promise me one thing, that you won't do anything until we've talked it over."

"I'm so confused. What good would it do to promise anything?"

Considering Debbie's chaotic state of mind, the worst thing Lita could do was pressure her. "Why don't you use my bunk for a while? I need to get some milk and bread."

"But it's a couple of miles to the nearest store," she protested.

"I need the exercise." Slipping on a pair of espadrilles, Lita stepped out the door. A few hours of rest would do her friend a world of good. She inhaled deeply. The invigorating sea breeze felt good as she walked across the dock.

Thoughts tumbled through her head as she strode briskly down the palm-lined street. Deb would be returning to California in a few days with Ray. Perhaps if Lita was no longer a reminder of Jeremy, the frightened woman's anxieties might fade and she could come to terms with herself.

Lita was torn with remorse. She never should have mentioned the situation between herself and Cade. She'd be responsible if anything happened. Why did she have to be so honest? she wondered. What seemed a virtue was becoming a monstrous handicap.

At the store she purchased groceries and a newspaper. Sipping a soft drink, she walked over to a telephone booth, dialed the number for Hamilton Industries, and asked for Ray Hamilton. When he came on the line, she was momentarily taken aback by the gruffness of his voice. "This is Lita Jamison," she said. She had no idea how to approach him.

He seemed genuinely happy to hear from her. After a few pleasantries were exchanged, she could no longer contain her anxiety. "Ray, you were wrong," she blurted out. She heard the strangled gasp on the other end of the line. "Debbie isn't leaving. There's no one else."

Silence. Then, "Lita, are you positive? You're not just saying this to make me feel better?"

"No," she assured him. "Debbie needs all your love. Tell her over and over how you feel about her. I can't reveal anymore without betraying her confidence. If she ever feels she wants to tell you"—she paused to catch her breath—"be there for her."

"I will," he murmured, so low, she had to strain to hear him.

"And Ray?" she said after a lengthy pause.

"Yes?"

"Good luck."

"Thanks."

She hung up the phone, feeling numbness in her fingers from grasping it so tightly. Sitting down on a bench, she flipped through the pages of the paper. Not really seeing the newsprint, she sat back, allowing memories of swelling ocean currents, crimson sunrises, and the fiery sunsets to flow over her. There was an ache in her chest as she remembered the lovely things that made Cade a part of her universe.

She bit into her lower lip, rose from the bench, and tucked the folded newspaper beneath her arm. Her steps were slow and weary as she walked back toward the mansion. Arriving at the *Sea Sprite*, she found it empty. There was an indentation on the pillow, so at least it seemed that Debbie had taken her suggestion to rest.

Realizing that she hadn't eaten since breakfast, Lita prepared a cup of soup and a slice of toast. She managed to eat most of it.

As dusk shadowed the room, she flipped the light switch. If she was leaving in the morning, why not pack her clothes now? Dragging her suitcases from the locker, she filled one with underwear and shoes. A teardrop rolled down her cheek.

Would she be able to tell Cade? she asked herself. Could she bear to say good-bye?

Misery echoed through her body as she folded a pair of shorts and a shirt, smoothing the fabric to avoid wrinkles. Immersed in her crushing grief, she didn't hear the cabin door open or the footsteps move across the rug.

Cade studied Lita's slim form as she methodically packed her clothes. Pain gripped his chest. He was losing her—the one woman he had ever loved. The muscles in his face contracted; a nerve beat against his temple.

Clenching his hands at his sides, he wanted to shout, to demand. But he loved her. He wasn't sure if he could even speak.

"Going somewhere, Lita?" he asked hoarsely.

Twelve

Lita spun around to face him, a soft cry on her lips. Beads of perspiration broke out on her brow.

"Running?" His voice cracked and his body went rigid with emotion.

"Yes."

"I can't stop you."

"No, you can't." She wanted to die at that moment, to feel nothing but numbness.

"You promised," he reminded her, his voice ragged with anguish.

"I didn't say for how long." Her lashes fell, then lifted again as she fought for control.

"May I ask why?" He sounded calm . . . deathly calm.

"One reason." She tried to ignore how his gaze lingered on the thin material of her blouse where her breasts strained against it. "I'm convinced we won't make it together."

"Why not?" His eyes met hers and she couldn't look away.

She tried to swallow. "You'll never be sure about

Jeremy's death. If you can't trust me one hundred percent, how can a loving relationship exist between us?"

"It can exist and flourish because I love you. If you felt the same way, nothing and no one could come between us." He hesitated. "I want you. I think you know that. But I also want you to come to me of your own free will—without any reservations." He stared at the partially packed suitcase.

"Were you planning to go back to Puerto Rico and the safety of Aunt Maria's arms? Do you want to make the Mariposa Club your life's work? Do you want to go on exposing your beautiful body to all those lustful eyes? Is that what you're missing? Is that what I can't give you?" His gaze searched hers fervently. "I have only two eyes, Lita. I had hoped the love you must surely see in them would be enough."

He turned away, then halted. Pivoting, he faced her again and removed an envelope from the pocket of his slacks. "This is an invitation," he said. "I thought you might like to look at it before you leave."

She held out her hand to take the envelope. She stared down at it, then looked up in time to see him stride across the cabin floor. Without a backward glance, he stepped out the door.

Wanting desperately to call out his name, she was aware of a faint cry passing her lips. The envelope slipped from her hands. Slumping into a chair, she felt all strength drain from her body. Until that moment she had never known what real pain was. Sick at heart, she felt as though bands of steel were being wrapped around her chest. Nausea whipped through her stomach.

Cade was right. If she could not trust him completely, willingly giving of herself and accepting nothing less, then their relationship was truly at an end.

Cade toyed with his succulent lobster, his mind on Lita. If love hurt this much, he thought, why did people want it so desperately? He took a sip of Chablis, then rubbed one hand across his brow. How would he survive if she actually left? His mouth flattened into a straight line. He would, somehow. That was what was expected of a Hamilton. But he knew damn well she would never be out of his mind—or his heart.

It served him right, he chastised himself. He had thought the worst of her. Under false pretenses he had taken her from the only love that she could depend on and brought her here. If you were her, he asked himself, would you be able to love someone like yourself? She had never admitted her feelings for him, but there was something in those huge, jewellike eyes that seemed to say it all.

"I should go to her," he muttered aloud, "make her understand. Not allow her to leave the yacht until she admits her love for me."

He looked up as the butler entered the dining room, plugged a telephone into the jack, and handed him the receiver. "Your brother, sir."

Ray had better make this fast, Cade thought. He had to get to Lita. "Yeah?" he said into the phone.

"Can you come to the hotel right away?" Ray hesitated. "I can't cope with this."

"Is it urgent?" Cade asked.

"Definitely."

"I'll be there in ten minutes." Cade pushed back the chair and stalked toward the front door. "I won't be back for a while," he told the butler.

"Very good, sir."

He glanced across the lawn to the *Sea Sprite*. It was in total darkness. Had she left? If so, she had taken his heart and soul with her.

Ten minutes later Cade was at his brother's door, shifting from one foot to the other in his haste to find out why Ray had sounded so desperate.

"Thank God you're here," Ray said, his voice choked. "I don't know what to do with Debbie. She's hysterical, making crazy statements, staring wildly at me."

Cade wasted no time when Ray pointed to the bedroom. He charged toward the door, flung it open, and stared at his wide-eyed sister-in-law. He hurried to the bed and held her hands firmly, slowly lowering her on to her back.

"Easy now," he said comfortingly, rubbing her chilled fingers. For ten minutes he sat beside her, speaking in gentle tones, consoling her, reassuring her that whatever was wrong, he would stand behind her.

"Oh, Cade," she murmured finally. "You'll hate me. Ray will hate me."

"No, no," he promised. "Tell me what it is and I know we can straighten it out."

"I'll go to jail—maybe . . . maybe . . ."

Cade didn't allow his face to mirror his anxiety. What had Debbie done for her to react this way? "Slowly," he said. "One thing at a time. Tell me everything."

"Okay," she said, panting slightly. There was pleading in her eyes. "I shot Jeremy!"

Cade felt the inner jolt of his body, but he managed not to show any outward emotion. "You shot Jeremy," he repeated slowly, not believing the words that passed his lips. In that highly charged moment, he felt nothing as his body absorbed the shock of her statement.

"It was an accident," she said imploringly. "Even Lita said it was an accident."

Lita! Fear shot through him. "What does she have to do with this?"

"I told her." Debbie's voice rose. "I had to tell someone."

He brushed the dark curls from her face. "Okay, okay, calm down. Just tell me what happened."

Cade listened, dumbstruck at the story she related. He grimaced in pain as she described the actual scene with Jeremy. Debbie was sobbing softly. She told him what Lita had admitted, that she was the auburn-haired woman who had left in Jeremy's car. Cade felt his heart twist in his chest. Everything his darling had said was the truth.

"There's more," Debbie said, grasping his hands. "I'm pregnant." Tears slid down her cheeks. "I asked Lita what they do to women in jail who are pregnant. She said no one would ever know what had happened. She told me I would have to keep it a secret. But I couldn't. I couldn't."

Cade held her in his arms while she wept and confessed. He felt no hatred for this frail woman. Jeremy had driven her to it. It wasn't her fault that his brother had lunged for the gun. Why had he acted so irrationally? One thought tugged at his brain—the medical tests he hadn't heard about before.

A sound at the door caught his attention. He glanced up to see a white-faced Ray slowly coming toward them.

"Cade," Debbie said, her voice muffled against his chest, "I was so wrong to think Jeremy was the one I wanted. I really do love Ray. Have I lost him too?"

He heard Ray's heavy footsteps approach. "Have you lost Ray?" Cade repeated, the question aimed at his brother. "I don't know that, honey, but I think he'll be able to tell you himself."

He felt Debbie stiffen. As he gently eased her arms from around his neck and moved back, he saw the fear in her eyes as she stared up at her husband. Swiftly, he stepped away to allow his brother to take his place. Pausing in the doorway, he saw them with their arms wrapped tightly around each other, both murmuring incoherently.

"Oh, Lord," Cade exclaimed, pulling the door shut behind him. "We're in for one hell of a day tomorrow."

He pulled a handkerchief from his pocket and wiped the moisture from his brow. He was so absorbed in the nightmare of Debbie's confession, he was unaware of going down in the elevator or of walking through the lobby of the hotel. When he stepped outdoors he scarcely noticed the humid air. Beneath his feet the concrete seemed as unreal as the evening chirping of birds.

Debbie was responsible. The words echoed in his weary brain. Lita was probably already gone. But then . . . maybe not.

Unlocking the car door, he eased his body onto the sticky leather and turned on the ignition. Seconds later, the Maserati was humming along the streets. At a stoplight he impatiently gunned the motor, then tore across the intersection as though his life depended upon it.

After screeching to a halt at the mansion, he slammed the car door and walked briskly toward the *Sea Sprite*. His steps faltered as he drew closer. The yacht was in total darkness. The muscles in his throat tightened, but he climbed onto the deck and fit the key into the lock of the cabin door.

Make her be here, he pleaded silently.

Closing the door behind him, he walked softly across the rug. Stopping short in the galley, he saw what he had desperately hoped for. Lita, her arms thrown above her head, lay sleeping on her bunk. She had not closed the drapes in the forward section of the craft. Her lovely features were faintly caressed by the light of a sickle moon.

"Maybe our problems are over, love," he murmured as he stripped and placed his clothes on a chair. "Or maybe they're just beginning. There might be all tomorrows, or none at all . . ." Since the start of their relationship, there had been passion mixed with pain. Now was the time for passion alone.

His pulse beat faster, reacting to her tiny moan and the movement of her slender body beneath the sheet. How lovely she was, he thought. He stood above her, drugged by her beauty. His breath came quickly as he gently pulled the sheet to uncover her. There was barely room enough for him to lie down beside her.

He placed one hand on her bottom to keep himself from falling and leaned his head on his arm, the better to see her. Her lashes fluttered at the contact, but she seemed deep in sleep. With a contented little sigh, she nuzzled close to him, her arms slowly creeping around his neck. Her sweet fingertips grazed the hair at the nape of his neck, creating a friction along his nerve endings.

His lips pressed down on hers lightly, then he lifted his head to watch her reaction. He saw the slight twitch of her mouth, felt the movement of her feet. Was she dreaming? He grinned wickedly. Could he make her dream come true?

Drawing her more closely to him, he teased her parted lips with the tip of his tongue. He slid his hand over one softly swelling breast, rubbing the darkened nipple between his fingers. When she writhed against him, his hand slipped to the auburn core of her femininity. Her arms tightened around him as he gently caressed the arching body, her mouth becoming frenzied, seeking his.

"Cade, Cade," she moaned, her hands running over his shoulders.

"My sweet Lita," he whispered, taking her mouth in a soul-touching kiss. With sensual abandon, she swayed against his masculinity, her tongue moving in hot rhythm with his.

Sensations chased through Lita, like high tension wires, melting any lucid thought of resistance. *I'm dreaming*, she thought. She felt the tongue that was setting fire to the skin that had been caressed just moments ago by gentle hands.

"If this is a dream," she murmured, "I hope I never wake up."

"Wherever you are, I'll be there with you," Cade whispered huskily. "Whether it's a dream or reality, you'll never be far from me."

A tear trickled from her eye, but she hastily rubbed her face in the pillowcase. This was no dream. This was Cade. . . . Even if it was their last night, she thought, it would be the most romantic, the loveliest of all the times they had spent together. She smiled and pulled his head to her mouth.

When he rolled her on her back and buried himself inside her, she heard her own purring sounds and the passion-fed groans of her mate. There was pain and joy and desperation in her tormented movements as he carried her into his world of erotic glory, his thrusting motions filling her with a sense of exultation that dreams could never achieve.

In a state of intense bliss, she tightened her arms around him, clinging to his moist body. Cradled in the warmth of his embrace, she slowly, tantalizingly, trailed kisses across his face.

Through half-opened eyes, she saw the faint rays of the moon cast a sensuous glow over Cade's skin, shimmering on the drops of perspiration. Languorous with the intoxicating afterglow of his lovemaking, she felt the gentle surge of renewed need that teased her senses.

There won't be much sleep tonight, she thought. Her hand crept downward to the source of his manhood. He responded to her steady stroking, words of love spilling from his throat.

There was nothing lethargic about their lovemaking. It was wild, fierce, like the tempestuous spirit of the ocean in a violent storm. Her mind swam in the turbulent surf, her body quivered in the thrashing pulse of each wave of sensation.

The scent of his body, drenched in sweat, was a powerful stimulant that sent her emotions reeling. When her cry of fulfillment echoed through the cabin, he plunged deeper. A low groan was wrenched from his throat, his shudder filling her body with the tremor of the final spasms of his love.

Lita lay against him, spent, aware that a renewed ache for him would prompt her to seek him out again before the night was through.

Lita awoke with a drowsy sense of contentment. Her hand automatically crept to the pillow where Cade had rested his head after their final session of lovemaking in the wee hours of the morning.

It was so wonderful, she thought, sighing. Flipping the covers aside, she went to the bathroom. After showering, dabbing on lip gloss, and brushing her hair, she quickly slipped on underwear, sandals, and a pale aqua sundress.

Walking rapidly to the house, she hesitated at the massive double doors. No sooner had she touched the door chime when the butler appeared, greeting her warmly. She told him she needed to use the phone, and he gestured for her to enter.

She ran one finger down the list of numbers beside the hall telephone. The butler seemed to hover beside her. After she'd dialed the hotel where Ray and Debbie were staying, she looked up at him.

"Mister Cade left early this morning," he said. "He seemed deeply troubled. He left a message for you. He told me to ask you to wait."

"Oh?" Her brow wrinkled. "What was wrong?"

"I don't know, miss."

Receiving a busy signal from the hotel, Lita hung up and redialed, getting through this time. No one answered at Ray and Debbie's suite, and worry started to grow in Lita. Where was Debbie? She left word with the operator for Debbie to call.

Thoroughly upset, she called Hamilton Industries. Neither of the Hamiltons were expected. Replacing the instrument, she turned to the butler.

"Have you heard from either Debbie or Ray?" she asked.

"Mister Ray called last night," he said.

She nodded, deeply troubled about Debbie, and left.

Back in the cabin, she sipped coffee, staring bleakly at the paneled walls. If Debbie needed her . . . But she was certain that if anything was really wrong, she would have heard about it by now. The half-filled suitcase was still on Cade's bunk. She shook her head.

Cade means everything in the world to me, she murmured. I love him. I want him. So why am I doing this—getting ready to run again?

Everyone had to make a stand, sooner or later. You're an idiot, Lita, she admonished herself. You have to take love when and where you find it, no matter what might happen in the future. Tomorrow is uncertain for every human being. She couldn't leave Cade. *She wouldn't leave him!*

Straightening her shoulders, Lita smiled. She had been through so much lately. But Cade was worth it. If he still wanted her, she would go to him with open arms.

She stepped out the door, her feet weightless. The Atlantic breeze moved over her gently, caressingly. It lifted her hair and cool, silky strands whipped over her face. She stood on the deck, accepting the joy that swelled in her chest, allowing it to mingle lovingly with the light wind. She felt alive, thrilled, supremely happy. Her mouth curved in a mischievous smile. "Add devilment to the list of sensations," she said aloud, and laughed.

Perched on the edge of the fly bridge, she saw a pelican peering down at her. She felt the restless stirrings in her chest as the bird dove, entering the water in a burst of sea spray, bobbing back up seconds later. It floated on the surface, its bill pointed downward, waiting for the water to drain from its pouch before swallowing its catch.

As the pelican flew low over the shifting waves, Lita was fully aware of the freedom her decision had provided. She had liberated herself from the bitterness associated with her parents and Jeremy. Her spirit was as free as the bird which now seemed to be eyeing a new resting place. She would accept her inheritance and provide for Maria, she decided.

When she reentered the cabin, the envelope on the floor caught her eye. She scooped it up and pressed it to her chest. Cade had said it was an invitation. Opening the flap, she pulled out a white sheet of paper folded like a greeting card. The front had a single yellow rose drawn on it. The words "Be my love" were written in ink across the bottom.

She flipped it open. A gasp escaped her lips and her throat tightened. She read on, blood racing through her temples, thudding out the message:

CADE INVITES YOU TO SHARE IN THE JOY OF
THE BEGINNING OF A LIFE TOGETHER
WHEN HE AND THE WOMAN HE LOVES
EXCHANGE MARRIAGE VOWS
ONE GLORIOUS SUN-FILLED DAY
AT DAWN
IN THE CHAPEL OF LOVE
HONEYMOON, LASTING FOREVER, TO FOLLOW
ABOARD THE SEA SPRITE

"Oh, Cade," she whispered. "My darling. I'm yours—any way, any time." She set the card on the table and stared at it in both disbelief and happiness.

"He wants me—really wants me," she murmured, and wondered where he was, so she could tell him how proud she would be to become his wife.

Better yet, she would *show* him. She grabbed her purse and raced for the house. *Our* home, she thought proudly. She rang the bell.

The door opened. "Telephone, Miss Jamison?"

"Not this time," she said excitedly. "What I really need is a ride to the nearest shopping center."

The butler reached in a closet for his chauffeur's cap. "I'll leave word with the housekeeper."

Minutes later the limousine swept through the opulent neighborhood. Lita fidgeted, a flare of color brightening her cheeks, her heart pounding in a crazy rhythm. When they reached a row of stores, she didn't wait for the butler to open the door. She sped across the pavement on wings of love.

Obviously sensing her urgency, he was waiting outside the car when she returned fifteen minutes later, hugging her purchases. She sprang into the limousine, wearing an impish grin. "All set, miss?" he asked.

She laughed. "All set."

"Something good is happening?"

"Something *very* wonderful."

"Ah," he said with a knowing smile.

Lita had the distinct feeling that the man had as much knowledge of what went on in the Hamilton household as his employer had.

Arriving at the mansion, Lita went straight to the telephone. Again she attempted to reach the Hamiltons. This time, she left no message.

By four o'clock she had eaten a light snack, cleaned the cabin, and placed Scotch tape over the wall light switch. By five-fifteen, she had taken a shower, sprayed herself lightly with her favorite cologne, and tugged on a robe. Checking the purchases that she had placed in the refrigerator, she smiled gleefully. Yellow roses were in vases on every surface. Two champagne glasses, with yellow ribbons gracing their long stems, stood on the countertop alongside Cade's wedding invitation. Clusters of yellow balloons and ribbons were fixed to walls and cabinets around the room. Everything was ready. Well, almost . . .

Dusk was settling over the elegant Palm Beach neighborhood when she heard a car on the gravel. Cade! Watching him enter the house, she felt a moment of panic. Would he come to her?

The house and grounds were in full view from where she sat at the table. She was nervous. "Please make him come soon," she begged aloud.

Several minutes elapsed before she saw him leave the house, heading toward the yacht. He seemed to move slowly, deliberately, as though not quite certain of what he would find.

Lita pulled down the shade, ran her fingers over the taped wall switch, and opened the refrigerator door. Her hands trembled as she removed the champagne she'd purchased earlier. The robe dropped to the galley floor. She heard the door open and sucked in her breath.

"What the devil—" Cade exclaimed. He tried to turn on the light, but the tape prevented him.

"We won't need a light," she called softly.

"Lita?" He stumbled through the cabin toward her voice.

"Who else?" she asked seductively, putting the champagne bottle down on the countertop.

"What's going on?" He paused near the bunks.

"Sit down, Cade. I'd like to talk to you."

"I'm so tired." He sighed, sinking down on a bunk. "I've been at police headquarters most of the day."

"Police?"

He drew in a sharp breath. "I know all about Debbie and Jeremy. She confessed last night."

"Oh." A strangled sob was stifled. "Is she all right?"

"Ray took her back to the apartment. Our lawyers don't think the police have a case. Why are we in the dark?" Then, without waiting for a reply, he continued. "There's a new development."

"What?"

"Jeremy was going blind from a football injury that happened some years ago. The diagnosis was confirmed the day he told you to leave."

"Jeremy?"

"His safe-deposit box was opened today." He cleared his throat. "In it was a letter. He was planning to . . . take his life." He paused to control the emotions that were swirling through him. "He said . . . that if he couldn't see beautiful women and would no longer be desired by them, life was not worth living. Not without them, racing, and sailing."

"Oh, God," she murmured.

"He provoked Debbie to anger—so that she would shoot him. But I can't help feeling that at the last moment he changed his mind, grabbed for the gun. Did you see it on his desk?"

"Yes, I did. But I never thought anything of it."

"Poor Jeremy." Cade sighed. "He must have wanted someone to pull the trigger. I still can't figure out why he wouldn't reveal whether he had shot himself or someone else had done it."

"Perhaps to protect Debbie."

"There will probably be a hearing, but I doubt that Debbie will be prosecuted after the admission of that letter in evidence."

"I'm glad, Cade. We'll have to stand by her. She needs our love and protection."

"And I'm glad." His voice softened. "Do you and I still have a problem?"

"I don't think so," she said huskily.

"Is there a chance now that we can sort things out?"

"Oh, yes," she said breathlessly.

"I love you."

"And I love you."

"Oh, darling."

She heard him move closer. "Cade, would you please turn on the light over the bunks?" She heard the click then his gasp.

"Lita!"

He didn't miss her seductive smile as his startled gaze whipped over the rose-strewn bunk.

Cade wanted to laugh and cry at the sight of her lovely soft mouth, a long-stemmed rose held lightly between her teeth, Carmen-style. He knelt before her, feasting on the beauty that he now knew was all his.

"My love," he murmured, gently removing the rose from her mouth so his lips could take its place.

Lita clung to him, all of her love showing in the hungry way she returned his kiss.

"You saw the invitation?" he murmured against her lips.

She nodded. "Before I saw it, I'd already made my decision to stay with you. I would have come to you any way you wanted me. If you'd rather not marry—"

He cut off her words effectively with his kiss. Then he

pulled back. In one swift motion, he flipped off the light switch and opened the drape.

"Say you'll marry me as soon as we can get a license."

"One thing at a time," she teased.

"Your promise first," he insisted gently.

"Withholding favors before the knot is tied?"

"I might even tell you I have a headache, unless . . ."

"Oh, yes, Cade. Whenever you say."

"I'll give you a bouquet of roses, orchids—"

"One perfect yellow rose will be fine."

He shook his head solemnly. "The yellow rose signifies jealousy. And I was jealous of Jeremy the first moment I looked at you. From now on, according to the florist, you'll receive forget-me-nots. They represent what I want to see grow between us—true love."

She laughed softly. "You're speaking the language of flowers, Cade. And you seemed to think you had difficulty in communicating."

"Not any longer," he murmured. "For the wedding, we'll buy you the finest dress at the most exclusive couturier."

"Mere details, Cade. Not now. Not when I need you and want you so very much."

"Last night," he said against her ear, "I was afraid it might be the last time I would ever be able to make love to you."

She laughed softly. "It was a sneaky approach, coming in here like that. I might not have known it was you."

"Really?" he murmured huskily. "I thought I was unique."

She wrapped her arms around his neck and pulled his mouth to hers. "Unique is correct, darling. And I deserve you."

"Of course." He chuckled. Then, solemnly searching her eyes, he said, "Have you forgiven me for ever suspecting you? Can my love for the next fifty years erase the hurt?"

She placed her fingers across his lips to stop the words. "Love and trust and forgiveness flow together like a healing touch."

His kiss was soft, gentle, persuasive. "We've weathered the tempest of pain," he said, remembering. "From now on we'll ride the crest of passion together."

Joy sang through her body. "Ummm." She sighed in ecstasy at having found the love she had always yearned for.

As her sigh was caught and held by the magic of moonbeams, she nuzzled closer. "From pain to passion," he had said. There would be more of both in the future, a lifetime of sharing laughter as well as tears.

Lita lifted her mouth to his to seal their promise, unafraid of what tomorrow would bring.

THE EDITOR'S CORNER

Sandra Brown, Iris Johansen and all of us at Bantam Books are delighted by your response to **SUNSET EMBRACE** and **THE FOREVER DREAM**. We thank you most sincerely for not only buying the novels, but for letting us know through your cards and letters how much you liked them. Now, you may want to urge any of your friends who haven't yet got their copies of **SUNSET EMBRACE** to rush to their nearest bookseller to do so. Why? Because they will want to be ready for Sandra's stunning sequel to it, **ANOTHER DAWN,** which we are publishing in October (on sale early in September). Next month we'll run an excerpt in the back of the LOVESWEPTs of this wonderful historical novel that tells the love story of Jake ("Bubba") Langston. **ANOTHER DAWN** is a breathtakingly exciting romance novel that we are very proud to publish.

And speaking of being "proud to publish," that's exactly how we feel about next month's LOVESWEPTs.

That talented author Fayrene Preston is back with the sensual and evocative **RACHEL'S CONFESSION**, LOVESWEPT #107. Rachel Kirkland is a forthright and very lovely young woman. Wounded by a first love, she has vowed to marry for money and she candidly says so to Alex Doral. Very much a man . . . very much a wealthy man, Alex has just arrived in the town to which Rachel also has returned to live with and help take care of her grandmother and her younger sister. Soon, Alex is determined to marry Rachel for he yearns to possess her and to heal the hurts he suspects she carries in her heart. **RACHEL'S CON-**

(continued)

FESSION is one of Fayrene's most compelling romances and you won't want to miss it!

If you thought Billie Green's last LOVESWEPT was wonderful, can you imagine what she'll come up with after **A TOUGH ACT TO FOLLOW**, LOVESWEPT #108? Indeed it's going to be difficult for her to top this witty and touching love story between Dempsey Turner-Riley and James Halloran. Delightfully off-the-wall, Dempsey literally captivates James on first meeting. (I can't leave it at "captivates"; I must tell you that this couple is handcuffed to one another . . . and the key is lost.) And then this fascinating pair is drawn into a madcap caper that sends them on a wild goose chase . . . with the most enchanting prize at the end. **A TOUGH ACT TO FOLLOW** sure is!

We're very, very pleased to introduce you to a marvelous new writer, Laurien Berenson, whose heartwarming romance **COME AS YOU ARE** is LOVESWEPT #109. Gem McAllister is a sensitive, loving young woman whose occupation is the despair of her family. Playing the role of Emerald the Clown, she entertains at parties and on the streets of San Francisco. She could scarcely believe the name of the "boy" she was to awaken with balloons and songs on his birthday. Tom Tucker's name proved to be no joke . . . but "boy" certainly did for he was tall, handsome . . . and, indeed, adult. Together they began to celebrate more than his birthday, yet his rather stuffy background and profession seemed to loom between them. **COME AS YOU ARE** is a tender and touching love story from the zany first to the memorable last.

Last, but certainly not least, we have a beautiful romance from Joan Elliott Pickart, **SUNLIGHT'S PROMISE**, LOVESWEPT #110. Jill Tinsley is poor as a church mouse and proud as a peacock about her independence. When she meets Chip Chandler her life takes an abrupt turn. Chip wants to cherish Jill, to fill her life with all the things she's never had. But Jill finds it impossible to accept anything but love from the man she's fallen for. When her secret dreams begin to come true in her professional life, too, an emotional storm blows up! Watch the secondary characters in this book. One of them has his . . . er, or her own story in Joan's next LOVESWEPT, **RAINBOW'S ANGEL**.

Enjoy!

With every good wish,
Sincerely,

Carolyn Nichols

Carolyn Nichols
  Editor
LOVESWEPT
Bantam Books, Inc.
666 Fifth Avenue
New York, NY 10103

*A special excerpt of
the riveting historical novel
GAMBLER IN LOVE
by bestselling author
PATRICIA MATTHEWS*

THE morning was glorious, clear and sunny, heralding the approach of full summer. It was a day to match Cat's feelings. She woke late, and was for a moment puzzled as to why she felt so good. Then the memory of last night flooded back to her, and she stretched like a contented kitten.

She dressed quickly and went up on deck. Everything seemed sharper this morning—the air smelled like wine; the songs of the birds along the canal bank sounded sweeter than she remembered; and everything she touched had a different feel to it. It was as though her passage into womanhood had sharpened all her senses, and it was wonderful to be alive.

Mick, looking disheveled and hung over, was sitting by the tiller, sipping at a mug of hot tea. Timmie was exercising the mules along the towpath, but Morgan was nowhere to be seen.

"Good morning, Mick. Where's Morgan?"

"How should I know? I'm not the lad's keeper," he said grumpily.

"But haven't you seen him?"

"Nope. He didn't even sleep in the cabin last night. Leastways, he wasn't in his bunk when I came back, about midnight. Never did show up." He gave her a look edged with malice. "Maybe the boyo decided he'd had enough of canal life, and snuck away in the night."

Hiding her alarm as best she could, Cat said, "Did he take his things?"

"What things? All the bucko has is the clothes he was wearing." He gestured and turned away, without looking at her again. "I'm thinking it's good riddance if he is gone."

She opened her mouth to retort hotly, but she refrained, afraid that she might give herself away if she said too much.

She turned away and mounted the towpath, staring up toward the town. Her good spirits had vanished. Cat knew that if Morgan *had* left, she would miss him sorely. But would he just sneak away in the night? That was not like him. . . .

And then she saw him striding along the towpath toward her. Her heart gave a great leap of joy, but she had herself composed by the time he reached her.

"Good morning, my dear," he said gravely, his eyes searching hers. "How are you this grand morning?"

"I'm fine," she said in a neutral voice. "I was just wondering where you were."

"I had things to do. I've been searching for a cargo for the *Cat*."

"Did you find anything?"

He nodded, smiling. "Oh, yes, a load of grain. I took it at a price lower than the going rate. I hope you don't mind. I figured that was better than going back empty."

"I don't mind at all; I think it's wonderful. You're a born canawler, Morgan!" She experienced a sudden desire to reach out and touch him, and then he spoiled it.

"The wagons will be here in about"—he took out his watch—"an hour."

"You were pretty sure of yourself, weren't you?" she said testily. "I gave you no authority to make such decisions!"

"But you just agreed that it was a good deal," he pointed out.

"All right, all right. But next time you might consult me first."

"I had to act quickly, Cat. Two other canal-boat owners came in while I was there. If I'd left to consult with you, without an agreement being reached, the grain merchant might have given the cargo to one of the others."

Knowing that he was right did not wholly appease her, but she said nothing more; instead, she turned toward the boat, calling out, "Timmie, get the mules fed. We have a cargo coming, and will be departing before too long."

Soon wagons began pulling in alongside the boat. They all pitched in, and five wagonloads of grain were soon stored below. Cat was introduced to the grain merchant, a plump, harried-looking individual named Fredricks.

"This man of yours, Miss Carnahan," Fredricks said, "is a pretty convincing fellow. If he hadn't been, I might have given my grain to another hauler. One man there offered to haul it much cheaper, but I'd already agreed to let you have it. I hope I don't have cause to regret my decision."

Cat felt her face flush at the phrase *this man of yours,* but she returned the merchant's gaze steadily and said, "You won't have cause to regret it, Mr. Fredricks, I promise you."

As they got under way, Morgan came to Cat at the tiller and said, "You know who one of those other two canawlers was? I'm sure he was the one who offered the lower rate. It was Simon Maphis."

"Maphis? And you beat him at his own game? Oh, I could kiss you for that, Morgan!"

"Why not?" he said jauntily, glancing around. "No one's looking."

Cat turned to tilt her face up to his, and he kissed her full on the mouth.

Cat selected a small side-cut, and they tied up there shortly after sundown. She watched Morgan help Timmie stable the mules, while Mick went below to prepare supper. She studied Morgan covertly, watching his well-muscled body in graceful movement, observing the sure quickness of his hands; and she shivered slightly as she remembered those hands on her body last night.

For the first time in a long while, she felt relaxed, without concern about where their next cargo was coming from. She felt confident that Morgan would always manage to find them something to earn money. Although she had little faith in luck—in her opinion, a person made his own luck—she had the feeling that the presence of Morgan Kane on board the boat was a talisman of a brighter future.

Her thoughts were interrupted as she saw Morgan coming along the towpath toward where she sat by the tiller. He made the jump onto the boat easily; and watching him, Cat suddenly wanted him, a want that was a sweet ache. She wanted to be in his arms again; she wanted again what she had experienced last night. He stopped before her, and as she looked up, his face went still, his eyes staring down into hers; and she realized that her want must be naked on her face. At that moment she did not care; she wanted him to know!

"Cat ..." He reached out to touch her, and then the moment was shattered by the sound of a bell clanging on the canal. With a start Morgan glanced around at a small boat hurrying east, pulled by a team of four horses. A bell hung on the bow, and a man was standing beside it. Even as Morgan watched, he clanged it again.

"What the hell is *that*?"

Cat laughed. "That is a hurry-up boat."

"And what is a hurry-up boat?"

"Troubleshooting boats. There's either a breach upstream in the berm or the towpath. Or they could be going to the rescue of a 'mudlark.' And before you ask, a mudlark is any boat that has run aground."

Morgan's attention returned to her again, but before he could speak, Mick's head poked up from below. "Food's ready, folks! Shall we eat on deck, as usual?"

Struggling for composure, Cat nodded. "Of course, Mick." She started to rise. "I'll help you bring it up."

"No, you sit there." Morgan's hand closed on her shoulder, squeezing intimately, his burning gaze still locked with hers. "I'll help your father."

The wine and the simple but hearty food that Mick had prepared further relaxed Cat. She sat quietly, listening with amusement as her father told Morgan tall tales about the Erie, a sure indication that Mick not only accepted Morgan as one of them but that he liked the man.

"There was this mad sea captain," Mick said, "who spent good money for a dead whale that had been washed up on a Cape Cod beach. Now this bucko figured that he was going to get rich off'n that dead creature, by showing it to people along the Erie, charging a goodly fee, o'course. Trouble was, after the thing had been out in the sun for a week or so, it began to stink something terrible. Nobody would go within a hundred yards of this feller's boat, much less pay to go and see the bloody carcass. The captain tried to get rid of the stinking carcass by dumping it into the canal at night. But a canal walker spotted him, reported him, and the captain was fined two dollars for interfering with canal traffic. You know what finally happened?" Mick laughed uproariously. "He found a farmer about as mad as he was, and convinced him that the whale would make good fertilizer for his crops. He sold the whale to him for eight cents! Jaysus, no telling how much that captain was out of pocket, towing that great carcass all that way!"

Morgan laughed appreciatively, and Cat joined in, although she had heard the story many times. Morgan's glance met hers, and again Cat felt the stirring of desire. She moved restlessly, hoping that Morgan would make some move to get her alone.

When Mick had finally run out of steam, and had taken the dishes down to the galley, Morgan said, "Would you like to walk for a little, Cat? It's a nice night, and we might sleep better for a bit of a stroll."

Cat rose to her feet eagerly. "I'd like that very much, Morgan."

She took Morgan's arm, and they strolled along the towpath. There was a slice of a moon, which gave a little light filtering through the trees shadowing the path. Insects hummed in the warm darkness, and somewhere a frog croaked hoarsely.

Morgan said, "I do believe that Mick is coming around to approving of me, finally."

Cat smiled up at him. "You can be sure of it. When he banters with someone like he did with you tonight, he likes that someone."

"Well, the feeling is mutual, Cat. I like your father."

"I like him, too, most of the time." She sighed plaintively. "If only he'd ease off on the drink."

Morgan shrugged, "Well, we all have our faults, some to a greater degree than others."

"And you, you seem to have taken to canal life well enough. Have you given any more thought to how long you'll stay with us?" She held her breath for his answer.

"I think I'll stick around for a while." He squeezed her arm.

"But what if your memory comes back and you find you're ... Well, if you find you're an important man somewhere, with a good job and responsibilities?"

"Somehow I'm sure I don't have any responsibilities, nothing to take me away from the Erie, and you, if I chose to stay."

"I'm glad you feel that way, Morgan." Her breath was coming fast, and her heartbeat was erratic.

Morgan turned them back toward the boat, and he did not speak again until they neared the side-cut. "Shall we walk over in that direction, toward that glade?"

She nodded mutely, already anticipating what was about to happen. Her body turned soft and hot with need. She wanted this man with an intensity that she would not have thought possible.

"There's one bad thing about canal boats," he said in a low voice. "They're so cramped, there's almost no privacy."

"I know," she said, detesting the tremble in her voice.

He led her into the secluded area and under a spreading tree. Cupping her face between his hands, he kissed her, lightly at first. She came against him hard, returning his kiss with ardor, hands pressing his back.

"Dear, sweet Cat," Morgan murmured. "You have been

in my thoughts all day, and I would become passionate just thinking about last night."

"I know. Me, too," she said shakily.

He stepped back from her, and removed his coat, spreading it on the thick grass. Cat sank to her knees on it, and Morgan dropped down beside her, taking her into his arms again. They embraced like that, swaying back and forth in their mounting passion.

She quickly divested herself of her trousers, shirt, and undergarments, then lay with pounding heart while he undressed. His tall, muscular body had the look of a statue, dappled by the moonlight filtering through the leaves. Somehow, being out in the open like this, with the night like a warm pulse beating around them, made it seem more natural to Cat, completely without any coloring of shame.

Then he was beside her, his hands on her body, his mouth on hers.

She locked her arms around his shoulders, and held him imprisoned there, his wildness restricted by her women's strength. As her pleasure increased, Cat became abandoned, her wildness matching his own. Morgan groaned loudly, his arms tightening around her as he began to shudder out his ecstasy.

"Ah, my sweet Cat, my sweet wanton, how I love you!"

When he finally lay beside her, she said musingly, "You called me wanton, Morgan. Am I?"

"I think so, but I meant it in the nicest sense, and there's nothing wrong with that. It's as it should be, and I love you the more for it."

She stirred uneasily. "But, a wanton ... A woman who is that is not considered a good woman. Landsmen think of most canal women as wantons, or tarts."

He traced the line of her jaw with his finger. "Ah, but

wanton can mean many other things. It can mean playful, capricious, unrestrained, and you are all those things. Besides, names mean very little. It's a label people put on other people they don't like, or understand. It's what people feel about themselves that truly matters. Do you feel like a *bad* woman?"

She thought for a moment. "No, I feel good about myself, I feel good about what's happened to me." Blushing furiously, she hid her face in the crook of her shoulder.

"Then it's all right, isn't it? Besides, love, you told me, many times, that you care little about what other people think of you."

"But this is something different. I just didn't want you to think that I'm ..."

"Hush." He covered her mouth with his hand. "I think you're the best woman I've ever known, and I love you."

There was an expectant pause, and Cat knew that he wanted her to answer in kind; but she could not, not just yet. She stirred and sat up. "It grows late, and Mick and Timmie will soon begin to wonder. We'd best get back."

"As you wish, Cat." There was an edge of disappointment in his voice.

He got up, picked up his clothes, and began to dress. In a few minutes they were ready to go back, and Cat took his arm as they strolled back toward the boat, both silent, busy with their own thoughts.

Climbing up the towpath, they soon could see the *Cat*. The boat was dark, and Cat assumed that both Mick and Timmie were bedded down for the night, for which sh was glad; she was positive that there was a glow abou' and Mick could surmise from one look at her ' just occurred.

Then she stopped, blinking, and pul' arm. "What's that glow?"

Morgan followed the direction of her pointing finger. "Fire, it must be fire!"

He began to run, with Cat right on his heels. As they drew near, Cat saw a dark figure squatting in the shallow water by the bow. Even as she watched, she saw the figure toss a pail of liquid against the boat, and the fire flared. The *Cat* was on fire; someone was putting the torch to her!

By the year 2000, 2 out of 3 Americans could be illiterate.

It's true.

Today, 75 million adults… about one American in three, can't read adequately. And by the year 2000, U.S. News & World Report envisions an America with a literacy rate of only 30%.

Before that America comes to be, you can stop it… by joining the fight against illiteracy today.

Call the Coalition for Literacy at toll-free **1-800-228-8813** and volunteer.

Volunteer Against Illiteracy. The only degree you need is a degree of caring.

Ad Council   Coalition for Literacy

LWA

LOVESWEPT

Love Stories you'll never forget by authors you'll always remember

LOVESWEPT

Love Stories you'll never forget by authors you'll always remember

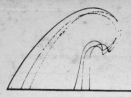

Love Stories you'll never forget
by authors you'll always remember

☐	21682	**The Count from Wisconsin #75** Billie Green	$2.25
☐	21683	**Tailor-Made #76** Elizabeth Barrett	$2.25
☐	21684	**Finders Keepers #77** Nancy Holder	$2.25
☐	21688	**Sensuous Perception #78** Barbara Boswell	$2.25
☐	21686	**Thursday's Child #79** Sandra Brown	$2.25
☐	21691	**The Finishing Touch #80** Joan Elliott Pickart	$2.25
☐	21685	**The Light Side #81** Joan Bramsch	$2.25
☐	21689	**White Satin #82** Iris Johansen	$2.25
☐	21690	**Illegal Possession #83** Kay Hooper	$2.25
☐	21693	**A Stranger Called Adam #84** B. J. James	$2.25
☐	21700	**All the Tomorrows #85** Joan Elliott Pickart	$2.25
☐	21692	**Blue Velvet #86** Iris Johansen	$2.25
☐	21661	**Dreams of Joe #87** Billie Green	$2.25
☐	21702	**At Night Fall #88** Joan Bramsch	$2.25
☐	21694	**Captain Wonder #89** Anne Kolaczyk	$2.25
☐	21703	**Look for the Sea Gulls #90** Joan Elliott Pickart	$2.25
☐	21704	**Calhoun and Kid #91** Sara Orwig	$2.25
☐	21705	**Azure Days, Quicksilver Nights #92** Carole Douglas	$2.25
☐	21697	**Practice Makes Perfect #93** Kathleen Downes	$2.25
☐	21706	**Waiting for Prince Charming #94** Joan Elliott Pickart	$2.25

Prices and availability subject to change without notice.

Buy them at your local bookstore or use this handy coupon for ordering:

Bantam Books, Inc., Dept. SW4, 414 East Golf Road, Des Plaines, Ill. 60016

Please send me the books I have checked above. I am enclosing
$_____ (please add $1.25 to cover postage and handling). Send
check or money order—no cash or C.O.D.'s please.

Mr/Ms_____

Address_____

City/State_____ Zip_____

SW4—8/85

Please allow four to six weeks for delivery. This offer expires 2/86.

THE LITTLE BOOK
OF WITCHES

THE LITTLE BOOK OF WITCHES

Dominique Foufelle

HALLOWE'EN

COPYRIGHTED BY RAPHAEL TUCK & SONS CO "??"

CONTENTS

Wishing You a Jolly Halloween

MAGIC THROUGHOUT HISTORY

Nowadays, claiming to be a witch is no longer dangerous. It might even be considered somewhat glamorous. At worst, it may be regarded as a harmless passing fancy. Self-proclaimed paranormalists, mediums and clairvoyants on the internet do not mean any harm. On the contrary, they claim to contribute to the well-being of those who use their divinations and ceremonies. Whether or not to believe in magic is a personal choice, entirely up to each individual, within the limits of public safety rules. It was however a very different story in the past.

Sorcery, revered and feared

In ancient times, people were sometimes troubled by the lack of answers to the legitimate questions they raised. How could natural catastrophes and disease be explained? What made the difference between an empire flourishing or suffering a disastrous fate? Science, still in its infancy, could not provide them with rational explanations. Even the few brilliant minds of the time remained in the dark. People were essentially at the whims of the gods and, in an attempt to change the course of things, they relied on those who claimed to be in contact with invisible forces. This state of affairs would extend centuries, until progress in scientific knowledge gradually replaced such popular beliefs. The ancient Greeks and Romans looked to Egypt as the land of magic with its high priests, miraculous papyrus

Une sorcière compose un médicament salutaire, à l'aide de simples
cueillis au clair de lune, quand sonne minuit.

and impressive rituals, but they also had their own magical rites that the whole of society could access. Greek mythology also includes characters endowed with exceptional powers, such as the sorceresses Circe and Medea.

People who claimed to be sorcerers or sorceresses were neither mocked nor questioned. They used all sorts of tools that have remained practically unchanged since the dawn of time: stones, plants, animals, amulets, tablets, incantations, songs... All of them could be used to cast spells, provided you knew how. However, sorcery, unlike religion, was not practised in public; it remained secret and aroused distrust. Sorcery has been practised all over the world: by the Native American peoples, the Celts, in the Far East and all the way to deepest darkest Siberia. Those who wield it inspire fear, for whoever can do good can also do evil.

Sorcery outside the law

In Europe, the rise of monotheistic religion would deal a severe blow to sorcery. The Old Testament condemned it. As the Catholic Church evangelized people, imposed its laws and quickly dominated the West, it hardened its stance, forbidding witchcraft. Of course, divination was still practised in high society, but so was palmistry and astrology. However, contact with the supernatural could only be made through a pact with God's archenemy, the devil. At the beginning of the thirteenth century, the Church created the Inquisition, tasked with enforcing its dogmas and trying all those who questioned them.

In 1326, Pope John XXII redefined witchcraft as heresy. There followed a succession of devastating wars in Europe throughout the Middle Ages, which were accompanied by plagues and famines caused by natural disasters and the shortage of farmers, driven away by conflict. People were living in appalling conditions. It was reassuring to know that the hand of the devil was behind this, and witches made convenient scapegoats.

Witch hunts are often dated to the Middle Ages, but they were still in full swing from the Renaissance through to the seventeenth century. They claimed a significant number of victims, with an estimated 30,000 to 50,000 lives being lost. Accusations or rumours almost automatically led to arrest, trial and burning at the stake. But who were those witches?

Persecuted witchcraft

In the Middle Ages, medicine was barely effective. To cure their ailments, whether mild or severe, the sick needed care from those who had mastered the use of plants, even if they were wary of these savants. Patients could not help but be suspicious of the use of supernatural powers and perhaps even the ceremonies that accompanied the healing.

Among the witches there were many healers. There were also midwives and those who performed abortions, which, while necessary, were strictly forbidden. In their own way, these people were rebelling against authority, refusing the duty of obedience imposed on women. In the case of the Salem witches, which is still renowned today, the first two young girls accused a beggar, a marginalized old woman and a slave. Important people were not blamed, only single women who had been alienated and isolated from society... There was, of course, some settling of scores. With the courts looking the other way, it was easy to do away with anyone you had a quarrel or dispute with.

Once this wave of bloodshed had passed, witches and sorcerers, no matter what they claimed to be practising, were no longer persecuted. As recently as the late nineteenth century, mediums became very popular among the wealthy, who loved to gather around séance tables and commune with the dead. In rural areas, there are still patients who place their trust in healers. And perhaps, the odd discreet witch or sorcerer.

HOW DO YOU BECOME A WITCH?

In the Middle Ages, it was believed that one irreversible act was necessary to become a witch: a pact with the devil. In exchange for the powers acquired, the aspiring witch renounced the Christian faith. The devil, now her absolute master, branded her with an identifiable mark. She willingly participated in carnal union with him because a witch's sexual appetite knew no bounds. The powers granted to her were evil: the ability to concoct poisonous potions, cast evil spells, summon malevolent beings, take possession of souls and harm them by any means possible. However, her two most valuable magical powers, flying and shapeshifting, could help her to do good deeds. But witches were rarely benevolent in fairy tales.

Today we have a different perspective as witches are no longer systematically associated with black magic. Nowadays, those who wish to reveal and exercise their gifts must be open to nature, the cosmos, others and themselves. Although their sacrifices today are different, becoming a witch has always required deep commitment.

WHAT DOES A WITCH LOOK LIKE?

Our popular imagination draws upon clichés from the children's stories that were all the rage in the nineteenth century. In them, witches are old, ugly and disheveled. They dress in rags, wear pointed hats and trap their victims with their claw-like hands. They have hooked noses, a feature that can be connected to the blatant anti-Semitism of the period, with Jews being depicted with prominent noses as a sign of greed. For centuries, we have imagined witches with pointed hats like those worn by heretics, yet this accessory has come to symbolize a witch's power. Black like the rest of her clothes, her hat is what gives her away. It emphasizes her malevolence. Indeed this unsightly woman would do well to use her powers of transformation to disguise herself with a more pleasant appearance. Besides, a witch must use her seductive charms to make her targets do her bidding. As Satan's reputed lover, she gives free rein to her loose morals. Her terrifying looks accentuate the diabolical nature of her sexual freedom, considered a terrible sin for a woman at the time this image was formed. However, if we consider other periods or cultures this has not always been the stereotype. For example, the beauty of Circe, a sorceress in Greek mythology, was just as awe-inspiring as her magical powers. Her niece Medea fell in love with Jason the Argonaut and used evil spells so he could capture the Golden Fleece.

RIE CRAMER.

YOU OLD HAG!

Calling a woman a witch is not a compliment. The repulsive image associated with witches since the sixteenth century has lent the term its meaning of old, ugly and wicked. We consider them to be bothersome, disturbing and menacing creatures. We even warn our children not to go anywhere near them. Witches are the female incarnation of the bogeyman, and their wide spectrum of actions (poisoning, curses and spells, kidnapping...) makes us all the more terrified. This sexist insult is more often aimed at older women than young girls, for whom insults with sexual connotations are favoured. Even so, in the days when people believed in witches, they were reproached particularly for their insatiable sexual appetites. They gave in to the advances of the devil himself, and God alone knew what debauchery they engaged in during their Sabbaths! Witches struck bargains with demons and their ability to surreptitiously spread evil knew no limit. Simple ignorance fed the public imagination, and frustration and hate sparked shameless accusations with tragic consequences for their victims.

Méchante comme une vieille sorcière.

THE EVIL QUEEN

The tale 'Snow White and the Seven Dwarfs' was published by the Brothers Grimm in 1812 in their collection of fairy tales, yet the image we have of the heroine's stepmother comes from the 1937 Walt Disney animated film. She is a particularly hideous witch: old, wrinkled, squat and hunchbacked, with a crooked nose disfigured by a wart and a saggy chin. She has messy white hair, deformed hands with crooked fingers and a trembling voice. Yet, before she used a spell to transform herself into the hag, the queen had been sublimely beautiful, elegant, haughty and very unkind. She was the archetype of the cruel stepmother. This figure was inspired by what was a common reality: high maternal mortality rates often led widowers to remarry, and blended families clashed over conflicting inheritance interests, causing strained relationships. The queen's wickedness is explained by her vanity. She unleashes her jealousy against Snow White, who is young, sweet, angelic and, above all, more beautiful than this woman who wants to be the fairest of all. After becoming a witch, the queen offers Snow White a poisoned apple, the symbol of lust and the forbidden fruit with which the serpent convinced Eve to commit the first sin. That is enough to make the evil queen an enemy of humanity. She is a temptress because of her beauty, frightening because of her powers and sinful because of her actions; she is a dangerous woman who must be hated for our own good.

THE WITCH'S KIT

If you see a woman flying around on a broom stick, you may be quite sure that she is a witch. In popular imagination, this item is her symbol. Its bristles come from six types of wood: birch, willow, broom, hazelnut, mountain ash and hawthorn. The witch attaches them to the handle with a flexible willow branch, holding it fast with a blackthorn twig. As her powers clean better than any household implement, she can use her broom to purify the air and trace her magic circle on the floor. Another essential accessory for all witches is the magic wand, made from elder wood. It must be cut with a golden sickle at sunrise or sunset, using the left hand. The witch scratches it lightly to add three to five drops of her blood, and then seals the opening with candle wax. A witch must always keep candles and candelabra in her home so she can draw a circle on the ground to perform her magic and protect the setting of her meetings with fellow witches. To prepare her spells, elixirs and potions, using the ingredients stored in bottles, she uses a preferably large cauldron in the fireplace. She keeps a record of her recipes and notes in a thick book of spells, which is kept safely hidden away. In her wardrobe is a simple accessory used in ceremonies: a braided rope to tie around her waist.

MIRROR, MIRROR ON THE WALL

Mirrors are one of the magical tools that mediums use to practice their craft, allowing them to see the past, present and future, and to make predictions. In ancient times, mirrors, or a pool of still water, were already being used for divination. The fact that mirrors reflect reality has little bearing, since soothsayers do not merely gaze at the surface: they go deeper, beyond appearances. Mirrors always tell the truth, as Snow White's stepmother learns at her own expense when her mirror reveals that her stepdaughter has surpassed her in beauty. However, witches do not limit their use of mirrors to divination, they also use them to ease pain. Used by a medium, a mirror can also summon a spirit who has watched over a family for generations. A witch, surrounded only by candlelight, will see her wish come true if she concentrates on a mirror. A magical mirror must not be used for any other purpose or to decorate a room. If it hangs on the back of a door, it diminishes the power of those who enter with bad intentions. Furthermore, before it is used for the first time, it should be magnetized for nine days by benevolent spirits who must be summoned.

Oh my! Do you you s'pose that's really him?

THE FORBIDDEN FRUIT

When Snow White encountered the witch in the forest, the frightening appearance of the woman did not stop her from biting into the apple offered to her. She may not have been so easily persuaded by another fruit as the apple is a symbol of temptation. It is an irresistible fruit. However, that which is forbidden comes at a price. The three Hesperides of Greek mythology braved the dragon Ladon so they could pick the golden apples that the goddess Hera intended for her husband Zeus. Eris, daughter of the Night, brought discord between the rival goddesses Hera, Aphrodite and Athena by throwing a golden apple on the ground during a feast. The apple had an inscription saying that it was for the most beautiful woman. In the book of Genesis, God banished Eve from heaven because she dared to taste an apple, the forbidden fruit. This act led her and her companion Adam to a life of suffering. Apples do not seem to be a woman's best friend. However, they are not always harmful. Golden apples that gave the gods eternal youth grew in the garden belonging to Freya, the Norse goddess of love. The apple tree symbolized fertility to the Celts, who decorated their rooms with its branches. The sacred land of Avalon, where Morgana the fairy lived, also abounded in apple trees. Arthurian legends associated apples with creation, death and rebirth, the most important stages of life.

SEE YOU AT THE SABBATH

Sabbath, from the Hebrew *Shabbat*, is the Jewish ritual day of rest. Sabbath is also the name given to a gathering of witches, presided over by the devil himself. It is no coincidence that the two words are the same, because Jews and witches have both been accused of causing misfortune. Why would witches attend a sabbath? On a practical level, to meet 'colleagues' and exchange professional tips. Perhaps to learn new recipes for potions, the incantations that make the potions work, new ways to cast spells... Even if the programme wasn't everyone's cup of tea, the sabbath was a joyful celebration. They would fly perched on their broomsticks, wands or, occasionally, animals. In preparation, they would coat their bodies with ointment, potentially made from the fat of newborn babies. Black cats and snakes could accompany them. The meeting would be held at night in a secluded place in nature such as in a clearing or atop a boulder. A banquet would be served, oaths of allegiance to the devil reaffirmed and, most importantly there would be dancing. At a time when modesty was expected of women, they were described as lascivious or frenzied dances. The witches' sabbath would end in the worst possible way: with an orgy involving demons. It would often feature crimes and sacrifices too. The finely detailed accounts of witches' sabbaths were firmly rooted in the popular beliefs of the fourteenth century. These were readily recounted during the witch trials, which were becoming increasingly common at the time.

WELCOMING BACK THE DEAD

On 31 October, it is customary to welcome witches, vampires and the undead. For the Celts, Samhain, today's Halloween (All Hallows' Eve), marked the end of the year and was celebrated over several days. There was no precise date because the Gaels and the Britons (including the Bretons) used a lunar calendar, setting the date to the closest night with a full moon in early November. In the ninth century, Pope Gregory IV established 1 November as All Hallows' Day, now known as All Saints' Day; in the thirteenth century, 2 November officially became All Souls' Day, to commemorate the faithful departed. These Catholic rituals led to the decline of the Celtic Samhain, until it was resurrected in popular folklore by the Irish in the mid-nineteenth century. In years past, it was believed to be the moment when the boundary between the living and the dead dissolved and the spirits of the dead returned to the places where they had lived. Today, it is when creatures of the night, mostly the stuff of legend, roam the streets. The night before the full moon, the Celts would put out the fires in every hearth before gathering around their Druid. They would light a new fire with sacred oak branches to celebrate the new year, and its embers were brought back to rekindle the household fires. Then feasts were held with generous quantities of mead and beer, and pork, the meat being thought to confer immortality. Ritual games and songs enlivened the gatherings.

ONE MISSION: TO DO HARM

Sorcery can be used for the good of others, or for one's own good. This is called white magic, and people have sought it out throughout history for its beneficial power. And then, there is fearsome, malevolent black magic, the magic practised by witches and warlocks, inspired by Satan himself. This magic is also called 'the left-hand path' (as opposed to 'the right-hand path' of good), demonology (belief in and use of demons) or *maleficium* (an accusation of witchcraft made by the Church). Practices such as hexes, evil spells, curses, Satanism, black masses, vampirism, enchantment, bewitchment and necromancy, which summon evil spirits, openly seek to harm. Practising black magic means venturing into a dangerous realm, and those who do so still today had better beware. Why do people risk it? To acquire something of interest, to seek revenge, to help those who wish to settle scores and earn a reward. This path requires complex rituals which are used to contact evil forces. The Church disapproved of black magic and could falsely accuse an individual or group if this was in its interest to do so, as was the case of the Knights Templar. The use of spirits is also a hallmark of white magic. The difference lies in the intention: black magic's mission is to do evil.

THE GODS DEMAND HUMANS

What wouldn't you do to gain the gods' favour? Research shows that since the Neolithic period no civilization has stopped short of human sacrifice. For witches, the goal is different: sacrifices are performed to earn favour with the demons. As a sign of allegiance and submission, Satan demands sacrifice, an act that inspires fear and horror. Performing human sacrifices was the most serious charge in witchcraft trials. It was also the one that most influenced public opinion because it meant the accused could potentially murder anyone. It was said that witches preferred children as their victims. They would strip fat from the children's corpses and coat their own bodies with it before celebrating at their sabbaths. Besides accentuating their cruelty, this choice emphasized the power of children, innocent beings who could enhance magical powers. Even today, sorcerers accused of practising human sacrifice in Africa demand children's limbs or organs for their ceremonies. Rumours periodically crop up around the world about ceremonies involving paedophilia and Satanism during which children die and some of these are well-founded.

LES DRUIDES. — SACRIFICE HUMAIN

AT NIGHT, TERRORS AWAKEN

When the sun sets and darkness falls across the earth, humans are tormented by fears. New noises reach the ears of peasants huddled in their thatched cottages. Owls hoot, bats awaken and flutter around the barn, red foxes rummage in the thickets and their prey shrieks. None of them are dangerous, but hearing these sounds makes our blood run cold, which is why they are said to have evil powers. Through a window, a will-o'-the-wisp is seen to flicker among the graves in the cemetery. Is it looking for a wandering soul? Or does it seek to lead the reckless individuals wandering after nightfall astray? Spirits emerge at night. If, by misfortune, mirrors have not been covered with a black veil during a wake for a deceased loved one, their soul might have become trapped in one, causing their ghost to return to haunt the living. Be wary of vengeful spirits wherever you are. Whether victims of injustice or violent deaths, or dissatisfied with funeral rites not worthy of their standing, they take the form they believe most fitting to torment those who have survived them. Even the moon can be a threat; in Brittany, its glow is said to have impregnated young virgins.

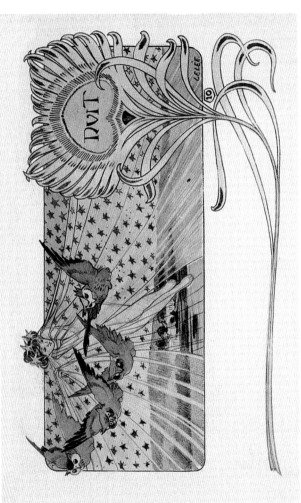

EXPERTS ON PLANTS

In 1862, Jules Michelet published the book *Satanism and Witchcraft*. This historian was criticized for dealing seriously with the task given to witches in the Middle Ages: healing. At that time, no distinction was made between medicine and witchcraft. Scientific knowledge, which was ever advancing yet subject to serious doubt, was not made public. Thus, ordinary people believed the ability to heal depended on power, not knowledge. The witches called to the bedside of a sick or wounded person healed with plants that they knew had healing powers. 'Healer' was therefore a real profession that could not be improvised, especially since witches took risks in practising homoeopathy before its time. They used tiny doses of potentially poisonous plants such as belladonna. 'What we know most assuredly about their medicine is that they often used a large family of questionable, very dangerous plants that served them well, for the most diverse uses, such as to calm or to stimulate,' wrote Michelet in the nineteenth century. Some of the potions boiling in their pots caused hallucinations and malaise, but for a good cause. They also used their knowledge to perform abortions, a procedure condemned by the Church, which did not work in their favour during the witch hunts between the fourteenth and the seventeenth centuries.

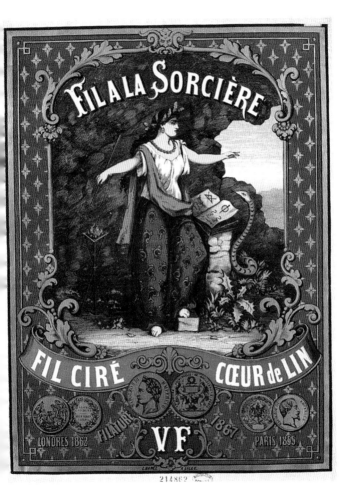

FIL A LA SORCIÈRE

FIL CIRÉ · CŒUR de LIN

LONDRES 1862 · FILATURE · 1867 · PARIS 1895

VF

THE POTION IN THE CAULDRON

What does a witch's potion contain? Mention is often made of toad slime, and also dragon blood, salamander saliva, bat hair, poisonous mushrooms, unicorn eyes, spider legs, snake venom and turtle shells. These ingredients are rather difficult get your hands on today, and they were no less difficult to find in the past. Moreover, legend has it that the witches of old included human ingredients in their potions where possible: teeth, nail clippings, blood, pubic hair and other appetizing substances. They were used to target the person for whom the concoction was intended. In order for the potion to work, the witches had to add other ingredients, which is where their extensive knowledge of plants played a crucial role. They had to harvest and measure the plants with care. For example, while low doses of hemlock could render a man powerless, high doses could kill him, so little mistakes could be extremely costly.

INVIGORATING
APHRODISIAC PLANTS

Nobody is more skilled at awakening dormant affections or arousing the most ardent passions than a witch. And just one potion is enough, because this lady knows all about aphrodisiac plants and their powers. It has been discovered that the effects of plants used to make love potions are not, strictly speaking, the work of magic. Aphrodisiac plants actually stimulate the libido because they have an effect on vitality. These include some very common plants, such as garlic, onion, oats, nettle, celery, rosemary, savoury and borage. Some others stimulate the senses with their aromas, such as vanilla, coriander, jasmine and violet. The desirable qualities of spices that remained rare and expensive for a long time, such as ginger, cinnamon, cloves, nutmeg, cardamom and saffron, are still highly valued. The mandrake owes its reputation as an aphrodisiac to its root, which resembles a human body – with its genitals, according to the most imaginative. This innocuous-looking Mediterranean herb is purported to boost fertility. It was also said that witches smeared their armpits with mandrake ointment so they could enjoy its hallucinogenic properties during their sabbaths. In the Middle Ages, its power was considered so strong that anyone harvesting them was advised to cover their ears with wax so as not to hear its agonizing cry, which would drive a person mad.

LES PLANTES
MÉDICINALES

MANDRAGORE
GENRE DES SOLANÉES
MANDRAGORA

Édition de la CHOCOLATERIE D'AIGUEBELLE (Drôme)

DANGEROUS PLANTS

Plants considered to be evil are simply common, naturally toxic plants. They can cause nausea, dizziness, vomiting, convulsions, asphyxiation, heartburn and even death. Such was the result of hemlock tea on the ancient Greek philosopher Socrates, who had been sentenced to death for impiety. Unfortunately for witches wanting to concoct discreet poisons, hemlock gives off a nauseating odour resembling mouse urine. Belladonna, highly prized in medieval black magic rituals, is more treacherous: its black berries are sweet, just like edible berries. Eating them, however, causes long-lasting pain that culminates in respiratory paralysis. Flowers can also mask their bad intentions with their attractive beauty. While the leaf of the oleander is very similar to a bay leaf, its effect in a stew is very different; wolfsbane, as slender and brilliantly purple as it may be, is a botanical source of arsenic; in May, the pretty lily of the valley will about serious heart problems rather than happiness not bring happiness; and the autumn crocus leads to poisoning symptoms that last for several days. As for mistletoe, it may decorate our houses, but it must never find its way onto our plates.

Ciguë.

BENEFICIAL PLANTS
TO THE RESCUE!

As healers, witches knew all about the properties of plants. But when it came to soothing hearts or bringing good luck, they could not rely solely on their knowledge. To get results they had to adhere to legends, honour beliefs and sacrifice their insight for customs. That meant that even the humble nettle offered protection: you threw a handful of it into the fire to protect the house from evil spirits and carried a full bag of it on your person to deflect curses. As for holly, it foiled the effects of poisons; making a herbal tea with it and sprinkling it on newborn babies would ward off the evil eye. Hanging a periwinkle, a plant of lunar influence, above your door fostered love, marriage and happiness in the home. In gardens, roses attracted fairies, and hawthorns were witches themselves who had transformed into plants. With iris root powder, you could spark and maintain love, or repel evil spirits by pouring it into bath water. The poppy symbolized fleeting pleasure in the language of flowers. It was customary to put a few poppy seeds into babies' bottles: the flower's sedative effect would immediately produce a peaceful slumber.

Pavot.

DEADLY POTION

To ensure that the happy and euphoric feelings of love at first sight lasted, there was nothing like a love potion. This imaginary herbal drink was not an aphrodisiac. It acted on mutual feelings, making them irresistible and indestructible. However, it did not guarantee eternal happiness, as demonstrated in the legend of Tristan and Isolde. Three centuries before its first written version, this tale based on a Celtic legend had been passed down in oral form by storytellers since the ninth century - three centuries before its first written version. And that version would be far from the last with studies of the tale and adaptations for stage and screen still being made in the twenty-first century. The twists and turns may vary, but the plot remains the same: Tristan, one of the heroes of Arthur's Round Table, is sent to Ireland to ask for the hand of Isolde the Blonde for his uncle, King Mark of Cornwall. Alas, during the trip, the two youths take a love potion that binds them inseparably together. Eventually forced to yield, Isolde marries Mark and Tristan weds a Breton princess. But Tristan's persistent love for Isolde the Blonde prevents him from consummating his marriage, pushing his wife to seek revenge. She forbids her rival to approach her husband, yet Isolde is the only one who can heal his lethal war wounds. The two lovers die, one because of his wounds, the other of grief. They are buried side by side, their graves linked by a blackberry bramble.

Triftan=Sage   Gg. Muhlberg pinx

THE WITCH AND HER FAMILIAR

After proving her worth, a witch was given a devoted helper, known as a familiar, for some of her duties. Sometimes it was a spirit or a minor demon, a gift from the devil himself, but it was often an animal familiar. Certain animals, known for their evil deeds, were used as a pretext for accusations. A witch would willingly carry a toad, for example, on her left shoulder and sometimes added it to her potions. They represented evil and a toad's presence near a house brought bad luck. Black cats, a more common animal, instilled so much fear that they were hunted down. People said that they participated in Satanic rituals. Any animal thought to be destructive was suspected of being a witch's familiar, such as rats, mice, hares, ravens, owls, spiders and bees. Their mistress fed them with meticulous care. She would offer them her blood or make them a porridge out of breast milk. In fact, it was believed that the infamous 'devil's mark' was actually a third breast for breastfeeding her familiar. It was in the witches' best interests treat their animals well; the beasts had the right to complain at the witches' sabbath if they felt that their mistresses were not treating them as they deserved. The accused witches were then punished.

THE PERSECUTOR PERSECUTED

Poor black cats! Elegant as they are, the colour of their fur has earned them a bad reputation – a dark fate, you might say. The story is an old one, dating back to the Egypt of the pharaohs. The ancient Egyptians worshipped cats as long as they were not black, with black cats being killed at birth. Even today, black cats are still believed to bring bad luck in a number of cultures. Indeed, black is a frightening colour because it is associated with shadows, bad luck and death. In Western culture, mourners have worn black since the time of the Roman Empire. In the Middle Ages, the black cat came to be regarded as the devil incarnate, offered as a sacrifice during heretical ceremonies. There are but two groups of people who would willingly associate with this animal: Satanists and witches, and they were often lumped together. Not only did witches enjoy the company of this cursed animal, with whom they are frequently portrayed, but they were also able to take on its appearance. Crossing a black cat was therefore equivalent to crossing paths with a witch! Writers, including Edgar Allan Poe in one of his short stories, have used this evil character to scare thrill-seeking readers. In Brittany, however, the animal is given a chance: one white hair is hidden in its fur coat, which will bring good luck to whomever finds it and plucks it out.

TOO WISE TO BE HONEST

What is it that scares those who take night strolls through the forest? Is that an eagle-owl or a tawny owl hooting? These two nocturnal birds of prey are distinguished by the presence of feathery horn-like tufts crowning the head of the former. With their pointed beaks, the ample grip of their sharp claws, their greyish-brown plumage and their sharp hearing, they can be scary. Owls are, of course, carnivorous, but while small animals should be wary of them, they pose no threat to humans, whom they do not attack. Yet we find these beautiful birds disturbing because they can see what no one sees and detect hidden thoughts. Athena, the Greek goddess of wisdom, sought counsel from her little owl companion. It must be that people do not like their thoughts to be seen clearly because they have turned owls into witches' horrible assistants, going so far as to nail them to barn doors to ward off bad luck. You had to hurry and throw salt on the fire when you heard a hoot. To please their mistresses, owls were said to fly ahead of them at night and inspect their destinations, and to suck the blood of children for their own pleasure. To further tarnish their reputation, owls were thought to haunt the homes of the dying.

Chantecler   La Chouette

(4)

ADORABLE BATS

Chiroptera, more commonly known as bats, are not considered a nuisance. On the contrary, they drive insects and pests away from crops. During the Renaissance, they inspired Leonardo da Vinci's drawings of the forerunner of the aeroplane. However, their strange appearance, their nocturnal habits, their habit of sleeping upside-down and their silence would trigger repulsion and fear in humans. They were given a notoriously vicious reputation that often costs them their lives. Until the beginning of the twentieth century, bats were nailed to barn doors to ward off evil spells. The Romans once associated them with the devil, who is often depicted with wings similar to bats' wings. Witches are said to love them because they could both make them their pets and a delectable part of their feasts. Because they hunt at night and avoid daylight, bats make an ideal partner for witches' sabbaths. People thought that bats supplied their mistresses with fresh blood. There are even species called 'vampire bats' that suck the blood of animals. But unlike giant mosquitoes, they would not dare to suck the blood of a human.

Halloween

No. 858

THE OMINOUS SNAKE

Silent and striking, the snake is perceived as a traitor. A snake was able to convince Eve to defy God's order and taste the fruit of the Tree of Knowledge. It is because of the serpent that humans were driven out of paradise and subjected to the torments of earthly existence. In many depictions, a snake encircles the body of Lilith. This demoness, whom the legends describe as a devourer of children, was Adam's first companion and his equal, since she too was made out of clay. The devil likes to take the form of a snake, so, when this beast assists a witch in her rites, one cannot be certain whether the evil being is the snake or the witch. However, we envy the snake for one unique feature: it sheds its skin. By regenerating its skin, it achieves the youthful appearance that has made it a symbol of health. Asklepios (Aesculapius to the Romans), the god of medicine and son of Apollo, carried a snake-entwined staff, which has become the emblem of the medical professions.

L'ENVIE

La Vipère

GODDESS AND SORCERESS

Isis is an ancient Egyptian goddess and sorceress best known for the deeds she performed in saving her husband Osiris. Her husband was also her brother, both of them the children of the god Geb and the goddess Nut. By becoming a benevolent and cultured king, Osiris attracted the hostility of his brother Seth, the master of the desert, who was dissatisfied with his lot. This jealous man led his brother into a cleverly orchestrated trap: during a feast, Seth showed Osiris an elaborate custom-made chest, declaring he would give it to whomever filled it. Unsuspecting Osiris got into the chest, which Seth promptly closed and threw into the Nile. Isis boldly set out to find her missing husband. She found the chest in Byblos, Lebanon, its final stop after floating across the sea. Although Osiris was dead, Isis managed to bring him back to life for long enough to conceive their son, Horus. Still seething with anger, Seth found the body, cut it up into fourteen pieces and scattered them. Isis had no shortage of helpers to find the pieces: these included Isis's sister Nephthys, who had married Seth, and Anubis, Nephthys's son, born out of adultery with Osiris, and Horus. But only thirteen pieces were found (his penis may have become fish food), and Anubis wrapped them in papyrus. That is how Osiris became Egypt's first mummy. The sorceress could not resurrect her husband, but she did make him ruler of the kingdom of the dead.

ISIS et OSIRIS
3. Complainte d'Isis

PRODUITS LIEBIG:
facilitent le travail culinaire.

KILLER FOR LOVE

Medea, priestess and sorceress from Greek mythology, was the daughter of Aeëtes, king of Colchis, and Idya, an oceanid. Her maternal ancestry made Medea a powerful sorceress who would not be separated from her magic chest. She was also a priestess for the goddess Hecate. In Colchis, a dragon guarded the ram bearing the golden fleece. Jason and his Argonauts landed their ship, the *Argo*, there to seize this marvel. Medea's life was instantly transformed. She fell madly in love with Jason. She put the dragon to sleep, tore her brother to pieces, then scattered the pieces in order to delay her father Aeëtes from going after the Argonauts. In return, obtained her desired reward: Jason married her and they had two children. However, Pelias refused to give up the kingdom that had been promised to Jason. Medea used trickery to persuade the usurper's daughters to slit their own father's throat, but it was in vain Banished, the couple took refuge in Corinth. Alas, Jason repudiated Medea to marry Glauce, the daughter of King Creon. Medea exploded with anger at this betrayal. She gave Glauce a gift: a robe that would burn her and her father alive. Medea then slit her own children's throats. Out of all her crimes, this infanticide is the one that has left the lasting impression. Nevertheless, because she was immortal, Medea escaped on a winged chariot pulled by dragons and continued her eventful life.

L.A SPEDIZIONE DEGLI ARGONAUTI.
5. Medea consegna a Jasone l'erba magica.

CIRCE, THE SORCERESS

Circe was a mortal goddess famous for her potions, used to make dramatic transformations. Using said potions she turned the wolves and lions living in her palace into docile creatures. She also turned her rival, the beautiful Scylla into a horrible monster, allowing the sorceress to steal her fiancé, the sea god Glaucon. King Picus also made the mistake of rejecting her advances and was transformed into a woodpecker. According to the poet Homer, Circe turned the companions of Odysseus into pigs when they landed on her island kingdom, Aeaea, using a potion disguised as wine. Odysseus only escaped by taking an antidote given to him by the god Hermes. He then turned his companions back into humans and lived with Circe for a year. During this relatively short time, they conceived several children whose number and names vary, depending on the author. Much ink has been spilled about Circe and many painters have illustrated her. Greek mythology created her and the Romans adopted her. To the ancient Greeks, she was the daughter of Perseus, an oceanid, and Helios, the sun god. She was also the aunt who gave Medea refuge with Jason after her niece had killed her younger brother, Absyrtos. The Romans made her into the daughter of Hecate, goddess of the moon, and Aeëtes, son of Helios. They said she poisoned her husband, the king of Sarmates, and fled to a deserted island.

BEWARE OF BABA YAGA!

In Slavic tales, particularly Russian ones, Baba Yaga is introduced as an old woman with bony legs. This deformity does not hinder her because she flies around in a magical mortar with a pestle for a rudder and a silver broom to erase her tracks. Fortunately, her presence is announced by a strong wind that makes the trees groan and hundreds of her spirit escorts whisper. Even though she is skinny, she has a ferocious appetite. Her favourite food is young children, whom she devours while flying with a mouth so huge that it stretches down to the ground and to the gates of hell. In some stories, however, she has as many as forty-one children, mostly girls. She lives alone in the middle of the forest in a Russian-style cabin raised on two giant chicken legs that can move if necessary. A wall of human bones topped with skulls with shiny eye sockets surrounds her hut. Some brave souls have ventured there, such as Vasilisa, the victim of a cruel stepmother. When the girl realizes that Baba Yaga wants to keep her captive, she runs away. But the witch has her chased by her servants: the White Knight, representing the light of day; the Red Knight, the personification of the sun; and the Black Knight, who symbolizes the night. Finally, the illuminating skull that Vasilisa steals from the wall helps to rid her of her evil stepmother. Baba Yaga sometimes does favours for others too.

WITCH OR FAIRY?

Befana is a curious character! Just like a witch, she is very old with a long, beak-like nose; she dresses in rags and wears a tall pointed hat; and she rides around on a broomstick. One detail that sets her apart, however, is that Befana always has a brilliant smile. She is generosity personified and has a heart of gold. Befana flies over the towns and villages of Italy on the night of 5 January, the eve of the Epiphany, when the Three Wise Men, the Magi, arrived to see Jesus. She fills the children's socks with sweets. But wait! Befana also distributes coal to children who have been naughty. That is the extent of this evil-looking fairy's cruelty. According to Christian legend, Befana was a woman who met the Magi in the desert and gave them directions to Bethlehem. Afterwards, regretful that she hadn't accompanied them, she prepared a basket containing cakes and small gifts for Jesus and set out. Although she was unable to find the Wise Men or Jesus, she continued on her way, distributing her gifts to the children she met.

GOD'S RIVALS

While the Bible condemns the use of sorcery and witchcraft, it does not deny their existence or even their effectiveness. Indeed, the supernatural calls into question the principle of Christianity, which is based on total and exclusive surrender to the one and almighty God. To practise sorcery would therefore be to question God's powers, to distrust His decisions and seek protection elsewhere. In fact, this would mean considering that sorcerers possess equal or even greater power than God. Worse yet, this means you accept the risk of surrendering to Satan, a fallen angel who is constantly on the lookout. And this is true regardless of the discipline practised, be it divination, prediction, magnetism, appealing to healers, interacting with the dead, hypnosis, mediumship, idolatry, etc.; the Bible does not distinguish between white and black magic. Both contradict faith, even when they are carried out with the best of intentions. This demand for obedience clashed with the customs of biblical times. Belief in the supernatural united every strata of the population. Kings themselves did not act without consulting their appointed sorcerers. God warned His chosen people in the Old Testament, saying, 'When you come into the land which the Lord your God is giving you, you shall not learn to follow the abominations of those nations.'

« Retire-toi, Satan ! »   MATTH., IV, 10.

BRINGING BACK THE DEAD

Saul was the first king of Israel, chosen by the prophet Samuel. One day, while besieged by the Philistines, Saul waited for an answer from God about what to do, but alas, he waited in vain. He finally decided to consult the witch of Endor, who conjured up the ghost of Samuel. The practice of necromancy involves invoking spirits of the dead, who are then asked for advice or a prediction. This was what a necromancer did, at least in ancient times. Necromancers could be found in Babylon and Persia, as well as in Greek mythology. Respected leaders whose opinions were valued, necromancers gradually became feared by disapproving Christians. The Bible had already warned of the danger of their services through the terrifying episode of Samuel's appearance and his deadly prophecy. Spiritism, shamanism and voodoo ceremonies also involve necromancy. The deceased who are summoned express their opinions and are sometimes asked to intervene in support of or against something. It is said that some necromancers were even able to control the dead they revived and would make them perform evil deeds.

CHOCOLAT
DES
GOURMETS
TRÉBUCIEN

La Magicienne d'Endor

DEATH TO HERETICS!

The primary goal of the Inquisition established by Pope Gregory IX in 1231 was not to punish witches. But at a time when new beliefs that deviated from Catholic dogma were being accepted, the Church wanted to protect its power by censuring the people it considered heretics. There were many heresies in that day and age, and by threatening papal authority, they also undermined royal powers. The Cathars, for example, whose influence extended throughout the Languedoc region, were a great concern for the King of France. Furthermore, the Church did not like the lords' propensity to conduct court cases according to their own interests. The creation of an ecclesiastical jurisdiction was therefore deemed necessary to control feudal law. So, in 1326, the papal bull *Super illius specula*, issued by Pope John XXII, defined witchcraft as heresy for the first time. Inquisitors were thus ordered to prosecute those who practised witchcraft, which was considered the result of a pact with the devil. At the end of the fifteenth century, after the Catholic Monarchs drove the Muslims out of the Iberian Peninsula as part of the *Reconquista*, the Spanish Inquisition turned violently on the Jews and Muslims who had preferred conversion to exile. The inquisitors appointed by the kings had many people burnt at the stake, especially wealthy ones whose confiscated goods enriched the royal coffers. The practice of witchcraft added to the case against the defendants.

33 Un sorcier conduit au bûcher. XIII_{me} Siècle.

Een toovenaar wordt naar den brandstapel geleid (XIIIe eeuw).

ALWAYS GUILTY

An immense wave of witch trials took place during the sixteenth and seventeenth centuries. During this period, civil courts rather than religious tribunals took charge of the matter. However, this change did not mean that justice was meted out with greater fairness. In fact, the methods used were worthy of the Inquisition courts of old. But where did these accusations of conspiracy against the Church and the State with the devil come from? Sometimes the accused were blamed for problems that had plagued the community, such as drought, epidemics and poor harvests. Personal scores were also at play, which made it difficult to find evidence that proved a suspect guilty. Wherever there was any doubt, it was up to the suspect to prove their innocence. Many defendants were put to trial by ordeal, leaving it up to divine judgement to determine guilt or innocence. Those who made it through the ordeal unscathed were exonerated. For example, a person who floated when thrown into a river was found guilty. In the absence of evidence, confessions from people who resisted had to be obtained through torture. Before their execution, the accused had to give the names of their accomplices, who would, in turn, be arrested and tried. This process led to serial trials that ravaged communities, such as the county of Namur in Belgium, where some 1,650 pyres were lit among a population of about 100,000.

Hausdrache

Strafe für böse Weiber.

JOAN, A POLITICAL WITCH

The trial of Joan of Arc began in the city of Rouen on 9 January 1431, presided over by Bishop Pierre Cauchon. Joan, a former shepherdess from Domrémy, in Lorraine, was nineteen years old at the time. She had won battles against the supporters of the Duke of Burgundy and their English allies, thereby returning France's throne to its rightful heir. Although she had made him king, Charles VII never expressed any gratitude or support for his imprisoned champion. Joan, however, did not hold this against him. She maintained that it was heavenly voices that were behind her heroic victories. She refused to say anything about the visions that had led her to Chinon, to convince Charles to go to Rheims to be crowned. She had told King Charles and would never mention them again. Though Joan was a military genius, she was not exactly skilled in diplomacy. She refused to renounce her beliefs, not even to save her own life. Moreover, she continued to wear men's clothing, one more charge against her. With the enemies reconciled, it was impossible to reproach her patriotism. The only viable accusations left were heresy and witchcraft. The girl's stubbornness and insubordination in an exclusively male court, as well as the fear of witchcraft at the time, made it an easy task. The trial lasted just five months. On 30 May, Joan of Arc died at the stake, remaining loyal to her king. In 1456, Charles VII convened a retrial that would prove her innocence.

Vie de Jeanne d'Arc

Jeanne devant les Docteurs

ÉDITION DE LA
CHOCOLATERIE POULAIN

7

POLITICAL SORCERERS

In 1099, the Crusaders took Jerusalem. Many pilgrims journeyed there, but there were bandits lying waiting along the way. To ensure their safety, Hugues de Payns and Godfrey de Saint-Omer founded the military monastic order of the Poor Knights of Christ and the Temple of Solomon. King Baldwin II of Jerusalem granted them part of his palace, built on the site of Solomon's Temple. Other knights joined the group, known by then as the Knights Templar, and they gained official recognition in 1128. Its members wore a red cross sewn on to their white cloaks. Protecting pilgrims was no longer their sole purpose. The order, which answered only to the Pope, also acquired earthly power. The legacies they received and the interest on the loans they made to the kings of England and France enabled them to build up an enviable fortune. In fact, people still search for the 'treasure of the Templars', which has remained a mystery for centuries. On their return to the West in 1291, King Philip IV of France, who was substantially in debt to them, suppressed the Knights Templar. Those soldier monks who were not slaughtered were thrown in jail, accused of a crime that was common at the time and difficult to refute because it was based on unverifiable facts: committing acts of sorcery. Under pressure from the king, the Pope abolished the order in 1312, removing all protection. They were punished as sorcerers by being burnt alive. Their last grand master, Jacques de Molay, was burnt at the stake on 19 March 1314.

SUPPLICE DES TEMPLIERS

WITCHES WHO MADE HISTORY

Angèle de la Barthe, a Cathar, is considered to be the first victim of a witch trial. She was said to have conceived a baby-eating monster by the devil. She confessed to this atrocious crime under torture and was put to death in 1275. Three centuries later, Ursula Sontheil died in her bed from natural causes – a rare occurrence for a witch – protected by the awe she inspired. Believed to be the devil's daughter, she made wild prophecies about the Great Plague, the Great Fire of London and the execution of Mary Stuart, all of which proved to be true. In 1628, the Duke of Lorraine accused his valet, Desbordes, of inducing serious illness, including that of his wife. Desbordes was also charged with making hanged men and tapestry characters move. Accused of sorcery, he was burnt at the stake. Catherine Montvoisin made her name in respectable society as a palmist and supplier of poisons. Her mistake was implying collusion with Madame de Montespan, a favourite of King Louis XIV. Accused of performing black masses and abortions, she was burnt alive in 1680. Anna Göldi was the last witch executed in Europe; she died in 1782 in Switzerland. Her employer accused her of trying to poison his daughter. Under torture, she confessed that a demon made her do it. Although she retracted her statement, she was beheaded. In an unusual turn, justice came two centuries later when it was discovered that her master had accused her to prevent her from revealing their affair.

A MEDIEVAL TRIAL

In the Middle Ages, rumours led the authorities to women who were suspected of witchcraft. One accusation could be enough. The arrests were carried out with many prayers for protection. Three charges had to be proven to definitively establish that a woman practised witchcraft: she should bear the mark of the devil, go to sabbaths and cast spells. The accused was shaved and her nails were trimmed before she donned a tunic sprinkled with holy water. She was also served food soaked in salt, a powerful purifier. During the initial interrogations, judges did not inflict physical violence on the accused. They urged them to confess, which no one did, knowing that death undoubtedly awaited them. The judges considered the accused's behaviour; if displeasing, it could be used as evidence. They would listen to testimonies from anyone, including children. The judges searched for the mark of Satan, which was said to be numb to pain, by pricking the accused with a pin in the most intimate places. If she didn't confess, they ordered torture. The commonly chosen method was called 'strappado': the accused's arms were tied behind her back and then she was lifted into the air using pulleys. Few women resisted these punishments. Almost all of the defendants were sentenced to death, likely a foregone conclusion from the moment they were arrested. They ended up being burnt at the stake in public squares in front of their entire family.

THE WITCHES OF SALEM

In 1692, the inhabitants of Salem, an American town near Boston, were suffering the after-effects of the war with France. The Crown of England was neglecting the area, which had been left in the hands of ministers who laid down the law. Inside the home of Reverend Samuel Parris, his daughter Betty and niece Abigail were fascinated by the stories of witchcraft told by Tituba, a Native American slave. A tide of panic gripped the city when the girls began to speak an unknown language, hallucinate and have fits. The strange symptoms spread to other young girls like an epidemic. The Salem elders concluded that they had been possessed by the devil and ordered them to denounce the people who had bewitched them. They gave names, specifically those of marginalized women, including Tituba. The accusations upset the surrounding villages, reaching all the way to Boston. A hundred people, including a few men, were accused. Those who were tried were never acquitted; the death penalty was pronounced and carried out. This turmoil lasted almost a year, until the governor intervened. The community of Salem was left scarred. It was weakened because daily work had been left undone, and it was divided because neighbourhood quarrels had exploded over accusations. There was already suspicion that the Salem witch trials were nothing more than a fraudulent hoax. More than three centuries after the events, the nineteen women hanged as witches in Salem were pardoned.

THE BLACK DOG, ACCUSED!

In the Middle Ages, the Church claimed that the devil could seduce humans by taking the shape of an animal. While it could not turn into an ox, donkey, sheep or dove, since these animals were present at the Nativity, it could possess any other species. As creatures of God, animals could also be guilty of crimes, just like humans. So, they too had to go on trial. They were accused of murder, robbery, dishonourable behaviour and practising witchcraft. Should a cockerel lay an egg, it was accused of cooperating with sorcerers, who adored these eggs that contained serpents. If a fly entered the mouth of a human, they became possessed. Dogs with black fur were suspects, as were parrots gifted with speech, goats armed with monstrous horns, and diabolically quick weasels. These animals were accused whenever there was an epidemic or inexplicably bad weather. Cats were tried for being the close friends of witches. Everything from locusts ravaging fields to rats causing damage in cellars were excommunicated, in absentia, of course. Rarely saved, even with the help of a lawyer, animals would also end up being burnt at the stake, like humans.

THE WITCHES OF *MACBETH*

Playwright William Shakespeare created three witches who have left their mark not just on the history of theatre, but also on the popular imagination. In *Macbeth*, old, ugly, bearded women gather around a cauldron, stirring the foul ingredients it contains. Shakespeare based his characters on the idea of the witch as it was understood in 1623. Shortly before, King James I had published *Daemonology*, which discussed the subject of witchcraft. He lacked sufficient words for 'these detestable slaves of the Devil'. Scotland's first witch hunt took place in 1590. The North Berwick witch trials lasted two years and involved nearly one hundred accused men and women, who made their confessions under torture. James I himself questioned one of the suspects, healer Agnes Sampson, who was later burnt at the stake. These events consolidated hatred for witches. 'Double, double toil and trouble; /Fire burn and cauldron bubble' chant the determined witches of *Macbeth*, proud of their work. They act at the bidding of Hecate, the Greek goddess of the moon, who is traditionally associated with demons and ghosts. However, these witches are not responsible for Macbeth's crimes. Messengers of fate, they predict his future when he asks, delighted by the cruelty of the events that are about to take place.

MACBETH. 1. Les sorcières prédisent à Macbeth qu'il sera roi.

VÉRITABLE EXTRAIT DE VIANDE LIEBIG.

REPELLING EVIL

Gargoyles were created in the heyday of Gothic cathedrals, the thirteenth century. Historians believe that Laon Cathedral in France was the first to be decorated with them. These sculptures had a very specific purpose: to drain rainwater as far as possible from the walls in order to avoid damaging them. Gargoyles were exempt from the strict rules applied to religious statuary and thus gave sculptors the opportunity to express their creativity. Sculptors were inspired by the creatures contained in bestiaries, works that depicted both real and imaginary creatures. They soon became increasingly elaborate and menacing fantastic chimeras due to their symbolic duty: to repel evil. Shouldn't they protect the house of God, which sheltered good? It was even said that gargoyles would scream if evil approached. The chimeras of Notre-Dame in Paris are often described as being remarkably beautiful and impressive. However, they do not date to the thirteenth century. We owe them to the architect Eugène Viollet-le-Duc, who led the restoration of French monuments in the nineteenth century.

VADE RETRO, SATANA!

Today, people who think they are in the devil's grip should not despair. The Catholic Church provides them with exorcists, priests delegated by bishops for this mission. However, the Church warns against the intervention of other exorcists and states that no payment should be made for this service. Be careful not to confuse oppression with possession. Oppression is when a demon can alter your will, but your soul remains free. Possession, on the other hand, deprives the victim of all control. In the case of the latter, expect the most unstoppable intrigues that could have come straight from a horror film. Priests who perform exorcisms instruct the patient to pray and observe their faith because heathen practices strengthen the devil's hold. Warding off Satan has been a human concern since ancient times, and people have turned to the practice of magic for this purpose: the laying on of hands, purifications, fumigations, sacramental rites, sacrifices, etc. A single person can harbour several demons with specific intentions, which is why exorcists try to discover their names and aims. The ceremony lasts for hours. Satisfactory results are not guaranteed, especially if the person supposed to be possessed is in fact suffering from psychiatric disorders, which medicine did not have an answer to until recently.

IN THE NAME OF SATAN

Satan was an angel before he became God's adversary. The leader of the fallen angels, he spreads evil and temptation around the world. Choosing to honour and serve him meant that you were working against all that is good and opposed the Church. In many rural areas, it was believed that witches become his wives. Accusations of practising Satanic acts, possession, bewitchment, black masses, witches' sabbaths and anything resembling a deal with Satan have all been brought up in witch trials which led to death sentences. If someone decided to devote themselves to the devil, they did so secretly. At the beginning of the twentieth century, Englishman Aleister Crowley brought the prince of darkness out of the shadows. Calling himself the incarnation of Satan, he renamed himself 'the Great Beast 666'. His Satanism ordained that a person satisfies their own needs above all else, even if it meant practising black magic. Crowley consumed large quantities of drugs and engaged in shockingly debauched sexual practices. He travelled the world before dying of a heart attack in 1947 at the age of seventy-two. In 1966, American Anton Szandor LaVey founded the Church of Satan and proclaimed it 'the Year One' of the Satanic Era. He wrote *The Satanic Bible* three years later. As well as hosting secretive gatherings, he blazenly conducted Satanic baptisms and funerals. His activities welcomed indulgence at a time when a return to spirituality was being advocated. Satanist sects continue to exist with few followers but much enthusiasm.

BOULETS ROCHEBELLE

UN FEU D'ENFER

IMP. BRABO.

Enfin je me repose!

A PACT WITH THE DEVIL

There was a German scholar called Johann Faust, also known as John Faustus, who lived in the sixteenth century. Generally considered to be a charlatan, he would turn up at fairgrounds, indulging in astrology and practising black magic. He was said to have made a pact with the devil, represented by one of his demons, Mephistopheles. Faust demonstrated the danger of becoming a heretical scholar, as opposed to a Christian scholar whose studies never deviate from the path outlined by the Church. Science, however, felt hampered by the limitations imposed on research by the religious authorities. The Renaissance, with its yearning for discoveries, managed to somewhat liberate attitudes. The Faust of legend, a sombre sorcerer associated with the devil, became a man who fell prey to the cruel uncertainties of his fate. In the nineteenth century, writer Johann Wolfgang von Goethe turned him into a learned old man desperate to discover the ultimate truth and frustrated at having devoted his youth to this goal. Mephistopheles traps him by offering him youth again in exchange for his soul. Faust consents and proceeds to lead a radically different life, seducing and abandoning the innocent Gretchen. But there is a demon in every human being. Now that few people still believe in the devil, stagings of scenes from the legend or the many literary works it has inspired have moved away from spiritual warfare and instead focus on struggles between the different human instincts.

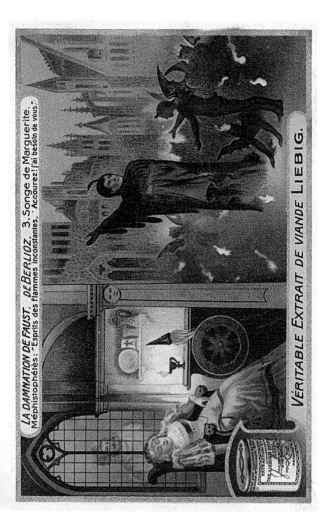

LA DAMNATION DE FAUST, DE BERLIOZ. 3. Songe de Marguerite.
Méphistophélès: "Esprits des flammes inconstantes, "Accourez! j'ai besoin de vous."

VÉRITABLE EXTRAIT DE VIANDE LIEBIG.

IT'S BAD LUCK

Superstitions give people the chance to practise simple magic in everyday life. Breaking a mirror carries a very heavy punishment: seven years of bad luck. In ancient times, mirrors were used for divination, so the destruction of this precious accessory was a bad omen. It is also important to count the number of dinner guests. If there are thirteen, misfortune will befall one of them, just like on the day of the Last Supper when Jesus feasted with his twelve apostles and was betrayed by Judas. At the table, placing the bread upside down attracts the devil, spilling salt brings bad luck and crossing two pieces of cutlery make the house prone to misfortune. Friday the thirteenth remains particularly ill-famed. According to Norse legend, the witches' sabbaths were originally held on Fridays. People avoid wearing new clothes on that day of the week. Some superstitions are a matter of prudence: don't walk under a ladder and don't open an umbrella indoors or put one on a bed. There are superstitions about cats in many countries, although they have different meanings: while black cats, the devil's companions, instill fear in many parts of Europe, in China, they drive away evil spirits. If resorting to fortune-telling to affirm or deny negative predictions, cross your fingers not to see spades, an unfavourable suit that heralds all kinds of bad luck.

IT'S GOOD LUCK

If you want to have a good night, just put your pyjamas on starting with your right foot! Many superstitious seem outdated and are met with laughter. Yet that does not stop us from performing them today. Whether or not they really believe in them, people cannot resist appealing to protective powers, if only to avoid the evil eye. All you have to do is knock on a piece of wood (preferably a crucifix) while making a wish, hang a horseshoe above your door, touch the red pom pom of a sailor's beret, or find a pin and pick it up. Lady Luck will shine on you if you pick a four-leaf clover, see a rainbow appear or watch a ladybird fly away. Unintentional clumsiness can magically transform misfortune into good luck if you break white glass, step in dog poo with your left foot, pour sugar instead of salt or drop a knife. Some animals save us from twists of fate, and not necessarily the cute ones. Pigs, for example, symbolize opulence in both China and Germany, where they appear on New Year's greeting cards. And even if you are afraid of spiders, it is better not to kill them because that brings bad luck too. Live animals, on the other hand, attract good luck. Be careful not to crush a cricket either: it will cease to sing its soothing song, which it does at the slightest noise, making it a wonderful guardian of the home.

Bekannt ist allerwegen
Dein Streben Fleiſs und Müh'n,

Mag deshalb Dir der Segen
Jm reichsten Maſse blüh'n!

THANKS TO THE TALISMAN

Keeping evil spirits at bay has always been one of humanity's major preoccupations. Wearing a talisman or amulet is considered one reliable solution. Either object can be made of wood, metal, stone, fabric or leather, with or without inscriptions. Their shapes vary widely, depending on the country and time period. But while amulets only provide protection or good luck, a talisman can give you powers. For example, by brandishing a cross or inverted pentagram you could be endowed with the ability to communicate with demons. However, a talisman or amulet should not be chosen at random. Whatever its material, shape, inscription or legend, each object bears a symbol according to the purpose it serves. A moon brings blessings in matters of the heart, while Saturn's image promotes wisdom. Wearing a diamond brings strength; an emerald, self-confidence; a topaz, inspiration; and a pearl, health. It is important to focus on the meaning of the symbol to benefit from it. If a talisman is bequeathed by a person who understands it and has acquired its powers, all the better.

WITCHES ON THE BIG SCREEN

Since the Middle Ages, witches have fascinated the general public, a fact to which many films can attest. However, witches are no longer necessarily presented as evil and repulsive. For today's woman, being a witch can be a way to bring an end to despair and assert her independence, as seen in the 1987 film *The Witches of Eastwick*. *Kiki's Delivery Service*, an animated film by Hayao Miyazaki (1989), melted our hearts. Karaba, the woman Kirikou has his eye on, is not very nice, but she is beautiful and her solitude is moving. However, most witches in cinema appear in gory and horror films where blood spurts and anguish abounds. *Witchcraft Through the Ages*, a Danish film released in 1922 full of striking scenes, gave birth to a genre that was destined to be a great success. In 1966, Hammer Film Productions maintained the classic English legend with *The Witches*. Dario Argento, a master of fantasy who knows how to produce bewitching images, treated amateurs with *Suspiria* in 1977. In 1986, Hong Kong's Ching Siu-Tung mixed romance, adventure and witchcraft in *Witch from Nepal*. In 2012, Tim Burton combined comedy and horror with *Dark Shadows*. That same year, a great classic revisited brought glamour to *Mirror Mirror*, in which Julia Roberts played the role of Snow White's stepmother, the evil queen. It is plain to see that witches are also talented at infiltrating every single film genre.

WE LOVED THEM ALL

In the early 1960s, the whole family would gather around the television set to follow the adventures of *Bewitched*. In the series, Samantha is married to a mere mortal advertising executive. Out of love, she decides to give up her magical powers. However, her change of lifestyle does not come without its difficulties, especially since her mother, Endora, disagrees with her choice and incessantly sets traps for her. The series was a huge success on both sides of the Atlantic. There is nothing frightening in this light-hearted family comedy. Released around the same time, *The Addams Family* tells the comic tale of a family of sorcerers who wish to go unnoticed but without refraining from doing their tricks and using magical objects. The youngest of the television witches appeared in 1996. *Sabrina, the Teenage Witch* was about a sixteen-year-old novice witch with a strange companion: a warlock who was turned into a talking cat. Teenage girls loved *Charmed* even more. This series, which came out slightly later, had young adult heroines and fuller plots. The characters had to face dangerous enemies, which added a delightful touch of terror to the scenes. The three Halliwell sisters in the series, witches just like their mother, became role models to the young girls who identified with them.

PAINTINGS OF
THE WITCHES' SABBATH

———————

Are witches stunningly beautiful, repulsive, or both? Ancient representations of witches highlight how fascinating they are to humans. Circe, who continued to inspire artists at the beginning of the twentieth century, appears on frescoes and pottery; her splendour is an excuse for those who could not resist her. Witches are just as respected as they are feared. Our traditional image of a witch was gradually established in the Middle Ages as an ugly woman riding a broom. We also saw witches tortured at the stake in fifteenth century miniatures, including Joan of Arc, the most famous one of all. Flemish painters from the sixteenth and seventeenth centuries, such as Frans Francken and David Teniers, painted witches' sabbaths with witches dressed as respectable middle-class women going about their business. At the end of the eighteenth century, Francisco de Goya's art became more spellbinding. The trials of the Spanish Inquisition were still being held and the ecclesiastical authorities suspected the painter, a notorious supporter of Age of Enlightenment ideas, of not sufficiently respecting their power. His scenes often depict emaciated women and skeletal infants, such as in his painting *Witches' Sabbath*. Lustful goats, distorted monsters and obscene nudity abound in his series of prints *Los Caprichos*. Goya exceeded - perhaps with irony -the fantasies that humans had about witches.

———————

EVERYDAY MAGIC

Magic played a major part in everything concerning life and death in ancient Egypt. It was neither taboo nor a secret: a supernatural intervention was indispensable for obtaining the favours of the gods. The Egyptians did not seek to seduce the gods, but to protect themselves against the potentially harmful consequences of their wishes. Most sorcerers were priests or scribes and they were endowed with special powers, thanks to their knowledge of writing. But they were not the only ones: women and men working as sorcerers were needed to select and prescribe medicinal plants in order to cure disease, protect children, and chase away snakes, scorpions and demons, etc. They reassured a population whose lack of explanation for natural phenomena made them vulnerable to constant trepidation about the future. These activities required equipment: amulets, figurines, papyrus scrolls containing formulas, in addition to stelae and statues. Archaeologists have discovered some of these elements. The priests were in charge of one fundamental matter eternal life after death. Mummification was not an aesthetic pursuit; it prepared the deceased for their journey into the realm of the dead and kept the body from decomposing. Opening a dead person's mouth allowed them to breathe and eat in the afterworld. The sorcerers' work ensured the link between humans, gods and the dead so that these three worlds would not be separated.

L'ALCHIMIE

1. — L'« art sacré » dans l'Égypte ancienne

LEADING THE CELTS

Druids occupied a predominant position in Celtic society. Archaeological excavations have confirmed that druids existed even though they left no written records. We rely upon Irish legends and stories by Roman authors for information on their role and practices. Julius Caesar endeavoured to describe his enemies' customs, at least as he understood them, in his *Gallic War*. Before the Romanization of Gaul and other Celtic territories, druids dominated the priestly class, with the most powerful druids prevailing over the rest, revealing it to be a hierarchical clergy. Druids maintained a privileged relationship with the gods and translated their will to the people through omens and prophecies. These practices were sometimes accompanied by human sacrifice. A druid's judgements and decisions were indisputable, and anyone who resisted them was banished from the community. Druids practised medicine through the use of plants. According to the Celts, mistletoe in particular, provided wide-reaching benefits if picked according to their rituals. Druids concocted potions, pronounced incantations and, historians believe, performed surgery. They also administered justice in everyday matters among private individuals as well as military conflicts involving the whole tribe. Their authority superseded that of the chief, who did not act without consulting his druid. You could not instantly become a druid - it took long years of study shrouded in secrecy.

CHICORÉE BLEU ARGENT

ARLATTE & Cie — CAMBRAI

LA RÉCOLTE
DU GUI
*Jour de l'An
chez les Celtes.*

3

IT'S ALL LEGEND

The myths and legends of the Celts of Ireland, Scotland, Wales and Brittany have not disappeared from the collective imagination, and they are steeped in magic. Above all, the Celts worshipped a sacred plant called the 'golden bough': mistletoe. Not yet identified as a tree parasite, mistletoe impressed them because it remains green all year and flowers in winter. To intensify its magical properties the mistletoe had to be picked from an oak tree – a rarity because this tree seldom plays host for the parasite. The druids used mistletoe for healing potions. However, the plant possessed other virtues: it allowed them to see and converse with ghosts, to purify souls and served as a talisman against evil spirits. The Celts were in great need of protection because there were some disturbing fairies lurking around. The Dearg Due, for example, haunted the Irish moors. This young woman died because she had been married against her will and was reincarnated as a vengeful vampire. Leanan Sidh, a beautiful redhead, seduced artists and made their talent blossom while sucking their life away, condemning them to an early death. *Banshees*, the fairies of fate, were messengers of death who sometimes appeared as owls. They would not kill you, but their horrifying screams could freeze your blood. These fairies were responsible for humans' passage into the other world, which the Britons called Avalon. Morgana and her fairies ruled that peaceful kingdom.

PALMIN

THE TORMENTED ENCHANTER

Merlin, the Enchanter, is a legendary character from Welsh mythology (by the name of Myrddin) and is also very popular in Brittany (under the name of Merzhin). A prophet, magician and impressive cultural figure, he is best known as the adviser of the Knights of the Round Table, a main character in the Arthurian legend, although it forms the context for only one of Merlin's many adventures. He was born covered in hair, the offspring of a demon and an abused young virgin. As a child, Merlin's wisdom and intellect already surprised people. However, his life was not a happy one because he was often taken by fits of madness. The forest became his domain. The first stories in which Merlin appeared were set in Great Britain, yet later he was associated with the forest of Brocéliande, in Brittany. He had taken refuge there with his scribe, the werewolf Blaise. He visited the forest animals, whose language he understood: the deer, which he adopted as his mount; the grey wolf, his winter companion; the wild boar; and the bear. He practised astrology, one of his well-known talents. Merlin was also a highly gifted builder. Legend has it that he was responsible for the megalithic complex Stonehenge. However, he was not immune to weaknesses; he was irresistibly attracted to women. In the legend of King Arthur, Merlin burned with desire for the fairy Viviane and in the hope of seducing her, he taught her the secrets of magic. She would later use this power to hold him prisoner.

LES LÉGENDES POPULAIRES – Merlin l'Enchanteur

THE MOST BEAUTIFUL GODMOTHER

First appearing in medieval European folklore, fairies have remained very popular ever since. Young and irresistibly beautiful, they know how to fly (and are often winged), shapeshift, cast spells with a magic wand, and bestow many blessings on those they protect. Having a fairy godmother has saved many fairy tale characters in dire situations, such as Cinderella, Sleeping Beauty and Donkey Skin, heroine of the eponymous French tale. Having a fairy for a lover is highly adventurous because she is elusive. Melusine, an ancient figure in European folklore disappeared because her husband Raymondin disobeyed her condition that he must not see her on Saturdays, the day she would secretly turn into a mermaid. Being tiny is no reason for a fairy not to offer protection. Tinkerbell, for instance, befriended Peter Pan, a fictional boy born into a nineteenth-century England that was particularly fond of fairies. Some fairies personify forces of nature including water (the Nereids of Greek mythology, mermaids, the Lady of the Lake of the Arthurian legends, etc.) or flowers and trees, such as those that haunt the forest of Brocéliande in Brittany. Others play dirty tricks, for example, stealing human babies and replacing them with changelings; belief in such substitutions even served as a pretext for infanticide. Carabosse, a character in Perrault's and, later, the Brothers Grimm's works, is a prime example of the 'evil fairy' archetype: old, ugly and, as her French name suggests, hunchbacked.

All Halloween Greetings

Dear Fairy will you join us
In our mirth and glee to-night,
And we'll dance away the happy hours.
Until the morning light.

A WEE TRICKSTER

Imps have been part of European folklore since the Middle Ages. These very small, human-like creatures like to come out at night. They live in groups and preferably in forests, where they hide without any difficulty, often in burrows. The creature's name varies according to place: generally interchanged with a gnome, goblin or dwarf, it is *lutin* in French, but *farfadet* in Poitou and Vendée, *fadet* or *gripet* in Provence, *nuton* or *sottai* in the Ardennes, *korrigan* in Brittany and *servan* in the Alps. It is also known as *kobold* in Germanic mythology, *nisse* in Scandinavia, leprechaun in Ireland and brownie in Scotland. Specialists say that these distinct creatures, to which local traditions attribute specific characteristics, should not be confused. However, they share many features in common. Imps have loose morals, hence the French term *lutiner*, which means 'to tease' in gentlemanly vocabulary. Although, because few imps feature in stories and depictions, one might imagine that these rascals are not bothered by their lack of success. Imps are mischievous and they love to play tricks on humans. They are not truly wicked and can even be helpful, but be careful not to offend their deep-rooted sensitivity. If you are fortunate enough to have imps in your home, inn or stable, you should treat them with respect. Pampering them too much, thus emphasizing their status as servants, irks them. Beware because, among other powers, imps can cast spells.

OF MICE AND TEETH

When children lose their baby teeth, they should not get too upset In France, as well as in other countries, if the tooth is placed under their pillow, a little mouse will come and replace it with a few coins or a small gift. The custom of rewarding children for losing teeth is quite recent; it only really became popular with the 1949 American story *The Tooth Fairy*. However, there are many legends around the world about baby teeth and mice, some of which overlap. The Vikings wore baby teeth on necklaces into battle because they believed they brought them invincible strength. The Egyptians threw them at the sun, representing the god Ra, and asked him to grant them healthy adult teeth. In medieval Europe, it was essential to hide these teeth from witches because if they took them, they could possess your whole being. Baby teeth had to be burnt, buried or placed in a snake or rat's nest, which witches hate. Making a mouse eat them was an excellent solution because this meant that the new teeth would be as strong as the rodent's teeth.

THE FLYING GIANT

Dragons never go out of fashion. Children are always fascinated by their reptilian head, long, sharp teeth, and wide wings. Their ability to breathe fire makes it difficult to imagine dragons having good intentions. In fairy tales, the dragon almost always plays the villain. In Greek and Celtic mythology, and later on in Christianity and local legend, the dragon is a beast to slay, especially if it guards a treasure or if you are granted magical powers upon killing it. In the Germanic tradition, Fafnir, killed by Siegfried, combined these two ideas. He protected the treasure of the Nibelungen from the mountain dwarves, and drinking his blood made it possible to understand the language spoken by animals. Saint George, a character inspired by a Christian martyr, gained lasting fame by defeating a dragon that was persecuting an entire village. There are many local dragons throughout Europe, each with their own names: Graouilli in Metz, fond of teenage girls; Grand'Goule in Poitou, defeated by Saint Radegonde; Lindwurm in Germany, who held young girls captive; Nídhögg in Scandinavia, who nibbled at the roots of Yggdrasil, the world tree; and the wyvern of Herefordshire, a terrible predator tamed by a little girl. Asians, however, do not consider the dragon to be systematically evil. In China, it symbolizes power, specifically the emperor's power.

LES ÊTRES LÉGENDAIRES. — 2. Le dragon.

IMAGINARY, BUT RESPECTED

The griffin has the front of an eagle's body and the back of a lion. Two of the animals at the top of the food chain have come together in this beast. It takes its ears from a third creature, one respected for its beauty and service: the horse. While the griffin might remind you of one, unlike the dragon, the griffin does not have a conflicted relationship with humans. On the contrary, it has been honoured since ancient Egyptian times. The griffin has served as a mount for deities, taken part in hunts and fights, guarded gold mines and competed against fantastic animals with comparable power such as centaurs. Griffins are depicted in many statues, mosaics and frescoes. Griffins seemed so familiar that the medieval Western world began to think they were real birds. Of course, nobody had seen one, but this didn't stop people from commenting on them in bestiaries, writing about them in novels or painting them. A griffin appears on the coats of arms of many noble families, cities, and even the provinces of Baden in Germany and Skåne (Scania) in Sweden.

Palmin-Post-
Sammelbild

Fabeltiere
Der Greif

79. Folge
Bild 6

NOT AS CUTE AS IT LOOKS

The legend of the unicorn is said to have come from the East. But when it settled in the medieval Western imagination, the animal was thought to be real. And why not? Nothing in its appearance suggests magic, because, as the Indian rhino proves, having only one horn is not unthinkable The debate lasted until the eighteenth century, when it could no longer be denied that no one had ever seen a unicorn. In the twenty-first century, the unicorn became a charming little mare who did good deeds. However, the bestiaries of yesteryear described it as a fearless and aggressive animal that we should be wary of. Accordingly, 'The Valiant Little Tailor', a traditional German tale transcribed by the Brothers Grimm, tells how the hero gained glory by defeating a ferocious unicorn. There's only one thing that quells the beast: the smell of virginity. This is why it is often depicted in the company of a young girl, such as in the Renaissance tapestry *The Lady and The Unicorn*. This also explains why the unicorn symbolizes purity. Unicorn horns, which were believed to absorb poison and cure all ills, were sold at exorbitant prices in the Middle Ages.

Palmin-Poſt-
Sammelbild

Fabeltiere
Das Einhorn

79. Folge
Bild 4

BRUTAL WEREWOLF

It is best to lay low on nights with a full moon; that is when the lycanthropes, more commonly known as werewolves, come out. The wolf is still a feared animal. As a carnivore, it has ravaged many grazing herds, especially during harsh winters when it becomes difficult to find food. It is no wonder that the wolf fills the role of predator in the European imagination. Zoanthropy, or therianthropy, the partial or total transformation of humans into animals, has played a role in myths and legends since prehistoric times. Likewise, lycanthropy, the transformation of humans into wolves, has spread terror far and wide, especially when they take on the traits of truly dangerous local animals, such as the tiger in India. Werewolves vary in appearance: they either transform completely or remain two-legged beasts with only the head of a wolf. Can you become a werewolf by choice? Yes, by making a deal with the devil. More often, being the victim of a curse or being exposed to the light of the full moon, a crucial factor, initiate the transformation. If the moon turns red, a lycanthropy epidemic can occur. An involuntary werewolf, on the other hand, loses control for three days during each full moon. It prowls, attacks and devours, with a special predilection for children. When the afflicted finally awakes, they are extremely weak and terribly depressed. They remember their misdeeds and woefully repent. This condition can last for seven years, unless it is hereditary, in which case it is permanent.

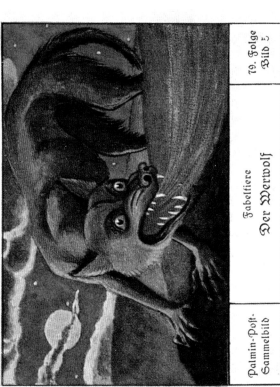

Palmin-Poft-
Sammelbild

Fabeltiere
Der Werwolf

79. Folge
Bild 5

THE QUEST FOR THE
PHILOSOPHER'S STONE

When picturing alchemy, it is easy to envision a secret, cavernous laboratory where, among nauseating burners, an elated scientist loses himself in endless calculations. This is how the alchemist was represented between the Middle Ages and the eighteenth century, when this occult science faded, though it did not disappear. Alchemists pursued ambitious goals: to create the philosopher's stone, an object that can manufacture a panacea, a universal cure and transform metals into gold. The art of alchemy incited greed – who has never dreamt of becoming immortal and fabulously rich? But it also sparked distrust because no one believed it could be done without magic. Moreover, alchemists wrote their texts in a complex esoteric language, which only fed the suspicion that they were doing deals with the devil. On the other hand, alchemists were respected because of their immense knowledge. From the time of Hermes Trismegistus, the ancient founder of the discipline, they were rather more successful at advancing science than accomplishing miracles. Alchemists were honoured in the Egypt of the pharaohs and in ancient Greece. In the twelfth century, the Arabs introduced alchemy into Europe, where at least the Church was not systematically hostile to it. It evolved freely and became increasingly similar to chemistry. At the end of the eighteenth century, self-proclaimed alchemists simply passed for eccentrics.

L'ALCHIMIE

3. — Raymond Lulle

LIVE, FROM MY PLANET

Astrology interprets the relationships between the positions and movements of the solar system's planets and human affairs. It is known today as a type of divination used by individuals to consult their horoscopes, which consist of predictions for the day, week, month, year or even their whole lives if they have their birth chart drawn up. All one needs to know is his or her zodiac sign, one of the twelve sectors of the circle surrounding the sun, moon and planets that passed through a certain constellation at their time of birth. The signs of the zodiac were themselves divided into three decans, each classified by one of the four elements: fire, earth, water and air. This rigorous system was established by the Babylonians some 1,700 years before our own time. At that point, the stargazers observing the stars did not have the intention of predicting a possible encounter with love. It was a more scholarly affair. In the fourth century BC, Hippocrates, the Father of Medicine, declared that it was impossible to be a good doctor without also being an astrologer. Prophecies pertained to a city, country, its present or its future, and were taken seriously by rulers. Prognostications were sometimes made very far in advance. For example, Nostradamus, a physician born in 1503, made predictions for the present day. Optimists prefer not to believe them, since they do not bode well for the environment and include armed conflicts.

L'ASTROLOGUE
QUI
SE LAISSE TOMBER DANS UN PUITS

TELL ME EVERYTHING!

Although there has never been any evidence that it is preordained, human beings have sought to know the future by any means since ancient times. And we have plenty of means from which to choose. The most popular divination practices in the West remain the techniques used by clairvoyants: chiromancy (also called palmistry, the study of the lines of the palm of the hand), fortune-telling (reading the future in playing cards), taromancy (use of tarot cards), crystallomancy (gazing into a crystal ball), and cafedomancy (reading coffee grounds). But diviners also use other tools or methods, which they may boast of as ancient practices: pendulums, runes, numerology (even Tibetan karmic numerology!), dream interpretation, spirit mediumship (communication with the spirits), dowsing (use of water-divining rods), clairaudience (ability to hear the voices of spirits), clairvoyance by illumination (called 'flashes of light'), or simply astrology. These are just a few examples of divination practices, for the future can also be explored with chopsticks, salt, animal (or even human) entrails, weather phenomena, a mirror, wax or candles, precious stones, molten lead, eggs, fire and many other elements. In this realm, the human imagination rivals our immeasurable anxiety.

LA VOYANTE

Choisis la demande et, au hasard, un des numéros : en tournant la roue de la Fortune tu auras la réponse.

Suis-je aimé 1-4-8-12-16
Serai-je heureuse ?
        2-6-10-14-18
Pense-t-il à moi ? 3-7-11-15-19
M'épousera-t-il ? 5-9-13-17-21
Aurai-je des rivaux ? 20-24-28-32
Deviendrai-je riche ? 23-27-31-35
Me sera-t-il fidèle ? 22-26-30-34-38
Suis-je trahi ? 25-29-33-37-41-45
Dois-je espérer ? 36-40-44-48-50
Le jeu me sera-t-il favorable ?
        39-42-43-46-47-49

IS IT ENOUGH TO BELIEVE?

What is to be done about a disease when it cannot be defined scientifically? This was a dilemma faced by humanity until very recently. Some people exercised strange practices that were similar to magic without calling them by that name. Practitioners sometimes performed daunting ceremonies but because they obtained results, they were not perceived as charlatans. They were called healers. In the Western world, being a healer means you have a gift, one which is usually passed from generation to generation, whether developed at an early age or discovered as a mature adult. These therapists use several techniques: magnetism, dowsing, massage, the laying on of hands, plant-based treatments, etc. The use of prayer has become rare and secretive. However, at the end of the nineteenth century, Christian Science, which claimed to have the power to heal, received official recognition. It was founded by Marie Baker Eddy, a fervent practitioner who, being very ill herself, was looking for a cure. The most famous mystical healer of all is Rasputin. This Siberian pilgrim managed to earn the trust of the last tsarina, Alexandra Feodorovna, by treating the haemophiliac heir to the tsar, Alexis, with some success. The power he acquired led to the court turning against him. He was accused of being a sorcerer and was murdered in 1916.

APPARITIONS:
HALLUCINATION OR TRUTH?

Do not confuse 'ghost' with 'apparition'. The former is a deceased person who periodically reappears to terrorize living people, poor things! The latter is a visible manifestation of a supernatural being to one or more persons. It might be Death coming to seek a living person at the end of his or her life or to remind them that they are waiting not far away. Reduced to a skeleton that is sometimes covered with a veil, the Grim Reaper carries a scythe, as his nickname indicates. He cuts lives short with a single, clean and irreversible blow. So it seems, anyway, because no one has yet to witness his appearance. Apparitions of the saints are different. The greatest number of these apparitions are attributed to Mary, the mother of Jesus. Accounts exist of hundreds of such phenomena. However, the Church does not recognize them all and the canonical investigation that follows a Marian apparition can last for decades, as it did in Giertzwald, Poland, where apparitions taking place in 1877 were recognized a hundred years later. In Mary's case, there are no predictions: her words (if she speaks) contain the message of the Gospel. Even if the Church recognizes the phenomenon, the faithful are under no obligation to believe in it. On the other hand, they are not prohibited from gathering at the scene of an unrecognized apparition.

UNFINISHED BUSINESS

We must be careful not to confuse ghosts with spirits. The former appear in human form, but are fuzzy, mobile and elusive. More infrequently, they take the shape of an animal, such as the monstrous canine in Conan Doyle's *The Hound of the Baskervilles*. Ghosts can appear silently any time and anywhere, and can walk through walls, seeming to fly through the rooms of a house. They rarely have evil intentions, but their simple appearance is disturbing. This is why the living seek to discover their secrets, often without success. We may not know anything about the ghosts that appear to us. They are identified by the local lore of the places they haunt since they usually return to where they once lived. They most likely suffered a terrible injustice or even a wrongful death, and their anger prevents them from finding peace. Even if unseen, at times you can hear a ghost, or a poltergeist. Poltergeists can move, throw objects, and turn on lights or electrical appliances – in short, disconcerting actions that can be perceived without seeing their perpetrator. Spirits, on the other hand, look the way they did in life. They have scores to settle or something they need to communicate. In the worst-case scenario, they are the undead, turned into a vampire who will not rise from the grave until nightfall. If a medium calls one, a spirit will manifest its presence. Deep concentration is required to spot its return among the living.

SPIRIT, ARE YOU THERE?

In the mid-nineteenth century, France was swept by a tremendous albeit brief wave of interest in spiritualism (lasting about fifteen years). 'Turning tables' invaded living rooms. This was when Hippolyte Rivail, better known by his pseudonym Allan Kardec, became popular. The movement came from the United States, where it had originated with two teenage girls, the Fox sisters. They claimed to have heard the ghost of a secretly buried traveller through the walls of their house. Although it later came to light that they had lied, belief that the spirits of the dead surround us and that we can communicate with them spread. A former schoolteacher, Allan Kardec took the name of the druid he claimed to have been in a previous life. Kardec theorized his doctrine in *The Spirits Book*. His philosophy, which he called 'spiritism', gained adepts around the world, particularly in Latin America. He was believed to have nearly half a million followers. Communicating with the inhabitants of the afterlife requires the intervention of a medium who is sensitive enough to contact them. Kardec and his disciples did not approve of groups using special turning-tables. However, these sessions even appealed to renowned intellectuals such as Victor Hugo, who hoped to reconnect with his daughter, Leopoldine, who had died tragically in her youth. Arthur Conan Doyle, the creator of Sherlock Holmes, was one of the most ardent supporters of spiritualism.

Les Esprits frappeurs (Spiritisme)

HOUSE SEEKS PURIFICATION

Ghosts haunt not only castles, but also charming thatched cottages. When supernatural manifestations are unpleasant, ill-intentioned, or the presence of ghosts is too strong or frightening, the residents will flee. This is the case of abandoned buildings where murders have been committed in Dunkirk or Lambersart in the Nord region of France, and The Cage, in England, built on the ruins of the prison where the famous witch Ursula Kemp stayed during the sixteenth century. On the other hand, the owners of the Château de Fougeret in France's La Vienne region have actually attracted curious overnight guests who want to experience the strange atmosphere of their home, which is haunted by a family of ghosts. In the absence of apparitions, a haunted house can nevertheless be identified by suspicious noises, voices, slamming doors or icy draughts. The wisest thing to do is to enlist the services of an exorcist. Only they will be able to convince the ghost or ghosts to leave. Yet it remains a difficult task because ghosts tend to have good reason to haunt a place, which they will not communicate willingly. How does one satisfy a ghost seeking revenge? It is not easy to reason with a ghost and several exorcism sessions will certainly be required. For heightened safety, you can rid your home of negative energy by cleansing it with sage or coarse salt flakes every week.

GHOST, SHOW YOURSELF!

The invention of photography founded a new activity: ghost hunting. Showing a picture of a returned spirit or one caught wandering was a way of proving it existed. The hunt for ghosts has grown with the advent of the internet and the ability to broadcast videos containing strange images and sounds. Hunters go alone or in groups to haunted places including castles, of course, but also houses or locations in nature. In addition to cameras, tape recorders and night vision cameras, they equip themselves with devices that enable them to measure electromagnetic fields and temperature differences as well as to capture electronic voice phenomena (EVP) and movements. Once the equipment is up and running, they edit videos with an impressive commentary and then broadcast them via social media with varying degrees of success. Some tricks have been unmasked, or their authors have confessed to them, justifying that they did not want to disappoint their thrill-seeking followers. In the United States, the activity has given rise to television series. Lorraine and Ed Warren started ghost hunting in the early 1950s and devoted their lives to the pursuit, becoming very famous. They were involved in high-profile cases such as the Amityville Horror case, involving a house, which, according to its owners, had been haunted since a boy murdered his entire family there.

There is a maid for every man
And every man be free
At this last hour of Halloween
By him to find the "She."

HALLOWEEN GREETINGS

THE HAUNTED SHIP

If you come across a large, old sailing boat that shows no sign of life and continues on its way unperturbed, there can be no doubt: it is the *Flying Dutchman*. The captain was murdered by his crew on the vessel, but before he died, he had time to curse them. The plague broke out on board and, refused mooring, the ship wandered endlessly over the seas. The legend was inspired by a Dutch captain who covered routes so swiftly that he was said to 'fly', and who disappeared without a trace. The ship inspired Wagner to write the theme for an opera, *The Flying Dutchman*. All over the world, sailors tell each other stories of ghost ships that appear from out of nowhere at any given moment, all sails out. Sometimes they are empty and sometimes poor souls wander on board. Crossing their paths is a bad omen. Such is the case of the *Caleuche* which is said to sail off the coast of Chile with a crew of sorcerers and demons. Numerous witnesses have attested to the vessel's bright, ephemeral apparitions, which were still being reported in the second half of the twentieth century. A disturbing fact: radars cannot pick them up. Sometimes ships can also become haunted. During a storm, the fishing vessel *Charles Haskell* unintentionally sank another vessel. The following season, men saw ghost sailors boarding their ship to later return to the water.

Qu'en puis-je faire hé-las, sans femme, sans enfant,

Héros des Opéras de Wagner. Le Vaisseau Fantôme.

ENIGMATIC WHITE LADIES

They all dress in white and have white hair. They usually appear on nights when there is a full moon, but will sometimes appear on other nights. They rarely make an appearance during the day. Those who come across them are surprised but not frightened. White ladies, also known by their French name *dames blanches*, disappear without leaving a trace, except for a deep sense of uneasiness in those who have witnessed them. None of those who have seen a white lady say they have been intimidated or abused. They arise from out of nowhere for some unknown purpose. The suspected reason: they died in tragic and troubled conditions, an accident or an unsolved murder that did not allow them to rest in peace. Such is the story of the dame blanche of Lessay in Normandy, highlighted in *The Bewitched* by writer Jules Barbey d'Aurevilly. She was murdered and returns to haunt the moor near her castle on nights when there is a full moon. Or there is the white lady who was buried alive in the eighteenth century. She appears on the roof of the Château de Trécesson castle in Morbihan, France. In this day and age, white ladies mostly manifest as mysterious hitchhikers. They always ask for the same directions from whoever stops. Silent, they get agitated as they approach a bend, begging the driver to beware. That is the place where an accident cost them their lives. The danger passes and they vanish into thin air. But beware: it is said that serious harm can come to anyone who passes by without stopping for them!

La Dame Blanche

ON A BED OF NAILS

Fakirs are members of a Sufi brotherhood of Muslim mystics. Their Hindu equivalent is called a *sadhu*. As ascetics, they adhere to strict poverty, living on alms. In the West, a 'fakir' is typically associated with seemingly superhuman powers: lying on a bed of nails, piercing one's body with a dagger, walking on hot embers, charming snakes, etc. These abilities are not the main activities of Indian fakirs but proof of their spiritual strength, gained through asceticism and meditation. These ascetics captivated Westerners with their amazing feats, which seemed to involve magic and later led to the invention of fakirism, performances similar to sleight of hand tricks. Fakirism became fashionable in the Interwar years and during this time some Frenchmen became particularly renowned. Among them was Charles Fossez, born in 1901, who styled himself as Fakir Birman and was the first astrologer to make a name for himself with press advertisements. He became famous on stage and on the radio. In 1939, banned from practising his clairvoyant activities, he reinvented himself in the women's lingerie business. Another was Léon Goubet, born in 1931. Under the stage name Ben-Ghou-Bey, he was feted by audiences worldwide for such astounding feats as being crucified more than seven hundred times and having his tongue nailed for four days straight. He did not claim to have any paranormal powers, but simply pursued continuous physical and mental preparation. He assisted medical research on pain.

SCÈNES DE ROYAUMES DISPARUS.

Ruines de
Golconde.

AN IN-DEPTH CONSULTATION

According to the World Health Organization, eighty per cent of Africans regularly consult traditional practitioners, commonly referred to as witch doctors. This is sometimes necessary due to the scarcity of health services. African medicinal notions differ radically from the ideas of Western medicine. In the former, illness results from a spiritual or social imbalance. In order to make a diagnosis, a healer looks for the cause through incantations, by throwing small bones and shells, or examining the entrails of a chicken. The use of magic is justified because the illness may arise from the displeasure of the gods or ancestors, or from a wrongdoing committed that the patient is unaware of. In addition to possessing clairvoyant powers and the ability to find the root of a disease, the healer also knows how to use medicinal herbs. He or she uses plants for massages, ointments, herbal teas and vapours. About four thousand plant species are used, chosen as much for their spiritual significance as for their medicinal efficacy. Nowadays, teams of Western researchers are interested in these treatments and are working to improve the production of traditional herbal medicines, while warning against species with harmful effects. Rather than contrasting the two medicines, they seek to use the methods in complementary ways.

A. Austr. Anglaise **UNION SUD-AFRICAINE**
Une consultation de sorcier

INGRAINED BELIEFS

Belief in invisible forces pre-dated the European colonization of Africa. The notion of witchcraft and the word for it were imported by colonists whose monotheistic religion was at odds with the African vision of the world. Europeans considered conversion to Christianity indispensable to the progress they wanted to impose. Blanket missionary activity also vilified ancestral beliefs. The people they called 'witch doctors' were traditional healers, considered by the natives to be wise leaders who intervened in the public affairs of the village. The village listened to their oracles and trusted them to heal their bodies and minds. None of them claimed to be a healer or cult leader on their own. They would have to undergo an apprenticeship that covered traditional knowledge and healing plants, taught to them by elders. The healer had a responsibility to the community and the chiefs consulted them. This system had nothing in common with today's witch doctors, who often cater to financial or emotional personal interests in return for payment. Nor does it have anything to do with the people, often children, who are accused of causing unfavourable situations by casting spells. Witchcraft is banned in many African countries, but this does not prevent occult practices from taking place or disgruntled populations from lynching 'culprits' accused of being responsible for all their ills.

POSS. PORT.   ANGOLA
UN FÉTICHEUR DE L'ANGOLA

SHAMANS AND THEIR FEATHERS

Every Amerindian community has special individuals who are able to foresee the future, interpret dreams, and invite good and bad spirits to come and talk with them. They are usually called shamans. They do not choose this role nor acquire it of their own effort. Shamans are identified during childhood by their parents and the council of elders, and they are subsequently raised and trained for this role. The process is the same for medicine men, who practice natural medicine, which is similar to Chinese Traditional Medicine. The shaman calls upon the earth's energy. The earth is venerated by Native Americans, who do not seek to exploit its riches. Like the great chiefs, shamans wear feathered headdresses. However, warriors also receive feathers in honour of their feats because feathers spread positive energy. Each type of bird feather has its own meaning. The feathers of eagles, the most prestigious bird, are used in magical and religious practices. They protect the wearer and drive thoughts flying towards the Great Spirit. Associated with the peace pipe, dove feathers are used for peace rituals. Shamans have duck, nightingale and various owl feathers. Female shamans use swan feathers for fertility rituals.

Nº 14 - SORCIER

INDIANA

MYSTERIES OF THE EAST

Pre-Islamic Arabia did not scorn magic. During Jahiliya, the polytheistic period, Arabs feared spirits and called upon deities, stones and sacred animals. When Islam appeared in the seventh century, it did not strictly condemn these beliefs. Popular and scholarly traditions have lived on, incorporating a pre-Islamic figure of great importance: the jinn, also known as genie. The Qur'an attests the existence of this invisible creature, whose ability to adopt a human, animal or vegetable form as it pleases makes it all the more formidable. It seems impossible to escape the unpredictable jinn. They inhabit waterholes, deserts and forests. Although endowed with almost unlimited supernatural powers – including the very threatening ability to possess your body and soul – they do not abuse these powers. Jinns are distinguished from angels as being neither necessarily evil nor always good. Born from fire and not clay, the jinn are creatures of God, to whose law they too are subject. They can still choose to acquiesce or disobey, in which case they will be punished. Nothing is final because even if jinns have committed sins, they will be able to repent if they wish.

UN GÉNIE APPARAÎT A ALADIN.

THE WORLD OF SCHEHERAZADE

Scheherazade kept her life thanks to her agile mind. She made herself indispensable to Sultan Shahryar, who decided not to kill her as he had intended. For a thousand and one nights, she told him fascinating stories that were interrupted by the dawn, thus forcing him to wait until the next day to find out how they ended. Her tales were full of brigands and travellers, but also of genies and magic. A woman is turned into a doe as punishment for her evil deeds. A jealous vizier throws a prince into the arms of an ogress. The severed head of a doctor gives instructions to a king. Miraculous fish converse with a fairy. A queen keeps her dead lover in a state of unconsciousness. Realism was hardly the point. From Antoine Galland's first translation into French at the beginning of the eighteenth century, *One Thousand and One Nights* became a great success in Europe. The magic of the East had come to readers who had never heard of it before. Some stories are particularly intriguing. In 'Aladdin and the Magic Lamp', a poor young man finds fortune and love thanks to the genie contained in a lamp. 'Ali Baba and the Forty Thieves' tells how a woodcutter enters a cave full of treasures with a magic formula. In 'Sinbad the sailor', a sailor escapes from a giant monster, makes friends with an elephant and confronts humans transformed into birds.

VODUN RITES

Vodun, also known as Voodoo, originated in the ancient kingdom of Dahomey, now Benin, in West Africa. This is where most enslaved people were taken on board slave ships. They took their religion with them. Despite religious prohibitions, they passed their beliefs on to their descendants. Religion brought members of diverse tribes together and strengthened the identity of enslaved people. Today Vodun is still practised in Africa and it also brings together believers in Haiti, in the West Indies, and certain African-Americans in Lousiana – both places home to a famous variant of Vodun, Voodoo – and Brazil. Its traditional magical rites have been preserved, in which invisible forces present in the air, earth, water and trees govern the universe. The faithful invoke these forces for protection or ask them to intervene. Under the authority of the creator Mawu, the inaccessible supreme spirit, a large number of Vodun deities act in a particular domain such as war, love, land, wealth or prestige. To contact the Voduns, the faithful rely on a sorcerer, who organizes secret ceremonies. They enter into a trance by taking hallucinogenic substances and dancing wildly, which incites the spirits to take possession of the sorcerer, who can then cast or break spells and curses. The most famous accessory in Voodoo rites is the doll. Made of rags or knitted, the doll embodies its target: by pricking it with needles, spells are cast upon the person it represents.

FURTHER READING

Arnould, Colette, *Histoire de la sorcellerie*,
Tallandier, 2019.

Atwood, Margaret, *Graine de sorcière*,
Robert Laffont, 2019.

Auray, Christophe, *L'Herbier des paysans,
des guérisseurs et des sorciers*, Ouest France, 2019.

Chabrillac, Odile, *Âme de sorcière ou la Magie
du féminin*, Pocket, 2019.

Chollet, Mona, *Sorcières. La puissance invaincue
des femmes*, Zones, 2019.

Collectif, *Contes de sorcières*, Flammarion, 2017.

Delatte, Armand, *Herbarius. Recherches sur
le cérémonial usité chez les anciens pour la cueillette
des simples et des plantes magiques*, Trajectoire, 2019.

Ehrenreich, Barbara and English, Deirdre, *Sorcières,
sages-femmes et infirmières*, Cambourakis, 2015.

Federici, Silvia, *Caliban et la sorcière*
Entremonde, 2017.

Frances, Isabelle and Laporte, Florence, *La Magie
des druides*, Rustica, 2018.

Michelet, Jules, *La Sorcière*, Gallimard, 2016.

Miller, Arthur, *Les Sorcières de Salem*,
Robert Laffont, 2015.

NDiaye, Marie, *La sorcière*, Minuit, 2009.

Prolongeau, Hubert, *Et vous, vous y croyez ?*
Petit tour de France des pratiques occultes,
Mon Poche, 2019.

Van Grasdorff, Gilles (préface), *Le Grand et le Petit*
Albert, Archipoche, 2013.

Victor, Henry, *La Magie dans l'Inde antique*,
La Clef d'or, 2017.

ALSO AVAILABLE

ABOUT US

E/P/A publishes high-quality coffee table and reference books.

Combining a highly visual approach with well-researched content and the highest standards of production, E/P/A offers books on Music, Film, Transport, Nature, Adventure, Science, History, and Hobbies.

E/P/A also publishes gift books under its Papier Cadeau imprint.

E/P/A is part of the Hachette Livre Group.

For the original edition:

© 2020, Papier Cadeau- Hachette Livre
www.papier-cadeau.fr

For the current edition:

Editorial Director: Jérôme Layrolles
Editor: Eglantine Assez
Art director: Charles Ameline
English Edition: Ariane Laine-Forrest

Translation © Papier Cadeau – Hachette Livre, 2020
English translation and proofreading by Rebecca Reddin,
Theresa Bebbington and Rebecca Stoakes for Cillero & de Motta

Published by Papier Cadeau
(58, rue Jean-Bleuzen 92170 Vanves Cedex)
Printed in May 2020
ISBN: 978-2-37964-105-3
1309786